I0685922

Seeker of Fate

The Fate Trilogy

L.J. Kentowski

Copyright © 2012 by L.J. Kentowski

This book is a work of fiction. All names, characters, locations and incidents are products of the author's imagination. Any resemblance to actual persons, things, living or dead, locales or events is entirely coincidental.

ISBN: 978-0615725222

L.J. Kentowski
laurakentowski@yahoo.com
http://www.laurakentowski.com/

Editing by: http://www.editingfairy.com

More books by L.J. Kentowski

<u>Fate Trilogy:</u>

Guardian of Fate (Book 1)
Seeker of Fate (Book 2)
Angel of Fate (Book 3)

<u>Lexie Pearce Series:</u>
Descended in Vengeance (Book 1)

<u>Heart of Seeton Series:</u>

Love Owned (Book 1)
Full Potential (Book 2)

Learn more about these books at
http://www.laurakentowski.com/

Get a FREE Urban Fantasy Short Story!

When you sign up for my VIP Newsletter, you'll receive access to release news, upcoming events, and exclusive content and giveaways!

As a thank you for joining, you'll also receive a FREE bonus short story companion to the Lexie Pearce Series!

Get started here:

https://preview.mailerlite.io/forms/1675703/160480288 834586588/share

ACKNOWLEDGEMENTS

I want to thank my family for their genuine love and support for all that I am and all that I want to be. You've never given up on me and without that, I don't know if I'd have the motivation to do what I do. With you, I know my dreams can come true.

Miss Loni Flowers, you know you are my soul sister! You've braved this journey with me and without you by my side, I could not have made it. Thank you for all that you are and all that you do. You are beautiful and I will love you forever!

A huge thank you to all of my pro beta readers: Lindsay Lanier, Jessenia Marie Berdecia, Tif Olson, and the beautifully talented, Mae Clair. You've helped make Seeker Of Fate what it is! You all totally rock!

Teri Gibson of Editing Fairy, you've made Seeker Of Fate shine beyond my dreams of it! Thank you so much for using your wonderful talents to make it the best it can be.

And last, but so far from least, thank you so much to all of my fans. You are the reason I write, and your love and support blows me away! I hope you keep enjoying my fantasies because I couldn't have done any of this without you!

CHAPTER ONE

I am running through the familiar woods, fear pulsating through my veins. My eyes dart back and forth, scanning my surroundings, frantically searching for something in the dense foliage. My arms bleeding, I swipe at branches that feel as if they are made of pointed nails, but I forge on, slicing my bare skin. I will not stop until I find what I am looking for.

Finally, my fingers brush against cement beneath a feathery wave of vines that emerge from the mossy grass under my feet and extend beyond my sight. A pungent smell hits my nose, its smoky nature competing with the woodsy smell of the forest around me to overpower my senses. My heartbeat racing, my breaths cause short, quick plumes of transparent smoke to form. The tough vine stalks prove more tenacious than they appear, as I struggle to pull them from the concrete behind, using all my weight to bend and yank them away. After trampling the remaining pillared guardians, I step back to behold a huge mountain of stone, which to most might be confused with one of nature's natural formations, but to me, it is much more than that. I recognize the solid wall as the barrier that blocks the world we live in from the evil that lies below the surface of human cruelty and error. This evil has a home, one that is hidden deep inside the very forest I have been running through for years.

It is what I was looking for all along, but now that I've finally found it, my instincts conflict with my will to stay. Half of me wants to run from the mass I see before me, while the other half feels I belong somewhere beyond this wall. I place my hands against the cool stone, lightly rubbing its rugged surface, as if coaxing it into telling me how to enter its depths.

I close my eyes, imagining what I think Hell would look like. A ball of fire manifests in my heart, stretching, radiating heat throughout the rest of my body, until I feel like the flames will consume my skin. I know I have changed inside, I can feel myself hardening. But as I open my eyes, the only thing that appears to have changed is my impression of where I was going—home.

With pure force and determination, I pound on the wall. Slowly, it slides aside, accepting me, waiting for me to return to its fiery halls.

Hell welcomes me home.

***

I woke up the same way I always did upon having this dream: T-shirt drenched with sweat and stuck to my skin, while unruly, damp curls are plastered against my shoulders and face. Throwing the damp sheets from the bed, I got up and mopped the sweat from my forehead. Despite the perspiration glistening on my skin, my body trembled from chills that would stay with me for the remainder of the day. To most people, this type of dream would be unnerving, to say the least. But they would be fortunate enough to allow it to fade like the morning sun, with the comfort of knowing it existed purely on another level of consciousness. I didn't have that luxury. My dreams couldn't be forgotten. They were analyzed and deciphered because, in time, they would become my reality.

Two kinds of dreams controlled my world. My Guardian visions consisted of prophetic dreams, involving the death of a human, whose soul is stolen by the shadowy demons from Hell. As a Guardian of Fate, it was my job to take the information from these visions and use it to save victims from untimely and evil-induced deaths. Without my intervention, their souls would be destined to an eternity in Hell. I have learned to live with these kinds of visions. They are very much a part of my life, my responsibility.

There are other dreams that haunt my sleep. Even though they appear as deadly as the Guardian visions, they are more obscure to me and nearly impossible to comprehend. Just when the puzzle begins to unfold, they change, leaving me as confused as ever.

I went straight to the bathroom and shut the door to avoid waking my roommate, Nora. She was well aware of my visions, but since it was two in the morning, I didn't think it was a good time to bother her with my newest puzzle. Letting the water run cold enough to make me gasp, I splashed it on my face. Its iciness shocked my system from its fuzzy musings. After wiping my face with a towel, I gazed at my paled features in the mirror. The luster of my skin was no longer visible, as if it had washed out from everything I'd lost in the last year. The deep furrows weren't etched from an abundance of smiles, but rather, a hardened air I'd recently developed in my determination to get everything back.

Silently, I asked my reflection what this latest dream might be telling me. For the past few months, I was making plans to go to the very place my subconscious carried me. Did it mean I was on the right track? Or were my actions of late now dictating my subconscious? For years, I'd only dreamt of Hunter, and then one day he appeared in my life. But even that felt like a dream to me now.

"Stop it," I screamed at the mirror. "Get over him...it...and move on." Throwing the towel into the sink, I yanked open the door and walked face-first into a chin.

"Owww...*damn it*." I backed into the bathroom. "Caleb, what the hell are you doing lurking outside the bathroom door?"

"I wasn't lurking," he said, rubbing his chin. "I heard you get up and go into the bathroom, and then I heard you yelling." Concern came over his face. "Who were you yelling at, Cassie?"

Holding my forehead, which took the brunt of the impact, I looked at it in the mirror. I didn't really care whether a bruise formed or not, the bathroom merely seemed too small at the moment. I was searching for something to make me feel less claustrophobic.

Caleb came closer. I kept my composure in front of the sink, despite wanting to jump out of my skin and hightail it out of there. He was the only one who could help me with my plan, so I needed to keep him around. But when he raised his hand toward my face, I instantly flashed back to his rough touch months ago, and flinched away from his fingers. He held my gaze, but withdrew his hand. The look in his eyes told me he understood, although I didn't miss the sadness and regret that accompanied it.

"I'm not going to hurt you," he said quietly as he turned to leave the bathroom. "That's not me anymore. When are you going to realize that?"

"Look, it's going to take me a while, Caleb," I said. "I mean, it wasn't that long ago you were trying to take my soul to Hell and make me your love slav—" I slapped my hand over my mouth. I didn't mean for the harsh words to slip out. Everything that happened all those months ago was because he was someone different. But Caleb was no longer a demon. He'd been changed by my own blood, which now ran through his veins, and was a Guardian once again.

He swung around, stopping me mid-stride in the middle of the hallway. Leaning close, he grabbed my upper arm and whispered, "My soul status has changed, Cassie. *You're* the only demon here, but I've decided to overlook that. Maybe you can try and overlook what I used to be. And, by the way, I'm still working on making you my love slave."

His green eyes, recently changed from their *demon-blue,* stared at me while he waited for me to say...*what?* That I'd consent to become his love slave? No freaking way.

I pulled away from his grasp as I moved past him and out of the hallway. Nora's room was too close. I was afraid our banter would wake her before I had the chance to map out my plan to Caleb. He followed me into the kitchen. As I got a glass from the cupboard, I said, "Look, if I didn't trust you, I wouldn't have allowed you to stay here while we figure all this out. It's just hard for me to see you as a Guardian after everything we experienced. But I'm getting better." I moved to fill my glass with water and purposely brushed against him near the sink. It was a feeble attempt to show him I could still stand being close to him. "And for the record, I don't like what I am any more than you can endure thinking about what you used to be, so maybe in the future you could spare me the reminder."

"Deal," he said, leaning against the counter. "So, now that we've established once again who we are, will you tell me what you were doing yelling at yourself in the bathroom at two in the morning?"

Holding the glass in my hand, I leaned against the breakfast bar, blankly staring. I shook it just enough so the water swirled inside. I wasn't sure how much I wanted to tell him, this man, who deceived me once before, hooking me with his good looks, kindness, and charm. He was a Seeker then, whose sole purpose was to turn me into one of Hell's newest residents. As the last descendent of a high-ranking angel, I was a pretty hot commodity to the Underworld, so Caleb stood to climb substantially in the ranks if he claimed the turn. He was the epitome of evil, using my friends and family as bait to lure me into his trap. And he would have succeeded if I hadn't been half-demon already, another fact I'd only recently learned, along with my angel ancestry.

Thankfully, Caleb had since transformed back into a Guardian. He believed it was from tasting my blood the last time we fought. Was it be possible my blood, being half angel, was strong enough to transform the demons from Hell? Could their lost souls be redeemed by what flowed through my veins? With no proof he was right, I nevertheless desperately wanted to believe it because my plan depended on it. There was a chance, however, this was all some trumped-up scheme to lure me into Hell, and very possible that Caleb was performing his greatest role. For now, I'd have to take the chance.

"I had a vision."

"A Guardian vision?" He looked confused. "Why are you still here?"

"It wasn't that kind of vision. This one was about me. Specifically, me searching for Hell. I've had these dreams for the last few months and they're driving me crazy. Lately, when I wake up, I feel like I'm running out of time." I set my glass on the counter and got close to him, determination in my eyes, as well as my tone. "I have to go to Hell, Caleb. Soon. You have to tell me how to get in, so I can get my dad."

"Have you had dreams like this before? About you? About Hell?"

"No...well, not about Hell directly, but I dreamt about Hunter..." It was hard for me to think about him, even after so many months. Caleb's face fell after hearing Hunter's name. I knew it pained him to hear it almost as much as it did me to say it, only for a different reason. "I dreamt about him, and eventually you, before you came after me."

He looked thoughtful for a minute, then his face turned angry. "If you knew what would happen, why did you sleep with him?"

Hunter was another Seeker assigned to steal my soul. Although his mission failed, he did manage to claim my heart. I was still not quite sure how it happened, but I fell in love with him, and I believe he fell in love with me as well. At least, that's what he told me when our hearts bonded, along with our bodies. In the end, however, he betrayed me by not telling me my father was still alive and being tortured in Hell. After becoming intimate with me, he let me continue to believe my father was a Guardian, when he was, and always had been, a Seeker. My own mother, another Guardian, didn't even know. We discovered that fact together before Hunter was returned to Hell by the king of the Underworld. He was sentenced to an eternity of torture for abandoning his mission to turn me, not to mention sleeping with me, which was treason in the highest order to them. Ironically, he and my father held the same fate.

I didn't want to think about what happened to Hunter. It was too painful. Not because I regretted it, but because my feelings for him were still so strong. I wanted to hate him for deceiving me; God knows I did when I first found out. But for the last few months, it wasn't his lies that haunted my thoughts. It was the way he risked everything for me, the way he rebelled against everything he was to ensure I kept my soul—regardless of its purity. Although I'll never be able to forget his deceit, I learned to accept it. There was no rulebook for our love, especially for those who weren't supposed to ever experience it. Now, it was too late for me to tell him I understood everything, and the only way I could bear the painful knowledge that he was being tortured, was to keep my mind on my own mission.

I lifted my chin and stared into Caleb's accusing eyes. "Not that it's any of your business, but these visions don't work like that. I *didn't* know Hunter was a demon, just like I didn't know *you* were when we first met. The dreams are cryptic, and they never spelled out that you would both turn out to be liars."

"The difference being that you chose to be with him instead of me."

"No, Caleb. The difference being that Hunter tried to save me from Hell, while you did everything in your power to drag me there," I argued through gritted teeth.

Standing opposite each other in the kitchen, caught in our silent standoff, we glared at each other for our own reasons, both knowing nothing more needed to be said. We had become so used to preying on each other's weaknesses, knowing exactly how to hurt one another, that now the accusations flew easily. It would take more than the few months we'd already spent together to completely ignore the fact that we were originally trying to kill each other. At least, for me.

"Yeah, well, he's still in Hell," Caleb said. He closed the space between us and braced his hands on the counter behind me, jailing me between them. "But I'm here."

All I could do was watch as his face came down, stopping inches from mine. The Seekers were familiar with the use of seduction to lure the Guardians in. The power of attraction they held was undeniable and extremely hard to resist. Caleb still retained the beauty and charm that molded him into the sensuous weapon that originally attracted me to him. And during the last few months, he hadn't shown even an ounce of his previously evil self. But it wasn't any of Caleb's qualities that attracted me now, it was the position we were in that caused me to slowly close my eyes, and savor the body heat radiating from him. Behind closed lids, I pictured a time when Hunter and I were in the same position. I could feel his fingertips brush my face, trailing down my neck. My pulse quickened as I felt his breath against my skin.

"Cassie..." he whispered.

The way he said my name should have been enough to shake me out of my reverie, as Hunter would never call me that. With him, it was always *Cassandra*. And coming from Hunter's lips, it never ceased to tantalize my skin, as if his hands were caressing my entire body. But I didn't want the memory to stop. God forgive me, I wanted to shut my eyes against the reality of it all and pretend it was Hunter's lips now pressed against mine. So I did. I moaned when his tongue found its way into my mouth, and I sank into the arms that wrapped around me.

His solid body felt so familiar against me. I didn't notice his lips had abandoned mine, allowing me to breathe in his sweet, woodsy scent. It was another thing that should have reminded me it wasn't Hunter whose arms I felt around me, but I was too lost to care.

"Cassie, open your eyes," he whispered. "See me. I want you to know it's me you're with right now."

I tried to do as he said, but I didn't want my illusion to end. I didn't want to see the hurt in his eyes when he realized where I'd been. There were moments when I knew exactly where I was and who I was with, and I couldn't say I hated the feelings they evoked. I *was* still attracted to Caleb. Maybe I could pull it off. Maybe he wouldn't know.

I opened my eyes and instantly saw Caleb's face fall. He dropped his arms from me, turned, and stepped away. I reached out and put my hand on his arm in an effort to comfort him. It was all I could do, since I couldn't seem to find anything to say that would justify what happened.

"I'm not going to do this, Cassie."

"Caleb it's not you. I shouldn—"

"No, I mean I'm not going to help you get in to Hell."

"What?" I yelled as I forced him around to face me. "You promised."

"I promised to help you get your father, but I can see you're still longing for Hunter, and I don't want you anywhere near him. I'm sorry. The deal is off."

"You can't do this, Caleb. You're my only hope of saving my father. I can't do this without you."

"And I won't let you either," he said defiantly. "Not only won't I help you, but I'll do everything in my power to make sure you don't get to Hell any other way. I'll call on the Elders if it comes down to it."

The Elders were a group of top-ranking angels who oversaw everything the Guardians did, and the very ones who gave the Guardians their powers to begin with. I, however, had a special tie with the Elders, two of them anyway. Hadraniel and Anael were my ancestors. Their angelic blood ran through my veins, and I was the last of their line. Recently, Hadraniel explained to me that if I ever showed any demonic tendencies, they'd not only disown me as one of their own and lift any protection they previously provided me, but would also consider me a direct enemy of the angels. They already knew my father had been turned, and I was created with the bloodlines of both angel and demon; but they promised to watch over me as one of their own, unless I decided not to be.

"You can't do this. Over what? Your jealousy?" I glared at him.

He moved in closer, steeled in his reserve. I backed up into the counter again, but refused to break eye contact. "I'll do whatever I have to in order to keep you away from that demon. Do you understand me? I won't let him have you. Not ever again."

He wasn't going to budge. I knew that. I could see it. I could *feel* it. But I still intended to save my father. I never planned to seek out Hunter. Not really, but I left my options open to it. It was always in the back of my mind. Who was I kidding? It was in the forefront of my mind all the time. But right now I'd have to let it go for my father. He was what mattered most now.

"Okay, I'll do whatever you say, Caleb. I give you my word."

He studied my face, most likely looking for the loophole he thought I might have reserved for myself, but there was none. "You'll stay away from Hunter?"

"Yes."

"Alright." He reached up and caressed my cheek.

I flinched, trying to keep my emotions in check.

"I wish you could see how great we'd be together, Cassie. Maybe in time you'll finally realize I'm much better for you than he is. In the meantime, let's put together a plan."

"And what plan would that be?" Nora's asked from behind me.

Shit. I was so busted.

CHAPTER TWO

Caleb and I split apart like two teenagers caught in a romantic embrace by a strict parent. I turned to face Nora, who was standing at the edge of the room, arms crossed, leaning against the living room wall, looking every bit the part of the omniscient parent. I wasn't sure how long she'd been standing there, much less how much she'd overheard. There were no partitions to separate the living room and kitchen areas, only the breakfast bar Caleb and I were leaning against.

"Oh, hey Nora. What are you doing up?" I asked. Nora was my best friend, had been since we started college. Only recently did I find out she was also the person the Elders assigned to observe me and report any signs of demonic tendencies. We were close friends, but became even closer after the cat was out of the bag that we were both Guardians. With no secrets to tiptoe around, it was much easier to confide in one another; that is, until Caleb came back into my life as a born-again Guardian. After persuading him to help me get into Hell, I knew I'd have to tell Nora about him. Our plan entailed hours of plotting, and there was no way to spend that kind of time together without her knowing. Oh, and did I mention, he had no place to stay?

The last time Nora encountered Caleb, he was hell-bent on force-feeding us his demonic blood. So, after introducing the new and improved version of Caleb to her, I told her about our plan to get my dad back. Well, kind of. There was no way she'd go for me traipsing around in Hell, especially since it would require that I reunite with my demon heritage; so I told her Caleb was going in for me. She performed every makeshift demon test there was to confirm he wasn't trying to trick us, aside from actually dissecting him. Finally, she agreed to help.

Now, I just had to figure out how to keep her dedicated support without letting her know I was the one going to Hell.

"I thought I heard you guys arguing out here, but clearly, I was wrong," she said, her eyebrows raised. From the way she stalked toward us, I knew she expected an explanation. I couldn't say I blamed her; we probably appeared pretty cozy.

Caleb and I glanced at one another before I moved around the breakfast bar, as if distancing myself from him would disprove Nora's assumptions. He watched me nervously scramble away, chuckling the whole time. I glared at him before facing Nora.

"I couldn't sleep," I told her, "so I came out to get something to drink. I guess I woke Caleb in the process. Since we were both up, we started talking about our plan."

"At two in the morning?" Nora asked. When I nodded, she glanced at Caleb, her hands on her hips. "So was this the plan to get into Hell? Or the plan to get into Cassie's pants?"

"Hey," I yelled at her.

"Jealous?" Caleb asked at the same time.

Although Nora begrudgingly accepted Caleb's newfound purpose, she still had reservations about it, and she couldn't pretend to be happy having him around. In order to please me, she agreed to work with him, but never said she'd be nice about it. This wasn't the first time I had to intervene in one of their verbal battles.

"It's obvious, Cassie, he's still after you," she said, staring Caleb down. "Do you actually think she's going to forget everything you did to her? To all of us? Well, I won't. I don't trust you, Caleb, and I'm just waiting for you to step over that line. The second you do, I'll have the Elders on your ass so quickly, you'll beg to go back to Hell. Remember that."

"It's not your line to draw," he challenged. "Last I checked, Cassie took care of herself. She's the one who saved your ass in the first place." He was recalling the time I sacrificed my soul for hers, after he inadvertently captured her while trying to get to me. "See?" He flashed her a wicked smile. "I can remember a lot of things."

"Okay, that's enough." I moved in front of Nora, symbolically blocking their line of fire. I had to tread lightly. I needed to keep Caleb close without tipping my hand to Nora that something more was going on. "Nora, he's right. Even if I did feel threatened by him, which I don't, I can take care of myself. He didn't have to come back and help me, but he did, and that means a lot to me."

"Enough to let him touch you?" she asked as she glared at him with blatant revulsion. "How can you just forget what he was?"

Watching Caleb sneer back at Nora, I realized the answer to her question.

"Look at his eyes, Nora. See what color they are? I'm more the demon that disgusts you now than he is."

I felt horrible. Not only was I keeping things from my best friend...*again*...but I was using my status as a demon to do it. God, what had I become? Maybe my demon blood was more potent than I thought.

"Cassie, I didn't mean—" Nora started, but I raised my hands in surrender before she could say anything else.

"You know what? I'm going back to bed," I said. "Caleb, we can talk about this when I get up. Try not to kill each other."

I crossed the living room and made it to the hallway when I heard Caleb say, "Nice. I think you just hurt her more than I ever could. Way to go, *best friend*." Then the door slammed.

He's right, I thought, climbing back into bed.

***

The sunlight streamed in the room following patterns from the blinds I forgot to close when I collapsed into bed. I squinted from the glare, but couldn't resist looking directly into the brilliant rays. They reminded me of the light that radiated against the dark, concrete walls in my dream.

It was another dream of Hell, taking me further into its depths than before. *It begins in the open doorway, with the forest at my back. I stand, staring down the long, dank hall of what looks like an endless corridor of stone walls. There is an illumination barely visible and far-off in the distance, calling me toward it, not with words, but energy just as clear. I feel its invitation pulling me further in, but gripping the side of the doorway to hold myself back, I fight its magnetism. My heart pounds, sweat glistens on my skin, and I swear I hear my name being called from the shadowy depths. It's as if gravity forces me forward, and having no alternative, I venture down the uneven steps. A harrowing growl jolts me from my trance. Instinctively, I run back up the steps, into the forest, and ultimately wake up in my bed.*

I threw the comforter off me, feeling the warmth of the sun beating into the room, burning me up. My restless sleep left me more exhausted than when I hit the pillow. The dreams may have changed in content, but their effects on me didn't. Their cryptic nature always confused me, but I had a feeling I knew what this one was trying to tell me. I had to talk with Caleb. It was time to formalize the plan to get to Hell and set it in motion.

Standing, blood rushed to my head, and I had to lean against my dresser until the dizziness passed. When the room came back into focus, I spotted the sweatpants and T-shirt I'd haphazardly thrown to the floor earlier and put them on. Barefoot, I stepped out of my room and saw Nora heading into the living room from the hallway. She obviously hadn't heard me come out because when I called her, she jumped and spun around.

"Holy crap," she yelled. "Cassie, where the hell did you come from?"

"What do you mean?" I asked, confused. "I woke up and came out. Why are you so surprised? I told you guys I was going back to bed this morning."

Her eyebrows furrowed above her eyes as she stared at me, gnawing on her lower lip, like she was completely disoriented.

"Helloooo," I said, uncomfortable and nervous from her puzzled expression.

"Sorry, it's just that...well...I checked in your room and you weren't in there, or at least I didn't think you were."

"What?" I stared at her as if *she* were the one that woke up feeling the effects of some crazy dream. "You couldn't have, or you didn't look for me very well. I was in bed the whole time. I woke up, threw my clothes on, and came out."

She shook her head, her eyebrows still furrowed, continuing to battle with something in her head. Finally, with a half shrug, she said, "Maybe you were under the covers, or something, and I didn't see you. Weird. Anyway, I was looking for you because I wanted to talk to you before I go to work. I feel really bad about what I said last night."

I went into the living room and sat on the sofa. Nora followed. "It's no big deal. I know you didn't mean to hurt me." I tried to blow it off, even though it *did* bother me. Talking about it was a huge reminder I was a demon. Even though it would help me get my dad back, it was still hard to come to terms with realizing I was descended from someplace so evil...well, half of me was anyway.

"That's no excuse," she said, a sad look on her face. "You're my best friend, and you've always been so pure and kind-hearted to me. You've been a Guardian for as long as I've known you, and I can't see you any other way. The only demons I've ever encountered have tried to hurt innocent people, including us. Not too long ago, *Caleb* threatened to kill me and take you to Hell with him. That's all I've ever seen a demon do, you know, be...evil. But you're not. I know you're much better than that, Cassie, and it's why I love you."

She enveloped me in a hard, bear hug, like she was trying to squeeze the forgiveness out of me, or maybe the demon. Hearing her apology, I couldn't help but think of another demon we'd encountered she forgot to mention. One who didn't try to hurt us. In fact, he went against his entire nature to try and save us all. I contemplated bringing this to her attention, but chose steer away from that talk for now.

Still wrapped in her embrace, I told her, "It's okay, I forget too, sometimes." She pulled back, and I gazed into her beautiful green eyes. "I don't *feel* evil. As a matter of fact, I don't feel any different than I did before I found out what I am. I know you've been through a lot, Nora...because of me. I don't blame you for feeling the way you do about them. I still feel that way too most times. When Caleb first came back, it's all I could see him as. Even though I knew he'd changed, I kept remembering the awful things he did to me, to all of us. But he has changed. He's proven himself to me many times, and I have to give him a chance."

"Do you really have feelings for him then?" she asked.

Her question made me consider what I truly felt for Caleb. I knew the memories of what happened would never fully disappear, but I almost pitied him. He was like me, probably better. He couldn't change what he was back then any more than I could drain the demon blood from my body. More importantly, he was no longer the monster from before. Caleb was doing everything in his power to prove himself, and all I could do was cringe at every contact he tried to make with me. When we kissed, I definitely felt something good. But I couldn't be sure it wasn't me simply replacing what I'd lost with Hunter.

Hunter was gone, I had to face that fact. But could I actually bring myself to experience something new and exciting with Caleb? He was a Guardian now, and might very well turn out to be the best way to keep me on the good guy side. Maybe I should give myself the chance.

"I don't know," I told Nora. "It's like those feelings I had for him when we first met keep creeping back. Whenever we get close, I can feel something between us, you know?"

"Well, he's still hot," she said with a snide grin. "There's no denying that. And he hasn't lost his charm at all, at least not toward you. Me, however, he despises."

"You don't give him much of a choice, Nora."

"I know, I know. I haven't been the nicest person to him, but I've been trying to protect you. And I guess I have been a little bit prejudiced. I'll ease up, okay?"

"It would make it easier working together anyway," I said. "Right now, all I really want to do is get my dad back. I can deal with what happens between Caleb and me later."

Nora nodded. We sat in silence together on the couch for some time afterwards. Being lost in my own thoughts about everything that might happen, I thought she was too, until I glanced over and saw her quietly studying me.

"What is it?"

"What about Hunter?" Her question was blunt, normal for her, but it was so completely unexpected, my heart quickened. It was amazing how the mere mention of his name could still make that happen.

"What about him?"

"Cassie, you know what I mean. You can't act like nothing happened. You're still hurting. After he was taken away, you never let yourself grieve over it. You were too wrapped up in helping your mom. You've kept it all bottled up; there's no way you're over it all."

She was right. After Hunter was taken back to Hell, my mom went into a deep depression over her discovery that my father was a demon, still alive and being tortured in Hell. It was a hard thing to endure, so I threw everything I had into being there for her and doing my best to help her function. It took a long time for her to get back into life again. She still wasn't the same strong force I used to go to for refuge and fortification, but at least, she was starting to live. Her visions came back, and she was saving souls again. Once I was finally able to let her be on her own, Caleb came back into the picture, so I never had a chance to stop and think about my own loss. But at the time, that was a good thing. I didn't want to think about it.

"What does it matter anyway?" I asked, probably a little more forcefully than I should have, which only supported her allegations. "I mean, he's gone. There's nothing I can do about it."

"Are you sure?"

"What do you mean?"

She leaned forward and grabbed my hands. "What if you could get him out too? I mean, maybe you can change him like you did Caleb."

I thought about it. Hell, I'd thought about it countless times since discovering I'd changed Caleb. But therein lay the problem. There was no way I could get into Hell *without* Caleb, and no way to get Hunter *with* him.

"I can't," I said. "I have to let him go."

"But why? If you still love him, why wouldn't you try?"

"There's no way, Nora, okay?" I said, pulling my hands away. "There's no way I'm getting him out of there. I won't even be able to get near him."

"How do you know?" Her eyes grew wide as realization hit. "Caleb won't let you," she whispered.

"Right. Caleb would only agree to help me find my dad if I promised I wouldn't try to help Hunter too."

Nora became quiet...too quiet, deep in thought over what, I didn't know. It was simple enough to me—Caleb wanted to be with me so there was no way I could get near Hunter.

I couldn't stand her silence a second longer. "Yeah, well, so that's it..." I said as I got up from the sofa.

"What if someone else got him out?"

I spun to face her. "Who?"

"Me." She got up and stood in front of me. "What if I went with you and got Hunter out?"

Her words finally registered. "Are you crazy? No way, Nora. No. Freaking. Way. I am not letting you go down there."

"After all I've done, it would be my way of making things up to you."

"By giving up your soul? *No.* I'm not letting you, and that's final. He's not worth the loss of you. Promise me you won't even think about this again. I mean it," I shouted at her, grabbing her upper arms.

She winced, and I loosened my grip, but didn't let go. "Promise me," I said, my tone softer, but still firm enough to let her know I was serious.

"Okay, I promise."

We didn't say much after that. Nora eventually left for work, and I replayed her offer a thousand times in my head. While I wouldn't consider letting her get Hunter for me, I couldn't help thinking of other ways I might be able to free him myself.

CHAPTER THREE

"You know the TV's not on, right?"

I shot up from the couch, surprised by Caleb's question as he stood in the doorway with groceries in hand. Deeply immersed in thoughts of a plan I knew would never come to fruition, I didn't hear him come in.

"What?" I asked.

He nodded toward the TV as he set the groceries down on the breakfast bar.

I turned and realized I had been staring at the black television screen.

"Daydreaming?" he asked.

"Uh...yeah, I guess so."

"Anything good?" He started taking the groceries out of the bags and putting them into the cupboards.

"What?" I asked again lamely.

After a few moments of silence, I glanced up and noticed he was standing in the open refrigerator door, a jug of orange juice in hand, staring at me. "Cassie, what's up?"

I felt like a complete space cadet and forced myself to snap out of it. I moved to help him put the rest of the groceries away, averting my eyes, afraid he could somehow read my thoughts and discover what I'd been fantasizing about. I had to stop. I needed to face reality.

"Nothing," I said, reaching into one of the bags, only to find it empty. I had nothing else to occupy myself with, so I stared at my hands as my fingers tapped away on the countertop. "Nora just left and we were talking about going down to Hell. I was thinking about my dad and how I need to get to him. I don't want to wait any long—"

My hands were gently pulled off the countertop as Caleb turned me around to face him.

"Cassie, slow down. We'll get your dad, but we have to think this through," he said, bending so we were at eye level. "Come away with me."

"Where?"

"We need to get out of this apartment. Every time we try to talk, we get interrupted. I want to help you, but we need somewhere we can talk things through, somewhere private. Let me take you to dinner."

I noticed his thumbs were making brush strokes across the backs of my hands, but I didn't pull away. I studied him, looking for some ulterior motive, but all I saw was his sparkling green eyes gazing sincerely into mine.

"That's private?"

"Well, I didn't think you'd go for a motel room, so it's Plan B. Unless, of course, you're okay with Plan A?"

His beautiful smile was accentuated by deeply set dimples, which outlined both corners of his mouth. This was the Caleb I first met, in seemed like so long ago at a bar named Luke's. It was the old Caleb, who joked with me as we sat in the grass, eating greasy burgers in the park. The guy whose flirtations made me blush...*and* fantasize. Of course, that was before he turned into a monster.

"No, I think somewhere quiet for dinner will be just fine," I said returning his smile.

"Great. It's a date then." I opened my mouth to correct him, but he placed a finger over my lips. "Just...let me have my moment, okay?" I nodded, and his hands moved to each side of my neck, beneath my hair. "Now, go pick out a nice dress, and I'll make the arrangements. Can you be ready in an hour?"

"Caleb, let's just go grab a bite to eat somewhere. We don't need to make this a formal affair. We're not hitting the town, we're going to talk about getting into Hell." I pulled away from him and tried to hide my face, but his hand came back up, preventing me from escaping.

"Please, Cassie, let me have this night. I know what we're going to talk about, but...I don't know...I need to feel like I'm with you in more than a business relationship. What I did to you, what I was...that's not me anymore. Every day I've wanted to celebrate becoming a Guardian again, because it feels so good to know I'm no longer the evil thing I once was. But I can't because I still feel guilty about what I did to you. All I want is for you to see me for what I am now, what I can be to you. Not only what I can do for you."

As I studied him and heard his pleading tone, trying so hard to right the wrongs he had no control over, *I* started to feel like the evil one. Was I so hard now I couldn't forgive him for something that wasn't even his fault? None of us asked for this life. I, of all people should know our paths were chosen for us and we were simply along for the ride, doing what was necessary and expected. There were far greater forces at work here. He was playing my heartstrings, which sang a sad melody I felt deep in my soul.

For the first time, I could see him for who and what he was now. Even the worst incarnations of evil could change, and from this point forward, I would try to honor that. He was willing to put his life back in the line of fire to help me, and at the very least, he deserved my respect. Maybe even a second chance.

"Okay," I said quietly, connecting with his gaze. "Let's go on a date then. But you better make it worth my while if I have to put on a pair of heels."

Caleb chuckled and surprised me by placing a tender kiss on my lips before quickly pulling away.

"It'll be worth more than your while, I promise," he whispered.

He backed away and got on his cell. I stood somewhat stunned as I heard him make reservations. He gave me an impatient expression, waving me off to go get ready. I smiled to myself as I hurried to my bedroom to find a dress appropriate enough for a dinner I knew he'd make extravagant. I was giddy about it all of a sudden. Or was it simply nerves?

***

As I sat down in the cushioned chair offered me, I glanced out at the view of the city below in amazement. I completely missed the waiter's introduction, internally contemplating how in the world Caleb was able to pull off private balcony reservations in less than an hour. We were at one of the most sought after French restaurants on the outskirts of the city. When we walked in, I gave an audible sigh of relief to see there were others in the restaurant. Demons could make anyone disappear in order to be alone with their prey. Caleb had, in fact, done it to me before. But after seeing the other patrons, I berated myself for thinking he might be back to his old ways.

"Caleb, this is gorgeous," I said, staring out into the clear night. Off in the distance, the lights from the downtown nightlife illuminated the sky, imbuing it with an electric gleam amid the outlying blackness. Our balcony shone from the soft glow of a few outdoor dining chandeliers that dangled from the varnished wooden overhang, highlighting various hanging plants and beautifully adorned planters situated on the floor. There were several more private balconies like ours located along the side of the restaurant, all too far away to hear their occupants' conversations. Faint music from inside the restaurant was audible through the curtained patio opening.

I closed my eyes, listening to the soft music, relishing the tranquility of it all as a slight, warm breeze blew across my skin. Summer was only beginning to smother the damp chill that sometimes lingered in spring, and it was always a welcome change to the long, cold winters in the Midwest.

A murmur of voices broke me from my inner musings, and I opened my eyes to catch the waiter leaving. A bottle of wine was chilling in a bucket beside our table. A candle flickered inside a tempered glass between us, creating a romantic aura that lit up Caleb's face as he smiled at me.

His hand seemed to approach me in slow motion. Gently, he placed his fingers under my chin and brushed his thumb along the line of my jaw. "*This* is gorgeous," he whispered, as his thumb moved over to my lips.

The compliment rendered me speechless, whether it was because it was so unexpected, or because it had been so long since I'd gotten one. A silly smile took over my lips before I quickly took great interest in my wine glass.

Caleb chuckled, and then ice cubes tinkled against the bucket as he pulled the bottle of wine free.

"You have a beautiful smile. I wish I could see it more often," he said, filling my glass.

"I guess I haven't had a lot to smile about lately." I gazed at him across the table. His expression turned as his hand stopped on its way to putting the bottle of wine back in the bucket.

"I know," he said, turning back to me, his eyes locking on mine. "I'd do anything to change that."

I didn't mean to make him feel guilty over my unhappiness. In an effort to take my comment back, I reached out and grabbed his hand across the table. "You are. You're helping me now. Getting my dad back means everything to me. Thank you, Caleb."

"Don't thank me—"

"No, I *do* need to thank you. You've done everything you could to help me since you came back, and I've been horrible to you. I'm sorry."

"I don't want your apology, Cassie. I just want a chance. Do you think we can start over? I mean, *really* start over?"

As he gently squeezed my fingers, I realized I liked how it felt. When my eyes took in his face, I saw a beautiful man, who was willing to go into the fires of Hell for me. Most women would die to have a man like Caleb looking at them the way he was looking at me. I was over his previous existence as a demon. There was nothing else holding me back from giving in to him. God knows I was attracted to him, both physically and mentally. He not only knew what I was, but what I feared becoming. It was a relief to relax and be myself with someone.

I took his other hand in mine, squeezing them both. With a sincere smile I finally felt, I told him, "Yes. I'd like that."

"Great." He pulled his hands from mine and raised his glass, waiting for me to do the same. "Here's to new beginnings, then."

I picked up my glass and studied the red wine inside. "Wait. Do you really think I'd drink this, Caleb, without knowing where it came from?"

His eyes grew smaller as his expression turned grim, and I could see his anger building. Apparently, I'd gone too far with my teasing.

"Where'd you get all the money for this?" I smiled playfully. "There's no way I'm doing dishes."

"Ha-ha-ha. Drink up, beautiful. I got this covered."

"Yeah? How?"

"Hey, I have skills, you know. I've got an identity and a job now."

"What? How? When?" *And where the hell was I?*

"What did you think I was doing all those times I left the apartment? Which reminds me, I can start paying for part of the rent now. It's amazing how easy it is to create a whole new life. Not like it used to be."

I gaped at him. I never even thought about how he was going to filter back into society. Of course, he had to make a living. I simply didn't expect him to be working on it without me knowing.

"So what do you do? Wait. Should I even be calling you Caleb?" I realized I was practically attacking him with my interrogation. "I'm sorry."

"Don't be. We haven't had a chance to talk about this and it all happened quickly. I wasn't expecting to land a job right away, but the local clinic happened to lose their best practitioner a few weeks ago. They were only too happy to take me on." He mocked a bow. "Dr. Caleb Walker, at your service."

"What? You're a doctor? But how? That takes years of schooling and—"

"I have all that. I used to be an ER doctor before I became a Seeker."

I was blown away. Not only that he'd been a doctor at some point in time, but that he remembered his life from before he was turned. As far as I knew, Seekers lost all memories of their former lives as Guardians.

"You got your memory back?" I asked.

"Yes."

I assumed he'd be happy about remembering the life he'd lost, almost like an amnesia victim who finally regains his memory after awakening to a foreign world. From the look on his face, however, that was clearly not the case.

"My previous life ended painfully. It's a memory I wish I *could* forget."

I grabbed his hands across the table again, comforting him for whatever he seemed to be reliving. I felt horrible for bringing it up.

"I'm sorry," I said.

"There you go again, apologizing. Stop it."

"I didn't know. I just figured—"

"You couldn't have known," he said, squeezing my hands before pulling away. "But I think you *should* know. It's part of who I am...or was. It's how I became a Seeker, or rather, *why* I became one. I was engaged to a beautiful woman, to whom I was completely and utterly devoted. She was a kindergarten teacher with the heart of an angel, no pun intended. We planned to be married in a few weeks. At my bachelor party, I got a vision of her...she was going to die. She was going to be in a huge crash and crushed in her car, but would painfully hang onto life for far too long."

He stopped and I could tell he was mentally reliving it all again, choking up from the vision of seeing the love of his life in so much pain. I waited for him to continue.

"I knew I couldn't get to her in time because I had been partying heavily." His eyes filled with tears, threatening to fall. "I was too drunk to save the one person I would have given up everything for. I knew it even before I stole someone's keys and got into his car. But I wasn't the only one who knew. The Seeker who targeted me also knew. And that's when I agreed to let him turn me. I lost her, but at least, she didn't go before her time."

Caleb's story was so heartbreaking I was on the verge of tears myself. He sacrificed himself and was willing to spend an eternity in Hell for her. After knowing that, it was hard to imagine he'd ever been as evil as I once thought. I felt like running around the table and taking him in my arms, and I almost did, but the waiter showed up with our food, eclipsing the moment.

When the waiter left, I asked, "Have you looked her up?"

"No," he said, shaking his head as he placed his napkin in his lap. "That was a long time ago. She would have moved on by now, and I don't want to interrupt her life by coming back from the dead. She knew I was a Guardian, but Guardians die. At least, that's what she thought. No, that part of my life is over." He picked up his glass and held it out to me again, a fresh smile on his face. "I'm starting a new one, remember? And I could really use one of your smiles to help me get it going."

I gazed back at him, internally sympathizing because all he wanted to do was put that life behind him. I wouldn't drag it out with pity. I knew all too well how hard it was to try and forget, and how impossible it could be to move on.

With a genuine smile, I tapped his glass with my own. "To starting over."

We sealed our new relationship with unspoken words as we gazed across the flickering candle at each other. I saw him in a whole different light, and the image of him being a savior began to overshadow that of him being my predator. I knew I'd never be able to forget what he'd done, and my defenses would always be on alert after all the things I'd seen. However, I was even more willing to offer him a chance now, knowing who he once was, and could potentially be again.

The conversation turned much lighter as we ate, and the food was as delicious as the atmosphere predicted it would be. We talked about places we always wanted to see, our dreams of what our lives might have been if we hadn't been saddled with the fate of others, and destined to grow up as Guardians. I found out Caleb's entire family died on the day he graduated Med School in a fatal car crash. Silently, I wondered if this was why, as a Seeker, he often chose terrible accidents in an effort to get nearer to his victims. Maybe there was something that crossed over when Guardians were turned, without their knowing it. Perhaps, it was like bits of DNA passing from one existence to the next.

Personally, I hoped I never found out.

CHAPTER FOUR

I was finally enjoying myself, setting aside all the stress in my life for an opportunity to feel normal. Who would have thought Caleb would be the source of my happiness? I never realized how funny he was, and how easily I could laugh after all I'd endured. It felt...revitalizing.

"Have I told you how beautiful you are tonight?" he asked, bringing the lighthearted conversation to a serious halt.

"Only about a thousand times." I laughed, trying not to let his appraising eyes make me nervous.

"Well, then, I'm sorry for repeating myself, but I can't help it. That dress looks amazing on you."

I peered down at the dress, more to avoid blushing again than to remind myself of what I was wearing. It was sleek and emerald-colored. The matte material formed comfortably over the curves of my body. Only one side suspended a wispy drape of the fabric, while my left shoulder was bare

"It's Nora's. My wardrobe is lacking in the formal department, so I stole it from her."

"I think it's designed for you. It brings out the red in your hair." I held my breath as he reached across the table and caressed a lock of it that hung over my shoulder. His fingers brushed my bare skin as our eyes met, penetrating, fastening on mine. "And your eyes are practically glowing. Gorgeous."

My nerves won out as my mind raced for something to extract me from such an intimate moment. I wasn't ready for this. My defensive wall was not ready to come down so completely. The mention of my eyes brought me back to why I'd agreed to come out in the first place.

"Caleb, we really need to talk about—"

"I know, I know," he said, sighing as he leaned back in his chair. "There's only one more thing I want to do, and then we can spend the rest of the time talking about Hell, okay?"

"What is it?" I asked, wary, but still curious.

He held his palm up to me and called the waiter over. After whispering in his ear, the waiter nodded and took our dinner plates away. I was about to ask what he was up to when the melody of the restaurant music filled our balcony. I looked up and realized there was a tiny speaker above the curtained doorway to amplify the music being played inside.

"It seems a shame to hide that dress all night behind the table," Caleb said, bringing my attention back to him. He was standing with his arm outstretched in invitation. "Dance with me?"

I stared at his hand for what seemed like forever, rooted to my seat, contemplating the intimacy that came with what he was asking. This would be my first test of whether I could really handle Caleb's touch. The kiss we shared earlier that morning didn't register with me, as I was too wrapped up in another memory to realize whom I was with. But I knew now, and even welcomed his presence, which was more than I'd allowed myself to do since he returned. Could I take the next step? Or was it too soon? Would the images of him glaring at me with those devilish blue eyes, as if he intended to devour me, come flooding back, sending me running away as fast as I could?

I pushed the thoughts aside, concentrating on the man who made me laugh tonight, and died for someone he loved long ago. Standing, I smiled back and placed my hand in his. He led me around the table without a word, pausing as I came into full view. He eyed me over with an appreciative gaze. I thought I heard a barely perceptible moan before he continued leading me to the open space in front of the balcony rail. Moving in front of me, he gently rested his hands on the small of my back, and I placed my hands on his shoulders. I didn't know what to do with my head, so I leaned back awkwardly. Wearing heels put my eyes in line with his nose, and I was afraid to look up or down for fear of instigating some kind of reaction from his eyes or mouth. My body was already responding to being pressed against his. I quickly blew it off as nerves.

Caleb leaned in. "Relax, Cassie," he whispered in my ear. "Let your body go."

The pressure of his fingers in my back urged me closer, and I let myself lean into him, resting my head on his shoulder. We swayed slowly, making small circles together in what little space we had. My body eventually relaxed against his, and I got lost in the rhythm of the music as we danced. Eyes closed, I inhaled his fresh, clean scent that somehow soothed my senses even more.

"This is nice," he said, pressing his head into mine, while squeezing me gently with his arms.

"Yes, it is." I was surprised at how good it felt to be wrapped in his arms. It wasn't a new feeling, but it *was* with someone new. My hands went around his neck as we continued. "I can't remember the last time I danced like this."

He sighed. "Good. I like being the only one for you."

His words took my breath away, their intent not lost on me. The music ended, and I didn't have time to respond, when he started leading me back toward the table again.

"Thank you for the dance," he said, pulling out my chair. "It meant a lot to me."

I sat, and he moved back across the table. "It was nice for me too, Caleb. Really nice. But—"

"Yes, I know." He groaned. "It's time to talk business."

I really wanted to talk about what he just said to me, not exactly comfortable with the possessive nature of it, but decided to let it go and move forward with our conversation about getting into Hell as long as he was offering. I was probably reading too much into it anyway. That wall of mine seemed to come with all sorts of imaginary accusations.

"Right. So how are you going to get me in?" I asked.

"To be honest, I don't know if I can. I've never taken someone into Hell with me until they were turned. And you can't turn."

He was right, even after drinking his blood to save the lives of my friends and family, nothing happened. This was apparently unprecedented in the Seeker world. We assumed it was owing to the fact that I was already half-demon.

"So if you can't get me in, how did you plan to help me?"

He studied me, as if weighing what he was about to say next. Leaning forward, he said, "I'm going to teach you how to be a Seeker, so you can get in yourself. That is, if the Elders don't come and strike me down before I get the chance. This is serious stuff, Cassie. We're messing around with two powerfully guarded worlds here. Getting into Hell may be the least of our problems."

"I know. I've thought about that. A lot. I'm hoping Nora is their only source of info on me, but I doubt it. Anael could be another," I said thinking out loud. "But she helped me before, so maybe she won't be a problem either."

"Yeah, but Anael only helped you to keep you out of Sheol. Since she's back with the angels, we can't count on that."

He was right. After enduring years of life in Hell as Negal's queen, Anael had finally severed her loyalty to him to keep me, her descendent, from incurring the same fate as my father. I was still confused as to why Hadraniel, one of the most powerful angels, and her lover from which our bloodline was created, saved her from Nergal's hand at the hilt of the Sword of Final Death. Maybe he was finally willing to forgive her infidelity. I may never know. Regardless, her loyalty resided with Hadraniel again, and he made it quite clear if I ever showed any signs of my demon bloodline, I'd instantly be considered an enemy. In his eyes, the lines that distinguished the two worlds were clearly black and white, and I was to be monitored, so my gray blood never dripped over that line.

"I don't care who's watching me anymore. Where were they when my dad was being turned? No. If I changed you back, there's a chance I can do the same for my dad. Who knows? If this works out, I might become their greatest asset in this war."

"But if it doesn't?" he asked, playing the devil's advocate.

"If it doesn't, I'll deal with the consequences one way or another, but I'm sick and tired of sitting back and wondering *what if*. I've been a puppet for too long. Now that I know I have the potential to fight, I need to cut the strings and do something about it. There's a reason I was created the way I was. I have to believe that, and I have to seek out my purpose."

"Okay, okay," he said, both arms up in surrender. "You don't need to sell yourself to me. I already know how important you are. I'm on your side, Cassie." He grabbed my hands again and gave them a squeeze. "No matter what happens, I'm on your side."

His eyes told me he meant what he said as we gazed across the table at each other. I was shaking from the blood pumping through my veins, talking about what could come of everything we were setting out to do, but I found his firm belief in me very calming.

"Thank you." I smiled, squeezing his hand back.

"Anything for you. Now, let's get you into Hell. Every Seeker has a portal of entry. You're not going to find the doorway anywhere but here," he said, pointing to his head. "It's not just any doorway either. You'll feel a connection to it. It will draw you in and call to you. I don't know how it'll work for you, though. Mine simply appeared after I was turned and was there for me every time I wanted to go back. It just seems to know."

My mind quickly thought of the doorway I'd seen in my dreams. I knew it led to Hell, but never thought it would literally be the entrance. Could it be that easy? And why all of a sudden did it appear? It never did before. Had I unconsciously let it in?

"I think I've already seen it."

"What? When?"

"Remember I told you I'd been having dreams about Hell? There's a doorway, a big stone doorway I uncovered. When the door opened, I knew it led into Hell. I don't know how, but I knew."

"That's got to be it, Cassie," he said sitting straighter in his chair. He appeared excited about the news. "This is going to be easier than I thought. Have you seen it any other time? Besides your dreams? I mean, can you picture it now if you wanted to?"

I closed my eyes and thought about the large boulder in the forest.

"No," Caleb yelled, and I blinked my eyes open, frightened by his outburst. "Not now." His tone was softer, but his determination remained evident.

"Why? What's wrong?"

"Didn't you hear me when I said it draws you in?" He was angry, but reined it in after noticing he scared me. "If you call it on your own, I don't know if you can resist its pull, and you're not ready to go there by yourself. I have to figure out a way we can do it together. I want to be ready when you do. You'll be lost in Sheol without me, and I don't know if I'll be able to get you back."

"Okay," I said, overwhelmed that I was so close. I'd been itching to get this plan in motion, but now that I knew I could be in Hell at any moment, I was nervous. He was right. I would have no idea where to find my dad without him. Then another fear crept into my head. "But what about my dreams? What if it pulls me in without me even knowing it? Could that happen?"

"I don't know," he said. We both sat in contemplative silence. Scenarios of me aimlessly wandering through the corridors of Hell ran rampant through my head. I pictured different forms of torture designed solely for me, reaching out from doorways or pits, grasping at me wherever I went. Panic began to swell inside of me. Suddenly, I felt so alone.

"Cassie," Caleb brought me back, his eyes serious. "This is going to sound like a line, but I need to watch over you when you sleep tonight. If you go to Sheol again, that's the only way I'll know."

I eyed him skeptically. What he said didn't make sense. "But how would you know what's happening in my dreams?"

"When a Seeker enters that doorway in his mind, his body goes with it. You've seen us disappear before. That's what happens. Remember?"

There were several times I watched Caleb disappear before my eyes. They all did—angels *and* demons. It was pretty amazing to watch. I remembered my conversation with Nora this morning. I told Caleb how Nora thought I was gone because she didn't see me when she checked my bedroom, although I knew I never left the room.

"She looked completely baffled by it," I explained.

"That must be where you were. Okay, no arguments. I'm staying by your side tonight. We can stay on the couch if it makes you more comfortable, but I'm not leaving you alone."

Thinking of Caleb by my side while I slept made me uncomfortable on many different levels, but the thought of being lost and alone in the Underworld overruled any anxiety I had about him. I handled him before, even as a demon. I'd do it again if I had to.

"Okay, no arguments here. But if I do disappear, what are you going to do? How will you get me back?"

"I won't," he said with deadly calm. "I'll have to come find you in Hell. Explain what you see in your dreams as best you can."

I detailed everything I could remember for him. He made me describe what I saw, what I smelled, and what I heard. But my description of the loud growling in the passageway seemed to affect him the most. I saw it in the twitch of his eyes, the way his body tensed, and I knew there was something about this morsel of information that alarmed him.

When he noticed I was watching him closely, waiting for him to say something, and tell me why he had reacted the way he did, he nodded. "I'm pretty sure I know where it is. I've been there before. I'll find you."

I waited for more, but Caleb didn't continue. Instead, he picked up his glass of wine, took a long gulp, and waved the waiter over. After paying the bill, he stood. "It's late. Why don't we get going? We've figured out how to get you in, or at least, where you need to go. Tomorrow, we can go over what to do when—"

"Who was it, Caleb?"

He continued putting on his dinner jacket. "Who was what?"

"Who did I hear in my dream? Who was crying out down there? Was it my dad? Did I hear him being tortured? Please tell me. It'll only hurt worse if you don't."

"No, it wasn't your dad," he said. "There are many tortured souls in Sheol, Cassie. It's Hell, after all. It could be any number of different demons, but I know it wasn't your dad. He stays very close to Nergal, and Nergal is in the heart of the Underworld. You can relax. It wasn't him, trust me."

I sat in my chair for a minute, while he stood behind it, waiting to pull it out for me. I got up slowly, grabbing my purse from the floor as I did.

"Ready?" he asked, putting his arm across the small of my back.

"Yes."

I walked through the restaurant in a daze, reaching the car as if on automatic pilot. Caleb made small talk as we drove home, something about the weather or his new job. I listened enough to give sensible responses, but my thoughts were obsessing over what he said in the restaurant—*trust me.* I wanted to trust him, I really did, but the look on his face when I told him about what I heard in that corridor warned me he was hiding something. But why? If it were my dad, I already knew he was being tortured, and while it would have hurt to know it was him, it wouldn't have shocked me. Was that it? Was he trying to protect me because he thought I couldn't handle it? I had to find out.

CHAPTER FIVE

Pulling into the parking garage, I noticed Nora's spot was empty. It was disappointing, since I wanted to get her take on everything. I knew her first reaction would be to accuse Caleb of having some kind of doomsday plan for us, but I was more interested in what she thought about my experience in Sheol. In the meantime, maybe I could get Caleb to come clean.

When we made it up to the apartment, Caleb unlocked and opened the door with a silly grin. Stepping into the living room, I was bombarded by a strong, sweet fragrance, which the apartment surrendered to completely. Sitting in the middle of the breakfast bar was the biggest, most beautiful bouquet of red roses I'd ever seen. With wide eyes, I ran to them.

"How did you..." I inhaled their scent while I stood over them.

Caleb was next to me, picking one of the red beauties from the huge glass vase. He held it up to his nose, mimicking my actions, seemingly as drawn in by their enticing aroma as I. Our eyes locked, and I recalled our first *date* when he gave me a rose he picked from a garden in the park. I remembered feeling as if the flower held some kind of power over me, its fragrance more potent than any other. I thought it was a sign then; a sign Caleb was someone special. He turned out to be special, all right—a demon after my soul. Would I make the same mistake twice? I was determined not to be the naïve, love-struck girl I was then, but I couldn't jump to the other extreme and become some paranoid person who thought everyone was out to get me. I wouldn't live like that.

I smiled at him. "Thank you, Caleb. They're beautiful."

Eyes transfixed on my face, he moved the rose toward me, brushing it along my cheek. Closing my eyes, I sighed, relishing the feel of the soft petals against my skin as they made their way down my jaw. His hand came up to cup the back of my head. When I opened my eyes, I saw the longing in his, the green orbs sparkling as if to hypnotize me.

"They're my peace offering for starting over. I gave you one once before, only to deceive you in the most unimaginable way. But not this time. This time, I assure you, my intentions are pure."

"So, you're not trying to seduce me?" I asked, only to prolong what I knew was coming. I wasn't sure I was ready for it. His lids were getting heavy, and the sexual tension was building between us.

Gentle pressure at the back of my neck pulled me closer. His face was so close I could smell the wine we shared on his breath.

"I said my intentions were pure. That doesn't mean I don't intend to seduce you, Cassie."

His lips were on mine, kissing me tenderly at first, until his need grew. He teased his tongue against my lips, and I let it slip inside to mesh with mine. Shivers ran down my arms when his fingertips caressed my neck. I reached for his hair, tugging at the short, blond strands, attempting to convince myself I still maintained some control.

When his hands went to my waist, pulling my hips against his arousal, I gasped. My reaction fired his passion, and he pushed me back against the counter. After trailing succulent kisses down my neck, his mouth rested on the bare, sensitive spot between my neck and shoulder. I raised my heavy lids, indifferent to my surroundings, until I caught a reflective light shining in the framed picture on the wall across the room. After realizing there was no way the small light from the kitchen could have been the source of the glow in the frame, I strained my eyes to try and make out what it was. A dark silhouette appeared, and the light reflection became two small, glowing spheres.

Wait. Was that? Oh my God.

My body tensed and I screamed.

Caleb jerked away from me. "What? What is it?" he asked, his eyes darting around the room.

But what I'd seen was already gone.

I couldn't find my voice. I wouldn't know what to say, even if I could. *I saw Hunter glaring at us from the picture across the room?* Caleb would think I was nuts. But those were Hunter's eyes staring back at me. I'd swear by it. They made me feel ashamed, afraid, and deceitful all in the short glimpse I had of them. Maybe my subconscious was playing tricks on me, condemning me for my actions.

"Cassie, what happened?" Caleb demanded.

"I...I saw..."

The phone rang, and I jumped again. My nerves were static. I couldn't move, but my whole body was shaking. Caleb stared, waiting for me to react; to the phone ringing in my purse, to him, to *something*. He let out an exasperated sigh and reached in my purse to pull out my phone. It rang once more in his hand before it stopped.

"It was your mom." He set the phone in my palm and kept his grip on my hand. "Cassie, *what* is wrong with you? You're freaking me out. What did you see?"

Before I could answer, my phone went off again. My mom's name came up on the display. It had to be important if she was calling back so quickly. I gave Caleb an apologetic look before answering.

"Cassie? Cassie, are you okay? Where are you?" My mom's voice was frantic.

"Yeah, I'm fine. I'm at home. Why?"

"I had a dream about you." I could tell she'd been crying. "You were trapped in Hell, and I tried to get to you, but you were out of my reach. And then, when you looked at me..."

I waited for more, but there was only silence. "What, Mom? When you looked at me...what?"

"You had the eyes of a demon," she said in a breathy whisper. "And you told me you didn't want to come out. You said you belonged there."

I glanced over at Caleb. He was leaning against the counter next to me, listening intently.

"It was only a dream, Mom." I knew how real dreams could feel, especially to us. We didn't believe in coincidences, and paid special attention to the visions we had. I'm fine. I'm here in my apartment."

More silence. Then she asked, "Cassie, please tell me you're not going after him."

My stomach dropped. I didn't want her to know. She was finally getting her life together. Not only would it set her back emotionally, but she'd also fight me tooth and nail to prevent me from going. I hated lying to her, but it was for her own good.

"Going after who?" I tried to sound as ignorant as possible. "Hunter."

His name took me by surprise. I expected her to think I was going after my dad, something I promised her I'd do long ago.

"No, I'm not going after him." I'd gotten away without having to lie. After all, I was going in for my dad, not Hunter.

Caleb perked up next to me, realizing what the conversation was about. He gave me an understanding nod, as if he knew how hard it was for me to keep things from her.

"I can't lose you too, Cassie," my mom said, sniffling. "You're all I have left."

I hated this. The truth was, I was risking my life. There was a chance I'd never make it back out. And if that ever happened to me, would be left alone. The responsibility should have been enough to call the whole thing off. But there was something much stronger than guilt compelling me to carry out my promise, whether my mom remembered it or not.

"I promise. It was just a dream, Mom. Get some sleep. I'll stop over tomorrow after work, okay?"

"Okay, honey," she said, sounding more at ease. "I love you."

"I love you, too."

"Everything okay?" Caleb asked when I hung up.

We were both leaning against the counter. He reached over and brushed my arm with the backs of his fingertips, reminding me of what we'd been doing before my mom called. I glanced at the picture frame again, but saw nothing. Still, I turned to face him so his hand was forced away.

"Yeah. She had a dream of me down in Hell, and thought I might be planning to do something crazy."

"Like go get your dad?"

"Yes."

Why I was lying to him was a mystery. Maybe it was because I didn't want to get into it with him about Hunter again. Or it might have had something to do with the chills I still couldn't shake from seeing Hunter's image in the picture frame.

I stared at the floor, trying to avoid Caleb's eyes, but he leaned in, forcing me to make eye contact.

"I'm sorry you had to lie to her. I know how much you hate doing that, but she can't know you're going to Sheol."

"I know."

Shuffling toward the sofa, I watched the picture frame along the way. I kept expecting the glowing eyes to reappear, but there was nothing. I was starting to doubt it even happened. How could it? Hunter was trapped in the depths of Hell. But even if it didn't happen, he was in my head. Would my memories of him ever let me forget?

I dropped onto the sofa cushions, exhausted, my body a dead weight I could no longer hold up. Caleb followed, sitting close by. I leaned my head back and closed my eyes. Feeling his fingers brush my cheek, I let out a sigh.

"What did you see, Cassie?" he asked.

I opened my eyes and met Caleb's gaze. His head was tilted, making him appear like a concerned parent over his child. Taking his hand in mine, I brought it down between us. Even with all of my trust issues, he was the only one I could confess my fears to. I wanted to reveal all of my emotions to him; I was terrified of going to Hell, never coming back and crushing the feeble remnants of my mom's heart, never seeing Nora again. But most of all, I was scared to death of becoming evil, and Caleb was the only one who could relate to that fear. Still, I didn't want to bring up what I thought I saw. He would know I was thinking of Hunter, and I couldn't shove it in his face.

"I honestly don't even know, Caleb. I think it was my mind playing tricks on me. It's nothing. I'm over it."

"Are you sure?" His brows furrowed as he examined me. "You were freaked out by something. Was it me? What we were doing?"

"No. No, it was nothing like that. I saw a shadow or something, but it was probably the lighting in the living room. Really, Caleb, it wasn't that. I was as into it as you were."

He relaxed, and a small smile brightened his features. I returned the sentiment.

When he moved closer, I realized he'd taken my declaration as an invitation to pick up where we left off.

I put my hand on his chest. "I'm really tired, Caleb. Do you think we could just lie here together? Maybe watch some TV or a movie?"

Disappointment flashed in his eyes, but he quickly recovered with another smile. "Yeah, of course. What kind of movies do you guys have?"

I groaned. "Nora and I are kind of the classic horror type, but I don't think I'm in the mood for anything like that, what with Hell right around the corner."

He laughed. "Well, then I guess it's up to me to find something on TV to lighten the mood. But before that, we need to come up with a plan in case you end up in Sheol tonight."

"Okay, what do I do?"

"Nothing."

"Nothing?"

"Nothing. If you end up at that doorway again, you stay put. I'll watch over you here. If I see you disappear, I'll go in and find you. Wait right in the doorway for me. Do not go any further without me."

"Won't I be a sitting duck? What if Nergal or one of his crony demons finds me before you do? How do you know you can still get in?" I felt helpless again and didn't like it. As a demon, I was stronger than Caleb and shouldn't require his protection. Technically, he probably needed mine. When it came down to it, he was merely a navigator. "Why don't you tell me which way to go, and I can meet you halfway? You're going to need me as much as I need you."

"No." His tone was adamant. "If you stay by the doorway, you can always run back out if you don't see me, or worse, if you see someone or something else. They won't come after you outside of Hell. They chance a war with the angels if they do. If we play this right, no one will need anyone, not for what you're implying anyway. We'll slip in and out without anyone knowing. Don't forget, I was right under Nergal's wing. I know all about his routines and how he thinks. I know exactly how to get to your dad without being caught. And if we do get caught, I know how to get us out quickly. If that happens though, we're going to need a lot more help than what you can provide."

I realized then, breaking my dad out was a no-win situation, and I shivered at the thought. Nergal wouldn't hesitate to come and destroy everything around me, and I wouldn't have the protection of Hadraniel's almighty angels anymore. We could come up with a thousand different plans, but the end result would always be the same.

Unless...I gave Nergal something in return. I ran the idea through my head, debating its success, but in the end, I knew it would work. I knew exactly what I would give him.

CHAPTER SIX

After agreeing with Caleb to remain wherever I found myself in dream Hell to wait for him, we tried to ease the tension of what might possibly be the most dangerous night of our lives by watching silly comedies that dated back to when humor wasn't as dark as it was now. Simple innuendos and non-life-threatening accidents made for hours of laughter back in those days. A small smile was harder to come by now that people no longer had the time to stop and appreciate the little, quirky things in life. I, however, never had a simple life to ever miss it.

Thoughts of what might happen once I closed my lids were enough to keep my adrenaline pumping and my body wide awake. But when Caleb snuggled in close, wrapped me up in a blanket, and urged my head in his lap, it was harder to fight the insistence of the darkness.

The stone door silently slides open. A needling feeling warns me not to go any further, to stay where I am and wait. But wait for what? There seems to be no rational reason. No, I have to go deeper. The pull is too strong. I walk down the stone steps that lead into a long hallway made of the same colorless cement as the door. The walls vibrate with a radiant orange glow that flickers in the reflection of an unseen fire. Coming down the steps, my eyes straining, I search in the distance for a door, an opening, something, *but see only a hallway.*

As I walk further, the eerie silence echoes down the length of the passage and back, ironically emphasizing the sense of nothingness surrounding me. Shivers run up my neck, causing the hairs on my naked arms to stand on end. Looking back toward the entry, I see the door sliding shut, threatening to close me inside. I turn, feeling the need to get out of the empty void, determined to get through the door in time, but as I reach the steps, the terrifying sound of a man screaming causes my heart to stop. The torturous wails are haunting, but somehow familiar, and I am frozen in place by them long enough to watch the door shut in front of me.

"I'll kill you," yells the man from behind me, his voice clear.

I turn back toward the corridor, surprised to see a torch attached to the wall at the end of the hallway, revealing an old rusted door on the right. Neither were there a second ago. I run toward it, the angry cries getting louder as I draw near. Chains are rattling, as if an animal is struggling to free itself. Loud growls and moans accompany the clanking noise. Large, open slats line the top of a heavy metal door, allowing me to peer into the darkened chamber. At first, I can see and hear nothing. It seems as if everything was a dream, until I hear him yell again.

"I'll kill you."

I jump from the threat that seems to emerge from out of nowhere, until I see a projected light against the back wall. It appears to be some kind of home movie playing out. The scene is set in my apartment, and Caleb and I are playing leading roles.

The sound of more clanking draws my attention away from the strange film and toward the man in the middle of the room. His naked body is illuminated from the projector's light, which slightly shadows his backside. Each arm is outstretched, held up by short chains attached to pillars that run from floor to ceiling. Sweat glistens on his skin, trickling down his muscled back. His hair hangs nearly to his shoulders in wet strands, much longer than it used to be.

I watch as Hunter's hands clench against the shackles. Slowly, the muscles in his arms, shoulders, and back bunch and harden as he pulls at the restraints holding him captive, a feral growl forming in his throat.

Watching the film, I see myself standing at the breakfast bar, smelling the roses on it. The growl grows louder as Caleb moves closer with a rose in hand. The timbre echoes off the walls, and the chains strain until I think they might snap under any more pressure. When Caleb and I kiss, Hunter's screams deafen me. The pain they cause as they rip at my heart takes my breath away.

This is Hunter's torture—forced to watch Caleb have his way with me, just as Nergal promised.

"Hunter," *I cry out.*

His head jerks to the side, straining to turn toward me against the chains. His silvery-blue eyes reach mine, and I gasp at the familiar pull they hold over me. He appears wild with fever, completely unlike the self-controlled man who at one time frustrated me to no end, and eventually won over my heart. I shatter into a thousand pieces seeing him like this, knowing this torment is because of me.

"Cassandra? Is that really you?" *His breaths are heavy.*

"Yes, it's me. Hunter, I'm here. I'm going to get you out of here."

I grab for the door handle, but my hand finds only air. I look down to see there is no handle. There's no lock. There's nothing. This door was never meant to open. This is Hunter's eternity in Hell.

"No," *he yells.* "No, you can't be here. Go back."

"I can't leave you like this."

I pull at the metal slats on the door in a feeble attempt to force it open.

"You have to leave. There's no time." *The voice comes from beside me, and I jump away from the large man standing next to me.*

"Eric?" *I hadn't seen Hunter's loyal ally since Nergal's army captured Hunter and took him back to Hell.*

"Cassie, this is a trap," he says. "You have to get out of here."

As he reaches out to touch me, I jerk away.

"Hunter?" I peer back into the cell, wanting him to reassure me and tell me what to believe. He is still straining against the chains as he glares at me through the slats of the door.

"Do as he says, Cassandra. Leave. I don't want you here."

I study his features for a sign; relief that I'd found him, perhaps longing, love? All the emotions I am feeling I want to see on his face, but even his eyes hold nothing more than anger and a piercing, demon glow.

Eric urges me from the door, as Hunter twists away. After seeing Hunter's reaction, I don't have the drive to resist Eric. He grabs my upper arms and shakes me, forcing me to meet his gaze.

"Cassie, listen to me." It is the first time I have ever heard Eric yell. "Caleb is near. You must get out of here before he comes."

"Caleb is near?" I ask, flicking my eyes down the corridor. "No, Eric, that's good. You don't understand. Caleb's not a demon anymore. I'm supposed to wait for him. He's going to take me to...my...father."—Eric is shaking his head—"But he's a Guardian. Look at his eyes He's here to help me this time"

"Then you're more naïve than I thought." The seething words come from inside the cell. "Or maybe you always wanted to be with him."

Hunter's accusation cuts like a blade to my heart. As much as I want to, I can't deny it. He saw us in my apartment. I can't lie to him; he's endured enough pain already. "You don't understand," I say breathlessly, staring at Hunter's back, grateful he doesn't see my shame. I want to explain everything; how I thought I'd never see him again; how Caleb threatened

*and made me promise to never come for him if I wanted to save
my father. He would understand, right?*

*Before I attempt to say more, Eric pulls me up the corridor,
toward the door. "There's no more time to explain. Get out of
here, and as far away from Caleb as you can." The door slides
open, and I know Eric has something to do with it from the
pointed look he gives it. "You were right about him being a
Guardian again, but his heart never left Hell. Talk to Nora when
you get back. I've explained everything to her. She's going to
help you, and so will I as soon as I take care of him."*

*I don't know if he means taking care of Caleb or Hunter,
and I am pushed out the door before I have the chance to ask
him. It slams shut behind me with a discernible clunk.*

Exhaling the breath I'd been holding, I step into the forest.

***

I woke up on the couch with a start, scaring Nora, who was
standing behind it, and myself. Nora had a crazed look in her
eyes as she stared back at me, her mouth hanging open. She
appeared ready to bolt at the slightest movement. Scared was
probably an understatement.

"Where the hell did you come from?" she yelled.

"Nora?" I shot off the couch and approached her.

Nora backed up and bumped into the kitchen counter.

"You...your eyes...Cassie?"

I brought my hands to my eyes, feeling for some anomaly.
"What are you talking about?" I asked when nothing felt out of
place.

"They're blue," she said, watching me closely. Squinting,
she leaned forward. "And they were glowing."

"Were?"

"That was incredible."

With mouth wide open again, Nora moved her hands to
the sides of my face as she peered into my eyes. I felt like I was in
some kind of experiment and Nora was the mad scientist.

"*Nora.*" I threw her hands off and stepped away. "What the hell? Would you please tell me what you're talking about?"

She managed to regain her composure, but was still staring at me like I was an unclassified creature. "Your eyes went from an iridescent blue back to green. *Crazy.* How did you do that?"

My heart was beating too fast in my chest. I may not have known *how* it happened, but I knew why. "I just got back from Hell," I told her, as if that were explanation enough.

"What? Eric came to warn me..." She glanced around the room, her eyes frantic. "Shit, Cassie, where's Caleb?"

"I don't know. But Eric told me—"

Nora grabbed my arms, squeezing hard enough to make me wince. "You saw Eric? Was he okay?"

I was surprised by her concern for Eric. "Yes, he was fine. He warned me about Caleb, told me to talk to you, and then pushed me out of Sheol. He said Caleb was coming for me. What's going on, Nora? What did he tell you?"

"They didn't get to him," she whispered. After a minute of watching her lost in thought, she finally refocused on me. "We have to get out of here...like, now." She pulled me toward the door.

"Nora, wait." I tried resisting, but Nora was on a mission.

"There's no time. Caleb could come any minute. I'll tell you everything on the way."

"Okay, okay. Let me get my phone. I need to call my mom."

"Caleb has been lying the whole time, Cassie," she told me as I grabbed the phone from the couch cushion and followed her to the door. "He made a deal with Nergal. He's luring you into Hell."

Opening the door, we both screamed. Caleb filled the doorway. His eyes zoned in on me. My skin crawled, as if his venomous glare was raking over me with a dull blade. I grabbed Nora's arm and backed into the apartment.

He was on me faster than I expected. "What did you do, Cassie?" He dug his fingers into the backs of my arms. I stared back at him, terrified and confused. "I told you to stay where you were, but you went to see him. Do you know what you've done? Do you know the kind of danger you've put yourself in?"

Either he was a great actor, or he didn't realize I knew. My anger, along with my backbone, grew, and I tensed my body against his hold. If Nora was right, I wasn't going to stand here and let him manhandle me after finding out what he intended to do. I was stronger than him and determined to make sure he remembered it.

"Get your hands off me, Caleb."

The power within me was threatening to erupt, and I flashed back to a time when I had to protect myself from him once before. An inner strength surged from me then, surprising both of us, but it was even stronger now. I was shaking with it.

Nora let out a gasp as her hand flew to her mouth. Caleb released me, his eyes wide as he stared. He backed away, his hands held up in surrender. "Cassie, calm down," he said, his tone soft and reassuring. "I'm here to help you, remember? Hunter escaped. You must have set him off. He got out, and he'll be coming for you. Come with me. I can protect you." He offered his hand to me.

Nora screamed, and a whirlwind blew in, throwing Caleb against the far wall.

"But who will protect you, brother?" Hunter was on him so quickly, it seemed as if his feet weren't even touching the ground. He picked Caleb off the floor and held him against the wall with an arm across his throat.

"I didn't think it was possible, but you look even uglier as a Guardian," Hunter taunted, after they glared at each other for a time. He leaned away and inspected Caleb from head to toe. "So pathetic and weak now, but it fits you."

"Yeah." The lecherous smile I'd become familiar with when Caleb was a Seeker made an appearance. "But not as good as Cassie fits me."

Hunter wailed so loudly, I was sure it could be heard throughout the apartment complex. His head snapped back and prepared to smash into Caleb's, but as he struck, Caleb disappeared. Hunter fell forward, smacking his head into the wall in front of him, leaving a gaping hole where Caleb's head would have been.

I stood paralyzed, adrenaline pumping through my veins, searching for an outlet. My ears were pounding from the rapid heartbeat that coursed through every part of my body. I saw nothing but the man in front of me, his broad shoulders seemingly larger than they were before. His hands were clenched into fists at his sides as he faced the wall. I wanted to go to him, but my body was frozen. I wanted to wrap my arms around his waist and hold him, reassuring him we were all okay.

Hunter had come to my rescue again.

Eric appeared in the kitchen, giving us another scare. Well, at least giving Nora and me another scare, as Hunter still hadn't moved. After taking in the scene around him, Eric put his hand on Nora's shoulder and looked at her in silent question. She nodded and motioned to Hunter.

Eric went to him. "Hunter? You okay, man?" he asked, after examining the hole in the wall.

Hunter nodded.

"We'll need to stay now," Eric told him. "They'll be back. Now that she's been in Hell, she'll have no other protection." He glanced at Nora. "None of them will."

Hunter turned and stalked over until he was towering above me, no longer the stricken, tortured man I saw chained to the pillars. There was no question he was powerful and strong again. Maybe even more than before he was held captive. His light touch under my chin was contradictory to his presence in front of me, and I surrendered to the slight pressure urging my face up toward his. His dark hair hung near his eyes, but didn't block his intense gaze. I fell into the blue depths, lost in them once again.

"Hello Cassandra." His voice held that familiar husky tone. "Miss me?"

CHAPTER SEVEN

I could only stare. It was hard to believe Hunter was standing in front of me as if nothing had happened, as if he hadn't been held prisoner for the last few months in that filthy dungeon, being tortured in ways only Hell could conceive. But here he was, a breath away, bearing down on me with his fierce presence. I never allowed myself to believe he'd get out. Maybe it was my way of not dealing with it at the time, but I was slowly finding out that demons always come back for you.

"You know what? Don't answer that," Hunter told me, his fingers tightening on my chin. "I wouldn't believe you anyway. You wear your new glowing blues well, Cassandra." His thumb came up and brushed near the corner of my eye. "Too well."

Apparently, my eyes had changed again. I could only imagine it was from the adrenaline rush I'd gone through, and was still going through. Anytime I fantasized about Hunter's return, I always pictured an explosive, emotional reunion, one filled with love and maybe a few lusty moments. Never did I imagine he'd be looking at me with as much disgust as he was at that moment.

"Hunter, I—"

His finger pressed my lips to silence me. "So, tell me, my beautiful little demon, how does it feel? Did you enjoy seducing Caleb to get what you wanted? Or were you so enraptured by the green of his eyes that you longed for his tongue in your mouth and his hands on your body?" I gasped, but he went on before I could respond. "Truthfully, I'd prefer the former, because it would mean since he's bailed on the deal, I'm the only one left to help you. I must warn you, however, it's going to take a whole lot of seduction to get me to help you now."

Oh God. It *was* Hunter I saw in the picture frame. They found a way for him to see Caleb and me while he was imprisoned in Hell. I wondered if it were only the apartment he saw. Not that it mattered, he'd seen the worst of it right here. How could I explain that I thought I'd never see him again? That most of the time, it was him whom I fantasized I was with? *Most of the time.* It sounded bad even to *me.* He'd never understand.

"I'm sorry you had to see that," I said, casting my gaze away from his, which only made me feel worse as it was now aimed at the grim line of his lips. "But you were gone, and I had to find my father. And you're right; Caleb was the only one who could help me. I was willing to do anything. I'm *still* willing to do anything."

Minutes passed without a word. I peered into his eyes, and found him studying me, as if gauging my honesty. Or maybe, in true Hunter fashion, how far I'd really go. Eric cleared his throat, but I didn't dare look away from Hunter. His eyes were riveted on mine.

"Uh, Nora, why don't we go somewhere and let them talk," I heard Eric say.

"Not if he's—"

"She'll be fine, Nora. I won't touch her," Hunter said, snatching his hand from my face and spinning away. "I promise you."

His words hurt. The true meaning behind them pierced my heart. The idea we'd been given a second chance to be together, and he couldn't even stand to touch me was worse than thinking he'd never escape Hell. At least then, he didn't have a choice. The worst part was I couldn't blame him. It was my selfish actions that made him feel the way he did. I didn't deserve the reunion I fantasized about. All I could do was accept the way he felt, and hope he would work with me to get my father back. I was determined not to lose sight of the goal that got me into this situation. If he refused to work with me, then I'd have to find a way to do it on my own.

I gave Nora a simple nod, letting her know I'd be okay. They left quietly, shutting the door with a soft click that echoed in the room, emphasizing the fact we were alone. It triggered my nerves. The tension in the room was so thick, I could barely breathe. I knew I'd have to be the one to cut it, but didn't know how to start.

"Why don't we just lay everything out on the table?" I said, ready to dive in, but only after moving around the couch to put some distance between us. "I never thought I'd see you again. I—"

"You didn't answer my question," he interrupted, leaning against the breakfast bar, arms and legs crossed. He looked like an interrogator of the worst kind—smooth, penetrating, and ready to get to the truth, no matter the cost.

"What question was that?"

His condescending tone irritated me. Yes, I did what I had to with Caleb, but I had my reasons. And the look on Hunter's face told me he didn't care what they were. I'd come up against his stubbornness several times before, and knew all too well this was a no-win situation...*unless* he decided to help me. It's all I could hope for.

"Did you enjoy being mauled by Caleb?"

"Look, Hunter," I started, straightening my back and squinting my eyes in an attempt to pull off the tough girl persona, unsure whether I was actually succeeding. "You were gone. I didn't think you'd ever be back." There was no way my body language was remotely comparable to his performance. If this were a pissing contest, I didn't stand a chance. His composure was impenetrable.

"I told you I'd be back for you. Did you think I'd let you go after spitting a few hateful words at me in anger?"

He was so damn calm. It amazed me how he could mask his feelings so well. Maybe it was a demon thing I'd eventually catch on to.

"You were imprisoned by the Devil," I yelled. "How was I supposed to know you could escape Hell?"

"I can escape anything to get what I want," he said, his voice calm. "I thought I'd proven myself to you...several times, in fact. You remember those times, don't you? Or maybe not so much anymore."

I realized then there was nothing I could say or do to erase what Hunter had witnessed. There was no point in arguing. I couldn't win.

"You know what, Hunter?" I moved toward the hallway. "I give up. I'm just a slutty demon who uses my body to get what I need. You've proven your point. You can go now. I'll go to Hell alone. Guess all I really need to do is give a little tongue, and they'll lead me to my father, right?"

A huge *whoosh* escaped my mouth when Hunter shoved me face-first against the wall, so hard I swore my lungs collapsed. I was caged, my hands trapped between the wall and my chest, unable to fight him off, even if I *could* catch my breath.

"Let...me go, Hunter."

His mouth was at my ear, so close his whispered words echoed. "Did you think of me, Cassandra?"

"Yes. Yes, of course I thought about you."

He spun me around so quickly I would have lost my balance if he hadn't held me up against the wall, his hands gripping my upper arms. Leaning in, his eyes nailed me in place, more than any physical weight could. My heart raced, and I panted in order to breathe, trying to keep up with it. Even through my anger at him, I couldn't help my yearning for his beautiful lips on mine. It had been so long.

"No," he said. "I meant while you were with him. Did you think of me when you were with Caleb?"

It took me a minute to wrap my head around what he was asking me, but once I did, I had to stop myself from blurting out the answer. I wanted to set his mind at ease, but I also wanted him to know I meant it.

I managed to free my arm from his grasp and raise my hand to his face. He pulled away, but I persisted, moving my fingers gently across his cheek, before finally cupping the side of his face with my palm. "My answer's still the same," I whispered.

His eyes closed and a silent breath escaped his lips, as if my simple words had saved his life. After his gaze was on mine once again, we stood for several aching minutes, reading one another. A force grew between us, pulling us closer, like polar opposites unable to avoid the magnetism. His eyes flicked to my lips, and I was sure he would kiss me, until his gaze moved over my shoulder.

"Were you with him in there?" he asked through gritted teeth and flared nostrils.

I peered over my shoulder and realized he was referring to my bedroom. My teeth clenched as I stared at him, appalled at his inference. I wanted to slap him for thinking I was so easy, but the scene of Caleb and me locked in each other's embrace flitted across my mind in warning. There was no way for Hunter to know how far we'd gone. I couldn't blame him for thinking the worst. I'd probably do the same.

"I never let it get that far, Hunter," I said, keeping my eyes on his. "I don't think I *could* have. What you saw was the worst of it. I promise you."

He looked toward the breakfast bar and sneered. I gave him space. I'd said all I could say. It was up to him to decide what he was going to do about it.

"I'm going to kill him, you know," he said, as if he'd seen it in some vision, and now, it was destined to be. When his attention was back on me, I could tell he was anticipating my reaction.

With my spine straight, I peered directly into his eyes. "Not if I do it first." It was true. The next time I saw Caleb, I'd find a way to kill him for all he'd done to me. After being deceived by him so many times, I had a lot of face to save. I vowed to be the one to drain the life from his eyes. I'd earned the right.

Slowly, one side of Hunter's mouth lifted into a devious smirk. "I think that might actually turn me on."

The tension between us lifted, and I somehow found comfort in his sleazy remark. It was a small reminder of the repartee we used to have. He'd make sexual insinuations and I'd roll my eyes—which is exactly what I did this time.

"You're still incorrigible." I chuckled as I moved to go around him, toward the couch.

He pulled me back before I got a few feet. One arm wrapped around my waist, while the other held the back of my head to face him. "And you're still beautiful." His lips were hard against mine, vengeful, punishing, but I gave in to them, granting him the revenge he sought. I opened my mouth, inviting his tongue to do the same. It found mine, and a battle ensued, a sweet, sensual battle, with neither side willing to surrender. His moan vibrated against my lips. It grew with intensity until it became a growl, and then he shoved me away. We stood face-to-face, the electricity stretching between us, but unable to snap. I couldn't move. My heart felt like it was going to explode as I stared at him.

"What the hell was that?" I tried to catch my breath.

"*That* is what it's supposed to feel like," he said through tightened lips. Moving in, he cupped his hand between my legs, making me gasp. "You feel that heat?" His lips were on my ear, making sure I didn't miss one word. "*That* is what my kiss will do to you every fucking time. Maybe the next time, you won't be so confused as to whom you're with."

His implication hit me like a blast of frosty air. It was meant to shock and take my breath away, and it did. But the frost melted in the hot flames of my indignation.

"Oh, I get it. You're punishing me," I said. "What for? Dishonoring you?"

Hunter glared back at me, his eyes squinted, his jaw clenched.

"I was with Caleb because I thought you were never coming back, and he was my only chance to get my father. You know...my father? The one you led me to think was dead while he was actually being tortured in Hell? The one who is *still* being tortured while you waste my time with your egotistical lessons? Save me your bullshit, Hunter. I don't need your tutorials anymore. I know what gets me hot, just like I know what gets you the same way. But right now, I really don't give a shit. So, either help me find my father, or go find some other Guardian to teach, because I'm not that girl anymore."

I watched him closely, searching for some kind of reaction to my tirade, but he was as calm as he'd always been. Typical. I give my best *badass* speech, and he didn't even give me the satisfaction of an eye-twitch.

"All right, Cassandra," he said, with the same cool demeanor. "Before I agree to help you get your father out of Hell, I want to get a few things straight, since you still seem confused about them. First, I stand by what I told you before with regard to keeping your father a secret—you were too immature to deal with the knowledge that your father was not the saint you thought he was. You also could not handle the realization of what that made you. You would have hated yourself as much as you hated me.

He waited for a reaction from me, but I didn't give one, wanting to let him have his say.

"Second, your irresponsibility continues if you think you have a chance of getting your father out of Hell on your own. The minute you step through that door of yours in your head, they will be waiting for you. Why? Because you were naïve enough to let Caleb in. He knows what you want, and he'll be ready. You may think you're strong enough with that almighty demon blood running through your veins, but you won't be able to take on what they have in store. What they did to me is nothing compared to the plans they have for you."

He moved in front of me, and I remained as I was, stiff and emotionless. His finger came underneath my chin, his eyes locking on mine to make sure he had my full attention.

"You *need* me," he continued. "I am the *only* one who can help you now. And if you think for a second I'm going to let you go in there alone, you are more immature than I thought. I didn't allow myself to be tortured for the last few months only to have you throw yourself into the fire. I won't help you unless you agree to a few stipulations first."

I listened to every word he said, and as much as I hated to admit it, he was right on all counts. There was no way I could do this on my own. And there was no one else to turn to. He was my only hope of getting my father out. His reminder of the torture he suffered on my account made my entire speech seem as he said I was—immature. It was time to grow up and accept what was being offered. The only problem was, I knew when it came to Hunter, there would be a big price to pay.

"Okay, I'll bite. What are your terms?"

He nodded, a silent *I told you so*.

"You will do whatever I tell you, whenever I tell you to do it. No arguments. And especially none of that Lone Ranger bullshit you pulled back at the diner with Caleb. Are we clear?"

"Yes, sir," I said sarcastically.

"Yes, Master will do just fine." He shot me a smirk.

I gave him another eye roll.

"Cassandra, I need you to agree that you'll do exactly what I say. This conversation is over if you don't." His expression was stern. There was no mistaking the gravity of what he was asking.

"Okay." I locked onto his gaze. "You have my word."

"Good. Then let's move past our animosity and concentrate on what we need to do to get your father out."

"I'm all for it. Where do we start?"

"First, we need to get out of here. Those angel relatives of yours could come looking for you anytime now."

"But can't they sense where I am no matter where I go? The last time I saw them, they showed up in the middle of no man's land, exactly where I happened to be."

"Yes. But I don't think I can look at that breakfast bar any longer without feeling like I need to mark my territory."

I nodded. To be honest, picturing what I'd done in the apartment with Caleb made me nauseous as well. I had no problem leaving those images behind.

We decided a hotel room would have to do for now. After throwing some things in a bag, we headed out.

"Oh, one more thing, Cassandra," Hunter said before I stepped through the door he held open.

"What's that?"

"When you said you know what gets me hot"—he wrapped an arm around my shoulder and cupped the side of my neck with his hand—"you have no idea. But I'd love to show you. Soon."

What was it with him and my ears?

CHAPTER EIGHT

We ended up in one of the busier hotels in the downtown area, relying on more people around, which would lessen the chances of encountering any unearthly armies on a SWAT mission. Sure, they could shut out the rest of the world no matter where they were, but I let myself believe it would be a pain in the ass to have to *poof* away over a hundred people rather than a few at some remote motel. It was enough to keep my paranoia in check, and allowed me to concentrate on coming up with a plan.

I called Nora on the way to let her know where we'd be. Hunter and I agreed we needed Eric's help, and I didn't want Nora alone, so they were both coming to the hotel. I wasn't sure what to do with Nora while we were gone. Caleb used her once before to lure me in. I didn't want a repeat of that catastrophe, but I also didn't want her coming with us to Sheol. We needed to go soon. I was afraid of what they might do to my father now that Caleb's plan had failed again. We wouldn't have enough time to get Nora to the Elders, and I sure as hell wasn't going to let her go by herself.

I thought about reaching out to Anael and asking the angels to watch over Nora and my mom, but there were more complications with that idea. I wasn't sure how to reach her, and if I did, I didn't trust she'd keep my secret rendezvous to herself. According to Hadraniel's rulebook, I was now their enemy because I defied direct orders to stay out of Hell. It was too risky, so I was counting on Hunter and Eric to help me come up with something.

Hunter paid for two rooms to accommodate the four of us for the night. They were located on the fifth floor at the long end of a hallway decorated with warm colors, soft carpeting, and floral paintings. It was designed to make both families and business patrons feel at home during their stay. The rooms were much the same.

When we went into the room, our reflections greeted us from mirrored closet doors on our left, opposite a marbled bathroom on our right. Glancing in further, two double beds with mauve-colored quilts and fluffed-to-perfection pillows, a small table in between them, lined one wall. An armoire, housing a TV and set of drawers faced the beds on the other.

Beautiful, paisley, floor-length curtains revealed a wall-to-wall window at the back of the room. Curious about the view we had, I went to the window and peeked out at the starry night. The moon was full, which seemed appropriate for the kind of hellish night I'd had so far, but it was beautiful, hanging beyond the downtown lights of the city, seemingly watching over everything.

"Nice desk," Hunter said from behind me.

Glancing to my right, I noticed the dark brown office desk against the wall. There was nothing special about the desk. It contained the usual hotel accompaniments on it, but the sight of it made my heart speed up, nonetheless. It was exactly the reaction Hunter was hoping for. I knew he wasn't admiring the rich, brown finish. He was referring to a time we used the desk for activities far from office-related. Remembering how he made me feel then sent heat rushing to parts of my body he'd made sure would never forget his touch.

My cheeks were flushed, but I was determined to show Hunter I would no longer swoon from his teasing insinuations. I was going to fight fire with fire.

Slowly, I skimmed my finger across the desk's surface, playing with its smoothness. Peering back at him through my lashes, I said, "Yes, it seems very...hard"—I pushed down on it with both hands—"and sturdy."

A grin spread his lips as he shook his head. "You must enjoy getting yourself in sticky situations, Cassandra." He stalked toward me.

My heart beat with anticipation, but I predicted his reaction. I prayed my plan would work. I had something to prove to both Hunter *and* myself.

I faced him as he came toward me, mentally preparing myself for what I was about to do. My body tensed, and I drew power from somewhere inside me, the same power I used on Caleb a few times. I needed to learn how to control it, and Hunter was a great guinea pig when provoked.

To my relief, I felt the strength building inside as I willed it into my arms. It was different from the times before, a burning sensation roiling up from my belly, like fireballs being set loose to my upper body, rolling slowly, then intensifying. The heat ran down the length of my arms as he reached me, and I held them out toward him. The energy surged from me as I pushed at his chest.

"Not so fast, cowboy," I said, quite sure I'd send him flying back, demonstrating my will, along with my strength.

Unfortunately, all my haughtiness was crushed, as were my arms against his chest. I had no idea what went wrong. It *felt* like it should have happened. Maybe Hunter was simply much stronger than I. Maybe I just didn't know what the hell I was doing.

Hunter grabbed my arms and held me away, glaring at me. I lowered my chin, wishing I could spot a huge rock to crawl under and avoid his accusatory eyes. I was going to catch hell for this.

"Did you just try to use your powers on me?"

"Umm...yes," I said, my voice sounding as mouse-like as I felt. "But it was with noble intentions."

"Oh, this should be good."

The whole point of the experiment was to show him I could be stronger, independent. Yeah, okay, it didn't work, but that didn't mean I was going to cower like a kid who'd been caught stealing a candy bar. I straightened my spine and fixed my gaze on his.

"Look, I'm trying to stop being the weak, dependent person everyone thinks they have to protect. I have power. I know I do because I've used it. I want to learn how to control it so I can take care of myself when I need to. Instead of standing there, gloating at me, why don't you make yourself useful and tell me what I need to do."

"So, you're asking me to teach you...like give you a lesson?" he asked, his hidden meaning not lost on me.

I let out an exasperated sigh. "Just tell me why it didn't work."

Hunter laughed. "Okay, but I don't think you're going to like the answer."

"Whatever. I'm getting used to not liking what I hear."

"Hmmm..." He brushed his knuckles against my cheek. "You've gotten spunkier since my absence. I like it."

I pulled my face out of reach, and his hand fell.

"The reason it didn't work is because pushing me away isn't really what you want to do with me, Cassandra," he said, not even trying to hide his grin.

I rolled my eyes. "Shut up, Hunter."

"It's true. If deep down you really wanted to push me away, you could have done it. Especially when I wasn't expecting it. Think about when you did it to Caleb. He had his hands on you, and you despised him. All you wanted was to get him away from you. Am I right?"

"Yes," I said, still trying to comprehend what he was telling me.

"A demon's power comes from here"—he placed his fingers on my temple—"Here"—he moved his hand and put his palm on my belly—"And here"—his hand covered my heart, with way too much emphasis on my breast.

I sucked in a breath on a gasp, causing my breast to press against his hand even more. My gaze darted up to his.

"I think this is the part that prevented you from pushing me away."

There was no sarcasm in his voice, no smirking. His eyes were soft, the words said in a whisper. He slowly lowered his head as his other hand came up to caress the side of my face. There was the smallest breath on my lips when his mouth hesitated over mine, as if waiting for my protest. When he didn't get one, his smooth, full lips gently pressed into mine, and I closed my eyes to savor the tenderness of their touch. The kiss was so different from the demanding one he'd given me earlier. It was...sweet. When he took his mouth away, I almost moaned with regret. He was only a breath away, watching me, when I opened my eyes, and I felt myself drowning in his beautiful blue gaze again.

"I missed you, Cassandra. What they did to me was nothing compared to the torture of not being able to kiss your lips, hold you in my arms, or feel your body against mine."

"Hunter, I—"

A knock on the door made me jump. I tried to twist my head toward it, but Hunter's hand on my cheek stopped me, forcing my eyes back to his penetrating stare.

Nora called through the door and more knocking sounded.

"Hunter, we need to let them in."

"This isn't finished." There was a warning in his tone. "We *will* continue our...talk."

Passion glowed in his eyes, telling me talking wasn't all he wanted to continue.

Nodding, I moved to squeeze by him, but he grabbed my arm to stall me.

"It's killing me, knowing you were with him, Cassandra. I need to *feel* what you told me was true. You understand what I'm telling you, right?"

Yeah, I knew exactly what he was talking about. He wanted me to show him Caleb meant nothing to me. Words were only letters put together until your actions gave them meaning. If my father's fate weren't on the line, I might have ignored the incessant knocking on the door, and showed Hunter right there and then what no words could describe. But sadly, it would have to wait. Words were all I could give him for now.

I rested my palm on his cheek and fixed my eyes on his. "It's always been you, Hunter," I said. "I promise, if we get out of this alive, I will prove it to you."

A dimple deepened as a sexy smirk took form. "Well, then I suggest you open the door, because if you look at me like that much longer, I may lose all sense of priority."

I ran over to the door and opened it before my hormones clouded my own sense of priority. *If only my demon powers could stop time*, I thought, at the same time chiding myself for getting so easily distracted by Hunter.

Nora and Eric charged into the room, their relief evident, but irritation quickly claimed Nora's features. "*Shit*, Cassie. What took you so long? I was about to make Eric break the door down. Didn't you hear us knocking?"

"Yeah, I'm sorry. We were just clearing something up," I said.

Nora's gaze darted between Hunter and me. My face flushed, knowing what she'd clearly see.

"Oh, stop looking at me like that, Nora. It's not what you think."

"Uh huh...so, I take it you've come up with a plan then of how we're getting your father out?"

"Well—"

"*You're* not going anywhere, Nora," Hunter said.

"I'm going with you guys," Nora countered.

"No, you're not. As a matter of fact, you're a liability to us, and therefore, we need to get rid of you altogether."

It took a minute for his words to register, but as Nora gasped, I let out a resounding, "What?"

I stared at Hunter, cognizant of the shock in both Nora's and Eric's faces in my peripheral vision. *What the hell was he doing?*

"Think about it, Cassandra," he said. "Nora's a spy. She told you she was. Do you think that's changed? *No.* The minute she knows our plan, the winged, *holier than thous* will be on us before we even get a chance to step one foot in Hell. She has to go. But since she's your friend, I'll give you a choice—we either turn her, or kill her. Eric, grab her."

Even though Eric appeared as confused as I was, he obeyed Hunter, grabbing Nora by the arms. As big and strong as he was, she was no match for him, but that didn't stop her from struggling to get free. I stood dumbfounded and speechless, watching Nora thrash about in his arms as he brought her against him.

How could Hunter possibly think this was the only way? He knew how much Nora meant to me. Hell, he even saved her life for me. There were so many emotions conflicting inside me. I was confused, hurt, and terrified at the same time, but I was also angry as hell. I'd practically confessed my love to him less than a minute ago, and now he was threatening to kill my best friend. My blood was exploding through my veins to the point I thought it would seep out of my pores. My heart was pounding, trying to keep up with the flow.

I spun to face Hunter, ready to launch myself at him, my muscles tensing. "Have you lost your mind? What are you thinking?"

"I'm thinking it's the only chance you have of getting your father back. Now choose, Cassandra."

"I will *not* choose, because this isn't happening. You will not lay a hand on her," I yelled, glaring at him.

"Well, if you're not going to choose, then I guess you leave me no choice but to decide for you. Personally, I have no use for another Seeker, so, Eric, snap her neck." He said it with such indifference, I could have been hearing it from a stranger, someone other than the man who had whispered such sweet words of love to me moments ago.

I swung around when I heard Nora crying. My heart dropped in my stomach, until I saw Eric staring at Hunter with wide eyes, clearly shocked by Hunter's order.

"Do it, Eric, or I will," Hunter warned.

Nora angled her tear-streaked face up to Eric's, her eyes begging him to spare her life.

I stood as if nailed to the floor, terrified one small move would set things in motion and I'd be too late. Then I noticed something in the way Eric was looking at Nora. There was tenderness in his expression, almost as if he were...

Relief spread over me when I realized that look was adoration. Eric couldn't bring himself to kill her.

Unfortunately, Hunter realized the same thing. "I guess I'll have to do the honors then." He stepped around me. "Say goodbye, Nora."

CHAPTER NINE

Nora screamed as Hunter neared her.

With a knee-jerk reaction, I hurled myself at him with everything I had. The power that had built up inside of me rushed out like a bulldozer driving into a brick wall, unable to stop until I took Hunter down. We flew across the room into the mirrored closet, glass shattering all around us. I landed on top of him. He didn't move, so I used his body to push myself up. Shards of glass sliced into my knees as I straddled him, but the burning fires within me dulled the pain. Hunter opened his eyes, and I picked up a chunk of glass, fully prepared to bury it into his eyes, his face, his heart. With glowing eyes he gazed up at me. Somehow, I knew mine were doing the same.

"Now, can you feel where your power comes from?" he asked.

His words sank in, and I couldn't move. I was kneeling over him, my arm poised with the glass cutting into my palm as I squeezed tighter.

He was playing me? This was all a test?

I glimpsed behind me at Nora and Eric. From the expression on their faces they were as shocked as I. But my surprise was quickly replaced with anger. I was furious Hunter had used us to prove a point. Granted, it worked, but it didn't excuse his callousness, or the way he'd toyed with our emotions, as well as our lives. The rage inside continued to boil my blood.

"You bastard," I screamed, bringing the glass down as hard as I could into his arm. It plunged deep into his flesh, causing the blood to spurt on him and me.

"*Owww, damn it.*" Hunter grabbed at the glass in his arm and bucked me off him. I fell to the side, but continued to glare at him. He winced as he pulled it from his arm and tossed it away. The blood rushed faster, and I noticed another gash on the hand he used to pull it out with. Not more than five seconds later, however, the skin began to mend itself. He sat up, and his eyes pierced me with their glow. He was mad, but I didn't care. I'd do it again.

"What the hell is wrong with you, Hunter?" I cried. "I could have killed someone. Although, right now, I'm still debating whether or not I'm sorry I didn't succeed."

He knew I was referring to him. The smile on his face as he stood told me so, but I refused to smile back. I was livid.

Getting up, I went to Nora, hugging her as she continued to shake in my arms. She stopped crying, but she was nowhere near over it. Eric didn't appear too happy either, but he remained his normal, quiet self.

"You wouldn't have killed anyone, Cassandra." Hunter came toward us. "I would have stopped you. But I'll admit, you're much stronger than I expected. That halo blood must give you an extra boost. I'd be careful, bro," he said to Eric with a laugh. "I think there's a chance she could take you."

Before I could stop her, Nora pulled out of my arms, faced Hunter, hauled her fist back, and drove it into his face. I could tell she put everything she had into the punch as she nearly fell over after doing a half-spin. The effect on Hunter wasn't as dramatic. It merely clipped his chin and knocked him back a step. More than likely, it surprised rather than hurt him. Regaining his footing, his glowing gaze targeted Nora.

I caught Nora from losing her balance, and seeing Hunter's rage, pushed her behind me. "Get back," I demanded. "You deserved that, and you're lucky it came from her. Mine would have hurt you far more than hers."

"Mine too."

I whipped my head around and gaped at Eric, shocked to hear him defying Hunter, but wishing I had a set of pom-poms to root him on at the same time. From the stunned look on Hunter's face, he wasn't expecting it either. Maybe that's what made him put up the white flag and concede what he'd done was wrong. We all stopped shooting imaginary bullets at him, but there was still a lot of tension in the room.

Nora and I sat on one of the beds. She was pulling herself together, but I could tell she was still leery. Who could blame her? She was a Guardian in a room full of demons. Technically, her enemies surrounded her, and if any of us were to go after her, she didn't stand a chance. Her power was no match to any of ours. I held her close to reassure her she was safe with me.

Eric busied himself by picking up the glass scattered around the closet. There was an awkward silence in the room as each of us seemed content to muse in our own minds. I noticed Hunter staring at Nora from the middle of the room. His eyes weren't glowing, but they were intense.

"Hunter, you need to get over it," I said, waving my hand between him and Nora.

"I am," he said with a shake of his head. "I was thinking. Maybe her spy status could benefit us after all."

We all regarded him curiously, each of us cautious after the last stunt he pulled. But when he explained how Nora could be the key to protecting herself and my mom, I jumped onboard. Instead of keeping it from the Elders, Hunter proposed Nora tell them I'd gone rogue demon after we left. She'd claim to be afraid for her safety, as well as my mom's. The Elders would take them in. They protected their own. Nora could make sure of it.

"No way," Nora shouted. "I'm not staying behind. I'll go crazy wondering what's going on. And don't even get me started about what your mom would do to me if she knew I let you go."

"Nora," I said, gently tugging her arm so she would turn to look at me, "this is the only way I can be sure you and my mom will be safe. I won't go unless I know you're going to take care of her. You don't have to tell her anything. Let her think it's real.

She'll know the truth once I get my dad out. They all will. Believe me, it kills me more than anyone for her to think I've turned, but it's the only way to keep her protected. If she knew the truth, there's a chance she'd come after me. I'm not willing to take that chance. Please, Nora."

We both sat staring into each other's eyes, mine imploring, hers calculating. She was gauging my desperation against her resolve to be involved. I could almost see the scales teetering in her green eyes. Finally, she broke the connection when she cast her gaze down at our clasped hands. I knew I had her before she even nodded her consent.

Eric came over and placed his hand on her shoulder. When she peered up at him, he said, "I'll come as often as I can to let you know what's going on. You have my word."

Their eyes locked, as silent messages passed between them. I wondered how and when they'd become so close. I was under the impression they'd only been around each other the few times they helped Hunter and me. Was I so wrapped up in my own needs that I completely disregarded those closest to me? All the times she talked to me about my own crazy feelings after Hunter was taken, I never once thought to ask her about what she was going through. Or whom she was going through it with, apparently.

"Thank you," Nora whispered.

I wanted to give them a moment, so I went over to Hunter and pulled him aside. "I don't have anything to worry about here, right?" I asked quietly so Nora and Eric wouldn't hear me.

He leaned against the wall and crossed his arms over his chest. "You mean, other than the spanking I want to give you for stabbing me?"

I gave him my best *give me a break* look, and he chuckled. "I mean about Eric and Nora."

His gaze darted their way, but he didn't appear surprised about what I was alluding to. "Yes, I've started to notice a few tender moments between the two of them. Are you worried he may try to turn her?"

"Well, that wouldn't be unheard of, you know. It is what Seekers do."

"Not all of them, Cassandra. Need I remind you that some have had the misfortune to come under the spell of their targets? Perhaps, I should warn him the end result has yet to prove anything other than pure torture, especially when the target seems to have mixed loyalties."

I sucked in a breath from the barb. It could have been my loyalties between being a Guardian and having demon blood he was talking about, but I had a gut-wrenching feeling he was referring to what happened with Caleb.

Straightening, I narrowed my eyes at him, defying his accusation. "I do *not* have mixed loyalties. I told you so before."

Nora and Eric turned our way at my outburst, but that didn't stop Hunter from pulling me into him. We were so close, I could feel every groove along the front of his body.

Leaning in, he whispered, "And I told *you* before to prove it."

I pushed at his chest, which got me absolutely nowhere, since it was like shoving against armored steel. He laughed at me, infuriating me more. I really needed to get a handle on the power thing. Not being able to knock Hunter on his ass on impulse was becoming increasingly frustrating.

Also increasingly frustrating was the smirk on his face at my expense. "Don't forget, your power has to come from your entire being. Obviously, parts of you want me right here." He rubbed his groin against me.

"Hunter," Eric called out. Hunter peered over my shoulder at him. "We really should get this plan down. I assume we are going soon?"

Hunter straightened and released me. I scrambled away from him, my legs shaking until I took a seat on the bed next to Nora.

Thank God for Eric. Hunter had a way of turning my anger into complete desire for him that made me lose all my senses. I hated being on a roller coaster ride of emotions, but I couldn't keep them in check when it came to him. As usual, he seemed unaffected by it all.

"We'll go tomorrow morning," Hunter said. "Other than a few things I still need to straighten out with Cassandra, the plan is simple. She will wait for me by her entry point. Once I get to her, we'll head straight to her father. Eric, you'll be in charge of locating Caleb and Nergal, and reporting to us where they are. They'll know we are there and come after us. Once that happens, I'll distract them while you move forward with Cassandra to get her father."

"That's your plan?" I asked as I stood to face him. "That's a *horrible* plan. I should be the one to distract them, and you know it. It's me they want. I agreed to do as you said, Hunter, but I'm not about to go on a mission I know is destined to fail. Give me some credit. You said yourself I was stronger than you thought. I know I can take Caleb an—"

"Nergal could kill you with a flick of his wrist," Hunter yelled. "Do you honestly think I'm going to let you set yourself up for a slaughter? No. You'll go with Eric."

From the stubborn set of his chin, I knew there was no way I could convince him. I glanced at Eric for a last ditch effort of support, but it was clear he wasn't ready to use me as bait either. I relented, telling myself if the opportunity presented, I'd follow through with my plans. No need to argue about it now. I'd only succeed in making Hunter overly cautious of every little thing I did.

Hunter eyed me suspiciously after my quick surrender, but said nothing more about it. "Nora, you'll go to Sara as soon as you see we've left. Call on the Elders the minute you get to her. Tell them Cassandra's been disappearing lately, and when you confronted her on it, she turned on you."

Nora nodded somberly, still not sold on the idea, but willing to help in any way we'd let her. I hoped she realized how important her role was. My mom's life would depend on her, not to mention her own. With the way Eric was regarding her, I was more convinced, at least, this part of the plan would go as intended. He'd make sure they were safe.

The plan as it was really wasn't a plan at all. It was more of a broad outline leaving ample room for things to go awry. But it only made sense to stick with basic goals as we were dealing with the most unpredictable realm there was, and one in which I imagined just about anything could happen. I expected the monsters of the Underworld to play dirty. But they weren't the only ones with dirty blood. I wasn't about to go down without a fight.

"Alright then," Hunter said. "Eric, Nora, we'll see you in the morning."

I snapped my gaze to his. "I'm going with Nora."

There were so many things my best friend and I needed to catch up on before this went down...just in case. I wanted to let her know I wasn't abandoning her, and how important she was to me, not to mention, finding out what was going on with Eric and her. I wanted to be Nora's friend tonight, something I'd forgotten to be in my determination to find my father.

Hunter eyed me back. "No. There are still some things we need to clear up, Cassandra." His eyes bore into mine with his true intentions, and they had nothing to do with our plans for going to Hell. "Besides, I need to make sure you don't fall asleep and go in too early. And I assume Eric and Nora have some details they'll want to go over for contacting each other as well. Am I right?" he asked them.

Eric looked to Nora, as if waiting for her reply. She turned my way, and I knew what her answer was. It was written all over her flushed face. She wanted to spend time with Eric. I wouldn't take that away from her, so I wrapped my arms around her. "Go, Nora," I whispered in her ear. "It's okay. We'll talk in the morning before I leave."

"You promise you won't leave without saying goodbye?"

"I wouldn't dream of it."

"Okay," she said.

Before they left, Nora stopped in front of Hunter. Standing tall, but still dwarfed by his size, she pushed a finger into his chest. "You be good to her, you hear me? Or I swear, I will find a way to kick your ass and make it hurt."

Hunter gave her a slow smile, in no way mocking her, more like one of appreciation. "Yes, ma'am."

Seemingly satisfied, she joined Eric at the door. After a quick goodbye from Eric, they left.

Hunter went to the door, opened it, and placed the Do Not Disturb on the outside knob before closing it. The sound of the deadbolt clicking in place set off a drop in my stomach. No matter how many times I'd been alone with Hunter, he could make me feel as nervous as a schoolgirl on a first date.

I bee-lined it to the compact refrigerator on a table in the corner. "I need a drink, would you like something?" I asked, opening the small door. It was a lame attempt at procrastinating.

"There's no need to be nervous, Cassandra," Hunter said from behind me. "I won't make you do anything you don't want."

With a bottle of water in my hand, I turned to see him on one of the beds, his back propped up against the headboard and his legs stretched out and crossed at the ankles. In his faded jeans and black T-shirt, he appeared comfortable, relaxed, and the complete opposite of what I felt. But I didn't want him to know. I'd already learned from experience it only excited him to taunt me.

"I'm not nervous. I'm just...thirsty."

"Mmm hmm." There was a moment of silence as I got lost studying him. His gorgeously dark features contrasted by the clear blue of his eyes easily drew me under his spell if I stared long enough. Those delicious lips begged to be tasted, while his incredibly hard body lured anxious fingers to stroke its contours.

"Cassandra," I faintly heard him calling, breaking me from my shameless fantasy. Was it the second or third time he called my name? I could feel the heat in my cheeks as he smiled. "Are you going to drink that water, or is there something else you're thirsty for?"

I opened the water and chugged a good portion of it down. Hunter laughed.

"So, tell me, once we get your father out, what on earth do you plan to do with him?" he asked.

"I don't plan to *do* anything with him. He'll be reunited with my mom...and me."

"You don't really expect me to believe that, do you?" My silence was his answer. "You're going to try and turn him back, aren't you?"

He sounded critical, making my defenses go up instinctively. "It's worth a shot. It worked on Caleb, why wouldn't it work on my father?" The argument may have sounded logical, but it also awakened the inner doubts I already had. Nothing had been easy up to this point. What made me think a wrench wouldn't be thrown into this as well?

"Ahhh, but answer this, Cassandra—what if your father doesn't *want* to be turned?"

There it was...the fucking wrench.

CHAPTER TEN

"What do you mean, *what if he doesn't want to be turned*?" I asked, as if the question were so far beyond the realm of possibility he should be institutionalized to even consider it. "He went AWOL from Hell long ago and is now a prisoner because he wanted to be with my mom. Why *wouldn't* he want to be turned?"

Hunter held up his hands in surrender. "I'm only making sure you're prepared for anything. He's been there a long time. There's always a chance they got inside his head. You have no idea what Nergal is capable of. He *is* the Devil, and the Devil has ways of playing with the minds of both humans and demons. Ways you can't possibly imagine."

I thought about the odds for only a moment before shaking my head in denial, refusing to let them sink in. If they were correct, my faith in fighting against the evil within me would suffer a tremendous blow. My father had allowed the love for his family to break through the demon armor that guarded his heart. If he couldn't fend off the call of evil after that, then I didn't stand a chance. I needed to believe he was still with us, that he still *wanted* to be with us. Trusting it was possible would help me get through everything.

Hunter sat quietly watching me. Gazing into his eyes, I replayed everything he'd done for me, wondering how different he was from my father. I braced myself as I asked him, "Don't you?"

"Don't I what? Want to be turned?" He paused. "No."

"No?" I asked, surprised. "But you're not like them. You care...you..."

He moved quickly across the bed, kneeling before me at the end of it. With his hand cupped on my neck, caressing my cheek, he said, "Love? Yes, I do love. I never thought it was possible. Hell, I never even *thought* about it as a Seeker. But you did something to me, Cassandra. You made me realize I still have a heart, regardless of what I'm made of. And you've stolen it, because there is nothing I wouldn't do to be with you. But that includes staying as I am, even if I have the chance to turn."

I stared, completely at a loss. It didn't make sense. If he wanted to be with me, why wouldn't he want to turn? He could be with me freely. No more running, no more hiding.

"After everything that happened, you still have no idea how important you are, do you?" He searched my face with such tenderness, I almost melted into the hand stroking my cheek. "Nergal will continue to hunt you down. He'll send dozens of Calebs after you until he gets what he wants, or is destroyed in the process. If I'm turned, I'll have no power to protect you. I will remain a Seeker until the day I know you are safe, if that day ever comes. I'm willing to stay this way for eternity if it means you are protected against their evil. I know what they are capable of, and there is no way in hell I'm going to let them get their hands on you. I told you once I'd fight Heaven and Hell for you, and that still stands. It will always stand."

I didn't realize a tear had escaped until his thumb wiped it away. In that moment, there was no doubt in my mind I was truly in love with him. And it wasn't merely because he used beautiful words to profess his love for me. It was because I knew if the tables were turned, I would do the same. Heaven and Hell no longer mattered when it came to being with Hunter. I would face any penalty or sentence imposed upon me just to be with him. Drowning in the blue of his eyes, there was only one world that mattered—ours.

I leaned forward, our eyes fastened by their bond. Our lips came together, and I felt as if we were sealing a union that would never again be broken. The kiss was light at first, the soft, lush feel of his lips resting against mine. We stayed that way, savoring the emotions, which silently passed between us until my heart surged up my throat.

"I love you, Hunter," I whispered against his lips.

With a deep, guttural moan, he wrapped his arms around my waist and lifted me onto the bed. His tongue sought mine in desperation, as if needing to brand his love for me on it. Our bodies twisted together until I was beneath him. As we kissed, I ran my hands down his back, the contours of his muscles revitalizing blissful memories of his bare skin against mine. The simple T-shirt was a barrier, an impenetrable wall keeping us apart. Frantically, I pulled at it, anxious to free it from between our bodies. Hunter lifted up on his elbows, allowing me to pull it as far as his shoulders.

Straddling me, he leaned back to take the rest of it off. His sculpted chest, now bared before me, drew me to it, my mouth watering in eager anticipation of sampling its taste. I pulled myself up and trailed tongued-kisses over the smooth, hard skin. Instantly addicted to the salty flavor, I wanted to sample every inch of him. His fingers tangled in my hair before his hands grasped the back of my head. He followed my movements across his chest while moaning my name above me, until he yanked at my hair, forcing me to look up at him.

His passion-clouded eyes followed my tongue as I licked my lips, in an effort to catch any lingering essence from him.

"Say it again," he said, his words coming out in a low, raspy breath.

I kept my eyes on his, my emotions for him so strong I didn't think the three words he wanted me to repeat were sufficient. But I said them anyway. His lids fell closed, as if absorbing my words and sealing them away in his memory forever.

I had every intention of continuing my feast on his chest, but he lowered his mouth to mine, relaxing me back into the bed.

He spread my legs apart with his knees. "Prove it," he said. My lips trembled as his arousal nestled itself against my core.

I smiled, running my fingers down his stomach. Making quick work of the button and zipper of his pants, we both gasped as I took him in my hand, slowly stroking him. His breaths came out in pleasured moans. I reached up with my other hand and grabbed the back of his neck, pulling his mouth onto mine, inviting his tongue inside. When it found its way in, I suckled it, matching the rhythm of my hand stroking below.

A roar vibrated from inside his throat, growing in intensity before he released it, along with a flourish of movement removing my shirt and bra. Holding my breasts, he tortured my nipples, alternating between tiny nibbles and apologetic kisses. He was setting my skin on fire, and the heat rose to its peak right between my legs.

Hunter kicked down his pants, and all I wanted to do was throw him off me so I could drink in his beautiful body. But I couldn't move. The sensations he was creating within me were too good to end. As his head began to lower and his hands smoothly peeled off my pants, I knew it was only going to get better. His mouth descended onto my body, and the memory of having him between my legs again put me in a euphoric bliss. But before he reached my urgently aching center, his words echoed in my head. *Prove it.*

I sat up, pushing him off me and onto his back with a strength I'd only used in anger before. We were both shocked by it, but I was less interested in my newfound power than seeing the long length of him before me. I smiled at him from a kneeling position between his legs and leaned over to taunt his nipples, using the same method he used to drive my body crazy with desire. He let out a half-laugh, half-groan, which encouraged me to venture even lower. I loved hearing him moan. Every time I heard it, it made me feel I was in complete control of his body. I wanted more.

His arousal rubbed against my stomach and slowly slid between my breasts as I continued my descent. When I ran my tongue over the length of his hardness, I heard him inhale deeply. Taking him in my mouth, he let it all out on a breathy murmur of my name. His hand gently rested on the back of my head as I continued to pleasure him, sucking, kissing, teasing him to heights accentuated by his growing cries of satisfaction, each one sending pangs of sweet tension to my core.

When I thought he was near the point of sensual oblivion, I increased my tempo over him, but then I was launched back onto the bed. He was on top of me before I knew what happened. Hands pressed into the bed beside my head, he smiled back at me, and I laughed at the battle of seduction we managed to come up with. It was a war I quickly surrendered to when I felt the hard tip of him pressing against me. My smile quickly faded. I all but bit my lip in keen anticipation of feeling him once again inside me. I squirmed beneath him, jutting my hips forward, trying desperately to drive him in, but he kept resisting, staying just out of reach, and tormenting me. I was about to beg him, when he leaned onto his elbows, bringing his face inches from mine. He brushed a strand of hair from my face and softly caressed my cheek, gazing deeply into my eyes.

"This is worth an eternity of torture," he whispered. "I'm quite certain I love you more than anyone I've ever loved in any life. I may have lost my soul when I was turned, but you, Cassandra, have replaced it. I'll never let you go." With that, he gently slid inside of me and took my breath away, both with his words and his body. Our pace was a slow and steady rhythm as we kissed with a passion barely imagined by our lips. It was a passion that could be felt deep in the heart with every electrifying embrace of our tongues. I was lost to my senses, the fire burning so hot where he was filling me, I felt like I would self-combust at any moment. His momentum picked up, and I knew he was there with me.

"Come with me, Cassandra."

As if on command, my body exploded, sending bursts of exhilarated lust throughout my entire being. I think I cried out, but I was so delirious with pleasure I couldn't be sure. As I rode the steady waves rolling through my body, he stiffened, right before he thrust deep inside me, letting out a loud roar that was only partially muffled by the pillow beside me. He was riding the same waves that continued inside me, as his moans grew quieter, but no less intense.

Running my fingers down his back, I turned my head to whisper in his ear. "I'll come anywhere with you, Hunter."

Tiny kisses trailed up my neck, my jaw, my cheek, until his face was directly above mine. He stared at me with passion-clouded eyes. I locked my gaze on his and brought my hand to his cheek. "Anywhere," I vowed.

He continued with his silent study, as if digging deeper into my soul to gauge the sincerity of my pledge. "I wish that were true," he said sadly. "Because if it were, I would steer you as far away from Hell as I could."

The verbal knife stabbed deep into my heart, but he was right. In the end, my family would always come first. As long as I had the power to ensure their safety, they would remain my first priority. I ran my thumb across his lips, following with my eyes as I felt their smooth shape. "But you'd never make me choose, right?" I asked with timid optimism.

The tip of his tongue shot out to sample a taste of my thumb, and I gasped at the arousal growing between us once again. "You make it hard to refuse anything you desire."

"Then don't," I said with a smile, rubbing against him.

***

I was exhausted, but Hunter found several ways throughout the night to keep me awake. I didn't put up much of a fight. Quite honestly, if given the choice between the sensations he awakened in me and a little shut-eye, there was no question. He did things to my body no amount of sleep could ever satisfy, not even my most lucid fantasies. But the light eventually started to creep in through the curtains, as if focusing a spotlight on us, and told us it was show time.

I stretched against Hunter's body, unable to suppress the loud yawn that came along with it. "How am I supposed to go kick some demon ass if I feel this drained?" I asked, my head back on his chest.

"Your exhaustion should disappear once you're in. Our demon asses, as you so eloquently put it, don't need sleep."

Another yawn escaped me as I peered up at him. "No wonder you're so wide awake. I can barely keep my eyes open." I stretched once again. It seemed almost reflexive to keep me from falling asleep.

"If you keep stretching against me like that, you're going to find out how awake I am." His low growl sent a small vibration through his chest that I felt against my cheek. I shot up, not sure my body could take more. I was already raw. I wondered if that would go away too once I was in Hell. In a way, I didn't want it to. It was a reminder of the night we shared. A night when nothing else existed, there was no danger, everyone in the world was happy, and all I had to think about was being with the most beautiful man I'd ever met. We loved each other with equal fervor, a love that would last an eternity. At least, that's what being with him made me feel, as sappy, romance novel-ish as it sounded. I may have been half-demon, but I had every right to a Cinderella fantasy too. There was only one problem—I wasn't Cinderella, and it was no ball I was headed for. No pair of glass slippers could change my reality.

"Do you think I can pull this off, Hunter?" I asked, desperately needing him to believe in me in order to reassure myself. The fantasy was over, and admittedly, I was afraid.

He pulled me over him. "If I didn't think you had the power to do this, I'd be throwing you over my shoulder and locking you up somewhere you'd never be able to escape. Then I'd make love to you every minute, so you couldn't sneak away in your dreams."

His words were playful, but the intensity of his expression proved he was deadly serious. Relief washed over me. It didn't wipe away my fear, as there were too many *what ifs* remaining to be completely confident, but it helped knowing Hunter thought I was strong enough.

"Hey." He placed his fingers under my chin, so I'd lock him in the eyes again. "I'm going to be with you every step of the way. I won't let anything happen to you."

"I know." And I believed it with all of my heart. All of the trust issues I had with Hunter in the past were gone. He'd proven time and again he would do anything to protect me. I only wished I hadn't waited so long to let down my wall. I don't know if we could have avoided the things that happened, but I wanted him to know I loved him all this time.

We shared one last long kiss, both of us knowing the time had come. Hunter told me he was going to check in with Eric and Nora to let them know we were ready. I decided to shower, not to keep myself awake, since my nerves had pretty much overtaken my exhaustion, but to keep myself from having an anxiety attack while thinking about what we were preparing to do. The water washed away all signs of our lovemaking, but I lavished in the smell of Hunter that emanated off me in the process. I pictured his powerful body and the way his strong arms enveloped me the previous night, symbolically protecting me. The shower spray and my memories gave me a new vitality and belief that we'd be successful in finding my dad. But Hunter's question still lingered in my head.

Would he want to be saved?

CHAPTER ELEVEN

One foot in the doorway of Hell.

That's where I found myself, appearing from nothingness, like a magician's assistant in a spectacular vanishing performance. There was no tunnel, no feeling of flying through space and time to get there, I was simply...there. The familiar forest loomed to my left, unchanged in its ominous, shadowy glory, but strangely comforting, as a more sinister scene welcomed me on my right. The entry into Hell was as dark and dismal as on my previous visit.

I took a deep breath and started down the steps leading into the bleak corridor, when I stopped. I remembered Hunter warning me to remain in the doorway until he came for me. The instructions were so similar to what Caleb said when he tried to set a trap for me, and I should have been more apprehensive, but I did not fear Hunter's intentions. Not anymore. I only prayed this was *not* one of those times when I would be proven wrong. I was determined to go with my gut instincts from now on. I should have been listening to the subconscious rumblings that were mingling with my thoughts all along. Then again, fate had a funny way of making you walk down a particular path of life no matter what you do. Lucky for me, I was part Guardian, so I did have the power to change that path when I needed to...in theory, anyway.

As I started back toward the entrance, a high-pitched scream echoed through the corridor. I spun around, the blood draining from my face while goose bumps pimpled my arms. My eyes were instantly drawn to the same door I peered through when Hunter was held prisoner. I knew without a doubt the scream came from inside those walls, but this time, it wasn't Hunter.

Dread filled my body as I heard the woman cry out again. I raced toward the familiar voice I'd heard my whole life. Reaching the door within seconds, my worst fear was confirmed as I looked through the slats in the door to see my mom in the very chains that previously held Hunter captive.

"Mom?" I cried out, desperately hoping the woman clothed in a flimsy white dress and shackled to the thick pillars would not respond and miraculously be someone else.

She turned her face enough that I could see her tear-stricken profile. There was no mistaking my mom's slender neck and high cheekbones. Sweat and tears distorted her usually bright green eyes, which were now red-rimmed and puffy. I gasped at the awful sight of her.

"Cassie? Cassie, is that you? Please help me." Her plea was filled with unmistakable terror, and my heart lurched.

"Yes, it's me," I told her, searching around for some way to get her out. Hunter managed to escape, so there had to be a way. "I'm going to get you out, just hold on. Hunter is on his way. He'll be here any minute. What happened, Mom? How did you get here?"

"It was Caleb. He tricked me. He told me you went into Hell for your father. He said you were in trouble and needed help."

"But how did he get you *down* here? You're not—"

"A demon?" a gravelly voice came from behind me, sending a shiver up my spine. I slowly turned to face it. From the moment I found out my dad was being tortured in Hell, I knew I'd be forced to confront the King of the Underworld again, but no amount of preparation could make the reality of it any less horrifying. It wasn't because he looked like the devilish creature all the horror movies portrayed. In fact, he was quite handsome to look at, as disgusting as it was to admit. What made me cringe was the fact I knew what he was capable of, and more importantly, I knew what his intentions were.

"No, not yet," Nergal said. "I'm not even sure if we'll turn her at all. We still have lots of playtime before we need to make those kinds of life-changing decisions. It's much more fun when she shows her petty human feelings."

I glared into his fathomless blue eyes, but my obvious hatred for him didn't seem to have any effect. His perfect, white teeth shone brightly in the leer he gave me. He was all wrong. There should have been ugly, pointed shark teeth set inside a hideous face, and horns protruding from a misshapen head. As it was, his appearance was symbolic of what he was—a deceptive, malicious demon. And I loathed him even more for it.

My abhorrence for him boiled inside me, and my power surged easily from it. I charged at him, expecting to meet the resistance of a brick wall, but managed to force him back. I feared he simply let me do it, but it didn't matter. I intended to take advantage as best I could. Pushing him into the wall, I braced one arm against his neck, while the other pinned his bicep.

"Let. Her. Go," I said with a menacing calm, as close to his face as I could get without touching.

"I'd let him go if I were you, Cassie."

Twisting my head without letting up on Nergal, I saw Caleb inside the cell, holding a dagger to my mom's throat. She was released from her shackles. He brought her up against the cell door so I could see both of them clearly. The tendons in her neck were strained, like she was trying to remain as still as possible. The blade of the dagger was pressed so deeply I was afraid the slightest movement might result in piercing her skin.

"C'mon, Cassie," Caleb taunted. "You know I don't care if she dies. She means nothing to us. I...*we*...want you."

"Yes," Nergal said as he slowly peeled my arm from his neck. "It's you we want." He kept his hand on my wrist and used it to spin me and face the cell door, pulling me back against his body, his arm crossed over my chest to hold me in place.

"I know what you're here for," he whispered in my ear, the wind of his breath causing a wave of tremors to pass down the left side of my body. I tried to lean away from his lips, but he held me too firmly. "And I can help you get what you want...painlessly. But you're going to have to cooperate, Cassandra."

I clenched my teeth together while I regarded my mom. Her eyes were closed, as if she wanted to void out everything around her. I could only imagine how hard it was to do with the blade still at her throat. Caleb's eyes, on the other hand, roguishly ran up and down my body while Nergal held me still. I felt like someone's dinner, and it made me mad as hell.

"Tell your dog to stop looking at me like I'm his favorite chew toy and we can talk." I gave Caleb my most disgusted look. Caleb licked his lips. I threw up in my mouth. "You know I'm going to kill you in the end, right?" I told him.

"Now, now, children," Nergal said. "You'll have an eternity to play with each other." Caleb smiled, and I bit my lip to keep from coaxing him into any more childish antics. "Are you going to talk nice now, Cassandra, or do I have to continue to restrain you? I can assure you either way works for me."

"I want him off my mom first. In fact, I want him out of her cell. Or her, whichever, but I want him away from her. I don't trust him."

"Caleb, take the knife off Sara and step away from her."

Caleb obeyed, and as he did, my mom's eyes opened. She was clearly relieved, but my heart jumped out of my chest when I saw her eyes were the color of blue steel—demon blue.

My own eyes widened in disbelief, and I sucked in a breath when I realized what had already been done. A warrior cry escaped my lips. I struggled against Nergal's hold on me, but his arms didn't budge. He was much stronger than when I threw him against the wall. My anger churned, power brewing inside me once more, but somehow, Nergal was containing it.

"What did you do to her?" I screamed, gaping at her devilish eyes as they stared back at me through the slats in the door. They were empty, as if a switch had turned, and she lost all emotion. My heart broke into tiny pieces knowing I'd done this to her.

"Well, now, how else did you think we'd get her down here?" Nergal's head bent close to mine. Thoughts of head-butting him crossed my mind, but I cast them aside, knowing it would be no use. "And here I thought we were doing you a favor. Don't you see the beauty of it? Now your mother and father can live happily ever after for all eternity. They are the same. Granted, they are both soulless and will work forever for me, but at least they'll be together, right? That is what you wanted, isn't it? For them to be reunited? You can all be a family again, Cassandra. Now, you have every reason to stay."

"You *bastard*." I struggled with all my will, only to be spun around and thrown back against the cell door. His arm pinned me across the throat. I spat in his face with all of the contempt I felt for him. "I will never work for you. I will fight you every day for the rest of eternity if I have to," I said through clenched teeth.

Nergal wiped the spittle from his face with his free hand and licked it off as he continued to bear down on me. "It doesn't have to be this way. You can still free them. My offer still stands. Work for me, and I'll free them both."

"What good are they the way they are? My mom would rather die, than be one of your brethren. And I would rather die, than see them this way. You've burned the bridge, Nergal. You have nothing to offer me anymore. Maybe you should have thought about that before you sent your flunky after her."

"Have you already forgotten about the reason you came here in the first place?" Nergal asked. "Do you think I didn't know what you planned on doing to your father once you got him out of here? Come now, I'm the King. I make it a point to anticipate my enemies' next moves. But we don't have to be enemies. I'll allow you to go through with your plans of trying to turn your parents back to their *holy* status as long as you agree to stay and work for me."

My inner bullshit detector was blasting me, warning me that this was the Devil, and there were always trip wires when it came to making deals with him.

"But why do you need me so badly? What do you want me to do?"

"I have big plans for you."

"Yeah, well, I like to know what kind of shit I'm about to put my foot into before I take the next step."

Nergal laughed. I didn't.

"Fair enough," he said after realizing I wouldn't give in to him. "You know, your stubborn resolve is delectable, and could prove quite useful once you bend to my authority." His hand caressed my face, and I quickly turned away from it as much as I could. "I was going to let Caleb pursue you, however, I may decide to keep you for myself. But there's plenty of time for all of that. Why don't we go sit comfortably in my quarters, and we can discuss all the details of our little truce, shall we?"

"I want to see my dad."

"Oh, you will. I keep him very close to me."

"And my mom comes with."

"You are very demanding for someone who doesn't have a whole lot of choices right now, Cassandra. I don't take orders well, so you'd do better to rein in your impulses, or your chance at any deal with me will quickly pass. You'll suffer the fires of Hell before you can say goodbye to those you so desperately want to sell your soul for. You're in *my* house. I suggest you try to be a more gracious guest for now." His arm tightened on my throat, and my windpipe was cut off before he let up again. "Do we understand each other?"

I could only nod as I gasped for breath.

"Good." He released me, and I bent over, not realizing how tense my body had gotten while he held me. "Follow me. Caleb, bring Mrs. Cosgrove along."

Nergal walked down the long corridor. Wall torches magically lit as he proceeded. I had the strongest urge to charge him while his back was turned. Images of crashing into him and using one of those torches to turn his body into an inferno of flames, melting him in excruciating pain, ran rampant until I heard the cell door click behind me. I moved away as it opened. Caleb led my mom out, her vacant eyes accentuated by her robotic movements.

"After you," Caleb said to me as he stood with my mom, his hand on her upper arm. She didn't pull away or even struggle against him. She simply stood and waited for him to direct her. I never felt so helpless in my life. But I would make it right. I had to.

"You know, Caleb. I'm kind of glad you don't die easily, because I'm going to enjoy ripping you apart—piece by piece," I promised.

"I'm going to enjoy *you* immensely too, Cassie," he countered, blowing me a kiss.

If it was the last thing I did in this life, I was going to make him suffer unending pain.

I followed Nergal down the corridor, banishing the thought that I was walking the green mile to an untimely death. Our plans may have been thwarted by this latest development, but I was getting used to winging things. My *mom turned demon* was a major setback, but I had much more faith in my abilities now, and I knew Hunter wouldn't let me down. I'd get my parents out of this, or die trying.

That was the new and improved plan.

CHAPTER TWELVE

I'm not quite sure what I expected the Underworld to look like. Countless images I remembered from Dante's *Divine Comedy*, with its nine levels of Hell, always popped into my head whenever I thought of it. But there were no half-man/half-goats, or wandering bodies toting their own heads in these hallways. At least, none I could see. There were many more prison-like cells lining the walls of the infinite maze of corridors we walked through, but we went by so fast I was unable to see any potential horrors they contained. Or maybe I was too afraid to look.

Each passageway was so similar to the last we could have been walking in circles without my ever catching on; all made of the same stone, dimly lit by torches hanging from the walls. I started out mentally leaving breadcrumbs for myself, but lost track after about the tenth gray, dismal path we followed. Once in a while, I'd spot a definitive scrape mark or smudge of something I didn't dare guess the origins of, but for the most part, there was nothing telltale or remarkable in any of the hallways we trekked through.

Having had enough, I was ready to call Nergal out for taking me on a wild goose chase, when we turned the corner and came to a steep set of stairs, leading to a huge set of double doors at the bottom. The doors were constructed of a polished heavy stone that ran from floor to domed ceiling. Like all the other doors I'd seen in Hell so far, there were no handles or modern-day keypads with which to open them.

The smell of something burning permeated the stairwell, and I prayed the sight of people being burned alive didn't await me inside. One could only prepare for the worst upon entering the Devil's lair. I stopped midway down the stairwell, geared up to make a run for it if I saw the first hint of flames on skin when those doors opened, but Caleb came up behind me, way too close for my comfort, so I proceeded slowly.

Nergal stood in front of the massive doors, and they began to gradually open inward. I thought of the sliding stone door through which I'd first come in. It too seemed to know when I was ready to enter. I'd thought my touch was the unlocking mechanism, but apparently, the doors in Hell were on some sort of mental telepathy system. I wondered how it worked. Who had access to what? What were the connections?

I was nudged from behind and realized I'd stopped while contemplating how the doors worked. Nergal had already gone in, and Caleb was making sure I wouldn't make a break for it. I gave him the evil eye over my shoulder before continuing into the room.

Upon entering, it was as if I'd walked into a whole different place and time. I expected a torture chamber of sorts, complete with every deadly instrument invented to sadistically torment individuals hanging from the walls, but I was way off the mark. The room was a palace of luxury; one fit for...*well*...a king. Maroon-colored walls gave the room a rich, dark atmosphere. My eyes were drawn to the paintings covering most of them. Depictions of men and women in multiple sensual situations appeared to be the theme. A shiver ran down my spine as I realized Caleb and Nergal saw exactly what I was looking at. I forced my attention to the tremendous fireplace centered on the wall on the other side of the room. The flames blazed, creating shadows that danced into the far corners of the chamber, dwarfing the soft, amber glow of the petite lamps, which sat atop small tables throughout the room. A beautiful, cushioned settee sat in front of the hearth, making the scenery appear more like a cozy cabin in the woods than the headquarters of the most evil being known to man.

All the furniture was lavishly outlined with gold, into which various symbols were etched, but I couldn't make out what any of them were. They weren't written in any language I'd ever seen. At the far end of the room, a long, mahogany dining table sat, surrounded by chairs made of the same material as the other furniture, all of which contained the same mysterious gold etchings surrounding the frames. Of course, the castle-worthy dining table wouldn't be complete without an extravagant candelabrum that magically lit as I glanced its way. I almost thought I had something to do with the mystical flames until I remembered Nergal was watching my every move.

I forced myself to stop checking out every lavish detail and settled back to observing my gracious host. I tried to appear bored, but it was a wasted effort since I practically spun around the room with my mouth agape already. Nergal gave me a knowing look before asking me if I'd like something to drink. In any other setting, it would seem like the respectable thing for a host to do, but considering my experience with demons and drinks, I passed.

"Look, Nergal. I'm not interested in dinner and a movie. I just want to see my dad so we can get on with this." I thought I heard Caleb chuckle, but I refused to glance his way.

"He's close, but there are a few details we need to go over before I reunite you with your beloved family. Why don't you have a seat?" He motioned me toward the settee in front of the fireplace, and I contemplated refusing, but figured it was only prolonging the inevitable. I was quite certain Nergal would wait me out much longer than my patience could tolerate. Plus, I had no idea if Hunter knew where I was. I expected he'd have shown up by now, but I still wanted to get to my dad before he popped in and all hell broke loose.

Taking a seat at the far end of the sofa, I silently admired how comfortable it was. Nergal sat in a throne-like chair near me. Caleb and my mom remained standing, but came into view near the hearth. My mom continued her comatose demeanor, seemingly ignorant of where and what she was. It was probably better that way. I hated it, but imagined if she were cognizant of what was happening, she'd be fighting my acquiescence.

"So what were those details you wanted to go over? It's simple, isn't it? You let me turn my mom and dad back, send them on their way, and I'm yours for all eternity."

Nergal tsked with a shake of his head. "There's one matter you seem to be avoiding, and I imagine you are doing it intentionally. What, my dear Cassandra, are we to do with your Hunter?"

Nergal's question threw me off. I wasn't expecting it, so all I could conjure up was a blank stare. Of course, he knew Hunter was there. It was naïve to assume he didn't. He'd anticipated every move up until this point. What would make me think he wouldn't know Hunter was with me...*somewhere*?

"I have a suggestion," Caleb interrupted.

"You couldn't if you tried," Nergal stated blandly. "You already know he's much too powerful for you."

"He caught me off guard." Caleb's tone was defensive. He looked like he was going to continue, but Nergal cut him off with a silent gesture.

"Why don't I get right to my point then," Nergal said, turning to me. "I don't trust you, Cassandra. I'm certain the feelings are quite mutual in that respect. Therefore, I'm looking for insurance."

"What kind of insurance?" A chill developed at the base of my spine despite the heat in the room from the fire blazing before us.

"If I no longer have your father here to keep you around, I'll need a replacement. Since I know Hunter will be relentless in trying to rescue you, I think he would be the perfect candidate."

"What?" I jumped up. "*No.*"

"Oh, don't worry. It won't be as bad as you think. I promise not to torture him this time." A devious grin took over his features. "In fact, I'd even allow you regular conjugal visits."

I was about to protest, verbally *and* physically, but I didn't get the chance before Caleb whined. "You said she was mine. That's why we brought *her* here." He punctuated this last bit of news by grabbing my mom's forearm and shaking her as if to emphasize his point. I had no clue what was going on. Obviously, there was some hidden agenda I was oblivious to and somehow, my mom was a part of it. Judging by the look on Nergal's face, Caleb had just spilled the beans.

"You idiot," Nergal yelled at him. They silently faced off for what felt like eons. The tension was so tight I was afraid body parts might start flying.

"I don't understand," I said. "What does my mom have to do with Hunter?" As much as I would have enjoyed seeing Nergal rip Caleb apart, I was afraid my mom might get caught up in the melee. It was scary enough being around two destructive forces, but being caught in the middle of them, hashing that destruction out was too risky for my taste.

Nergal regained his composure after he gave Caleb one last warning look. He turned to me. "I guess it's on to Plan B..." He paused and cocked his head, as if listening to some distant sound no one else could hear. "Ahhh, Hunter, you're just in time."

I spun to face the entry doors as Hunter walked through them. He eyed me over as if assessing whether or not I was hurt, before turning his wary eyes onto Nergal.

"What are you up to, Nergal?" Hunter asked, stopping near Caleb and my mom. Nergal met his gaze, the corners of his mouth slowly rising, as he enjoyed the strain of the moment. He was the magician and we were his audience. Apparently, we were destined for a nail-biting performance because he continued to draw out the suspense with his silence.

"Who is this woman?" Hunter asked, grabbing my mom from Caleb.

"Hunter, what are you—" I started before he cut me off.

"This isn't your mother. One of my men was just *with* her. She is safe and certainly not in Hell."

My head spun as if caught in a whirlwind of questions. *What the hell was going on? The woman standing with us looked exactly like my mom. It was all an illusion?*

The mental fog lifted, and I berated myself for believing in it. I should have known. The Underworld was *supposed* to be filled with deception and misdirection. The King easily achieved his role as the ultimate magician.

"Oh well, I guess the jig is up, as they say." Nergal laughed. "It was inevitable. You never would have cooperated, Hunter, and that is a problem. It was my attempt at being a nice guy, but as it is, you force my hand. It's just as well, I never could wear a halo fashionably."

He waved his hand toward my mom, who transformed right before my eyes. Before me stood a beautiful woman, with long, silky, raven curls that hung to her waist. Olive skin and high cheekbones accented her glowing blue eyes, which made her even more mesmerizing, despite what they represented. She was small, like my mom, but more toned, and her biceps while not big, were well defined. As unforgettable as her features were, I didn't have a clue who she was, and from the expression on Hunter's face, neither did he. While feeling relieved this woman was not my mom, I held my breath, waiting for another bomb to drop. I knew Nergal would never show his hand without some alternate plan.

The woman's demeanor changed drastically from the zombiesque disposition she held when she appeared as my mother. Caleb released her from his hold, and she stood at attention, as if waiting to obey her next order, a soldier fighting for a cause. There was no way this woman was a slave to the King; she had to be in on the ruse of her own free will.

"I'd like you to meet the latest addition to my growing family," Nergal said, putting an arm around her shoulders like a proud father. "This is Alison."

If the name was supposed to ring a bell, Nergal must have been greatly disappointed seeing the blank looks on our faces. With his arm, he angled Alison until she was standing directly in front of Hunter.

"Don't recognize her?" he asked Hunter.

My stomach became queasy. I had no idea what Nergal was up to, but it gave me a really bad feeling.

"Let's not play games, Nergal," Hunter said. "I have no idea who she is, nor do I care."

Guards appeared in the doorway, and then they tiptoed into the room, cautiously spreading out behind Hunter, as if readying themselves for attack. Hunter twisted his head only a fraction, tracking them in his peripheral vision as he continued to glare at Nergal. My nausea grew into a full-blown knot that ached with every deep breath I took. This was not good. Something really bad was about to happen.

"Ah, yes, I forget, you have no memories of your former life," Nergal said with a conspiratorial smirk. "Why don't we fix that problem for you?" Before the blood from my face had the chance to fully drain, Nergal made an almost imperceptible nod of his head toward Hunter. I watched Hunter, waiting for his reaction, wondering if this was even possible, but I knew with Nergal, anything was.

Hunter's eyes focused, as if they'd been clouded over all this time, and I knew the minute he recognized the woman. His eyes became more animated than I'd ever seen them, his emotions exposed, clearer than any words could describe. It was as if he were watching a movie play out before him, causing him shock, happiness, sadness, and then anger. His face contorted with each sentiment as he stared at the woman.

Whoever she was, she meant a great deal to Hunter, and I went through a myriad of emotions when I realized it. In all the times I worried about complications of being with Hunter, not once did I imagine having to deal with his past. Hell, I really didn't even consider his former life. Seekers couldn't remember their previous lives, so it was pointless to think about it. *Until now.*

Hunter stood frozen in place, except for his eyes, which revealed their murderous intent as they shifted from Alison to Nergal. I jumped and let out a scream as Hunter launched himself at Nergal with a loud warrior cry. The guards were ready for him and they pounced, tackling him to the floor before he could reach their master. My heart lurched as he struggled with the demons, but I knew there was nothing I could do.

The woman didn't appear affected by anything transpiring in front of her. There was no indication that she knew Hunter, as he seemed to know her, and no reaction to Hunter's explosive display. She simply stood as she was, awaiting her next order.

I faced Nergal, needing to help Hunter in any way I could. But I had to know what I was up against. What kind of twisted plan had he put in place?

"What have you done?" I demanded. "Who is she, Nergal?"

Death threats continued from the floor, even though the guards appeared to be getting Hunter under control. They had him face down with all four looking like they needed everything they had to hold him down. More guards waited in the doorway to guarantee he'd be restrained if need be.

"Of course, yes, how rude of me," Nergal continued with his performance. "Cassandra, it is my pleasure to introduce you to Alison—Hunter's fiancée."

There it was. The bomb that was ticking away, timed for the right moment to explode. That niggling feeling I had this whole time about being in love with Hunter just blew up in my face. He wasn't supposed to have a past. And it sure as hell wasn't supposed to show up in Hell with us.

CHAPTER THIRTEEN

Speechless—jaw-dropped, wordless, and bug-eyed speechless. That's how Nergal's introduction to Alison left me. Hunter's fiancée from when he was a Guardian was standing in the depths of the Underground as if she belonged there, blue eyes and all. They'd obviously turned her for this very occasion, and it chilled me to the bone to see the extremes they were willing to take to get the upper hand. Any hopes I had of making it out of Sheol with my father and Hunter were instantly deflated. I had no idea what was going through Hunter's head. To have all of his memories flood back to him in an instant, not to mention one of those memories standing before him, soulless, was too overwhelming for me to expect him to help. I couldn't imagine what he was feeling, but my heart ached seeing him so tortured. At the same time, my heart ached knowing there was someone else over whom he was agonizing.

Caleb's muffled laughter grated on my nerves, and I turned to him with an icy glare I felt all the way down in the pit of my stomach. "Shut. Up," I said through clenched teeth, standing as near as I could to him without having to feel his breath on me. My fingers twitched as I pictured grabbing his neck and breaking it with no less effort than snapping a twig from a tree. The power within me was pulsing in my veins, begging to be set free. My eyes felt electric, as if at any moment, a current would surge from them, sending powerful voltage into their target.

Caleb must have sensed my explosive air because he backed away. I took a step toward him, but was stopped by Alison's hand on my upper arm. Her fingers dug into my skin, making her intentions clear. After glancing down at the clenched fingers holding me, I trailed my gaze up her arm until it rested on her glowing blue eyes. Alison was defending Caleb all right. Either that, or she had a thing for me. There was definitely a malicious fixation on me in those eyes. Did she know what happened between Hunter and me?

"Alison, no," Hunter yelled from the floor. He was still pinned down, but able to raise his head enough to see Alison face off with me.

Alison didn't even flinch. Her eyes remained on mine. There was no emotion in them aside from the murderous intent she had for me. Her fingers clutched me even harder, and it was getting unbearable. I didn't care who she was. I wasn't going to let her manhandle me. Twisting her grasp on my arm, I pulled away and quickly grabbed her forearm in the process, wringing it around behind her, high against her back. I was surprised at how easy she was to hang onto. She seemed to have very little strength now that I had her in my grasp.

"Let him up," I yelled at Nergal, knowing the guards would only listen to him. He appeared bored by my command, so I grabbed Alison's neck with my other hand. "Let him up or I'll snap her neck right here, and then you'll have no leverage. You know I can do it."

"Cassandra," Hunter said tentatively, as if concerned one wrong word could trigger me to do exactly what I promised. I would never do it, but Nergal couldn't know that. I was taking a huge chance and counting on Hunter to know I would never hurt him like that, but I had to do something to get him free.

"As you wish," Nergal said with a nod at the guards.

They released Hunter, and he slowly got to his feet, watching me cautiously. My heart dropped from the look in his eyes, as if I were the enemy. Didn't he realize I was only doing this to help him? Or was he playing along in hope that maybe there was a way out of this mess? *God, why couldn't mind reading be one of the added benefits of being half-demon?*

"Alright," Hunter said, "you can let her go now."

I locked onto his gaze, searching for a hint of trust in me, but no matter how hard I searched, I could only see his trepidation and concern for Alison. I wanted to scream at him to remember who I was to him, what we were to each other, and tell him none of this changed the way we felt. But I couldn't show my hand to Nergal and Caleb. They had to believe I was willing to do anything to get what I wanted.

With my eyes still on Hunter's, I released Alison.

Nergal clapped his hands together. "Splendid. Now she's free to partake in the real reunion."

Confused, my gaze darted from Hunter to Alison, but I could only see the back of her head from my vantage point, so I watched him to gauge his reaction. His eyes were wide with surprise as he watched her. Her shoulders straightened and then fell forward, as if letting out an enormous breath. A smile came over Hunter's face, his eyes softening toward her. Instinctively, I knew—Alison had her memories back as well.

They crashed into each other, as did my beating heart into my chest while watching their desperate embrace. Hunter's eyes were no longer visible to me, as he buried his head into her neck, but I was thankful to be spared the sight. As much as I believed he deserved to have his life and memories back, I couldn't deny that it killed me to see him care so deeply for someone else, someone other than me.

After parting slightly, Alison's hands went to Hunter's face, her fingers running over his beautiful features, as if checking them to make sure they were real, while he stared back at her in awe. "Hunter," she said breathlessly. I stepped away from them, turning my back in a small attempt to tune them out. I couldn't stand it any longer. Witnessing their tender reunion, my heart felt like it was being ripped from my body.

With my back to the happy couple, I stepped to Nergal, my determination evident in my stiffened spine. Deep down, I was struggling to put one foot in front of the other. I had to banish all thoughts about Hunter and his newly rekindled flame clear out of my head. I was there to get my dad, and even though my heart was in pieces, I had to stay focused. With thoughts of never being with Hunter again, it was the hardest thing I had to do.

"I want to see my father." I held my chin up as I stared directly into Nergal's eyes. It irked me to no end that they held a sparkle in them. He was being entertained at my expense.

"What? You don't want to stay and watch—"

"No! I only want to get my dad out of here. Now take me to him, Nergal. Enough games." I was pushing my luck by making demands of the King in his kingdom. He had the upper hand. He knew it and so did I, but I was too pissed off to control my urgency of getting out of there, away from Hunter and Alison.

Nergal laughed, which pissed me off even more, but I knew I was lucky my disrespect only amused him.

"Very well," he said, turning to the guards. "Take them to Hunter's quarters, so they can get reacquainted in a little more private setting."

I heard shuffling feet, but didn't dare turn around to see what was happening. If I saw any more, I'd fall apart. Instead, I watched Nergal's eyes follow their movements until there were no more footsteps, and Nergal's gaze returned to mine. A breath I didn't know I was holding escaped my lips.

"Shall we?" he asked, offering his arm, as if we were on our way to some macabre prom. I glared at it in disgust. He got the hint, and motioned me toward a hallway off to the right of the room. Caleb fell into step next to me as I passed him. I wanted to cringe away from him. Maybe I did, because Nergal called him out. "Caleb, go and make sure Cassandra's chambers are ready. I want all the comforts we have to offer at her disposal. She should feel at home here with her new family."

That *did* make me cringe, but I continued down the hallway, determined not to let him goad me. He'd only enjoy it more.

Caleb let out an exasperated groan, like a spoiled child who was just told *no*. It was swiftly quelled, however, I assume by a threatening look from Nergal behind me. I didn't hear Caleb leave, but the air seemed less polluted to my senses, so he must have heeded Nergal's instructions. I shivered, thinking how close I'd gotten to him at one point. I'd do just about anything to be able to go back in time and have a *do over* on that occasion.

We reached a metal door at the end of the hallway. I wondered what the King had against knobs or handles, as this one also didn't seem to have one.

I turned toward him. "You're going to have to teach me that trick if you expect me to spend the rest of eternity here, you know. I would hate to keep bothering you for help every time I needed to go to the bathroom."

He laughed a rich, belly laugh. I didn't.

"You have your father's witty sarcasm, Cassandra," he told me, a smile lighting up his face. In any other circumstance, I'd say he had a *nice* smile, but seeing he was the Devil and I was in Hell, it only creeped me out.

"I'm sure he'll be very proud," I said. "Why don't we go and ask him?"

Nergal nodded, and I heard a click of the door behind me, along with a breeze on my back, telling me it was opening on its own. I sucked in a breath, expecting to turn back around and face my worst fears at seeing my father's condition, but I was surprised when I walked in. It was far from the cold, dark cell Hunter was held in. This room was large, so large that I barely saw the other end of it. The walls were gray, like almost everything else I'd seen in Hell, but the recessed lights in the ceiling brightened them to a lighter shade.

The door closed behind us with another click. I spun around with thoughts of being trapped surfacing in my head. Bringing myself back into focus before I had a panic attack, I realized the walls were lighter, not only because of the illumination, but because they were made of something different. I walked over and gently touched where the door now meshed in with the walls. It was soft, softer than walls should be. Pushing into it, I realized they were made of padded material.

I looked at Nergal curiously.

"Helps him sleep at night," he said with a smirk. "It can get pretty rowdy out there."

I shot him a glare, letting him know I was not amused. "Yeah, well, considering demons don't sleep, and there is no nighttime in Hell, I'm calling bullshit."

His eyebrows rose. "You've been doing your homework."

"I've got friends in low places. Now, where is he?"

Nergal glanced toward the back of the room and my eyes followed. Shadows lined the deepest part of the room, preventing me from seeing anything further.

"Troy, my old friend, you have a visitor," Nergal called out.

Leery but curious, I stepped deeper into the room, squinting in an attempt to see what was back there without going too far. Too many years of watching bad horror movies had my inner skeptic screaming at me that this was a trap. A creaking noise, like the kind that transpired from someone adjusting their weight on old furniture, came from the left corner of the room, where I could barely make out the outline of what appeared to be a bed. Maybe it was more like a cot, I couldn't be sure, but it didn't appear very big. It was too dark to see anything more.

"Go to hell, Nergal," came a deep voice from the area with the cot. "I'm not in the mood for any company today."

I gasped. It *was* my father. My memories were mere photographs, but I still knew it was him. Was his voice forever ingrained in my brain? Or was it only my heart trying to make the connection after not having him in my life all this time? It didn't matter how I knew. What mattered was I'd found him, and he could finally be released from his torture.

"Dad?" I called out tentatively, walking closer. I wasn't sure what I should call him. Doubts filled my thoughts as I realized I didn't really know this man...demon. He'd been there almost all of my life. What if it had changed him? Hell, I didn't even know who he was to begin with so how would I be able to tell? I'd grown up believing he was a loving man, a Guardian like my mom and me. But that was all a lie too. What if I were making a big mistake? *No*, I told myself. Hunter wouldn't have let me come if my father's heart had become hardened by this place. I had to believe that.

More creaking, and a shadowy figure shot up from the bed. "Cassandra?"

"Yes, it's me."

My silly, fairy tale fantasy of him rushing to pull me into his arms remained a dream as he inched slowly toward me. Instead of the amazed happiness I expected to see, his features shouted suspicion. With dark eyebrows furrowed, his squinting blue eyes examined me. My nerves gave way to trembling as I stood before him, suddenly worried what he might be thinking about me. All of those normal, human, *I'm meeting my long lost father for the first time* feelings came flooding through me. Questions like, *would he approve of what I've become*? Or *will he like me*? which, given the circumstances, seemed ridiculous and futile, still managed to wend their way into my thoughts. Forcing them aside, I examined him as well.

I had no idea what I expected him to look like after all this time. The only mental picture I had of him came from family portraits from when I was four. I must have expected him to age like any other human father, because I was shocked to see he looked exactly the same as in those old pictures. His black hair was as thick and wavy as it was then, without one strand of gray. He wore a pair of sweatpants, his muscled torso bare. I assumed his solid physique had nothing to do with a strict exercise regimen. Apparently, Seekers didn't age either, and managed to keep their appearances young and strong. I mentally slapped myself for hoping that was a gene I inherited. As I peered up, searching his features for more recognition, I realized my mom was right...I did look like my father.

"So you've come for me?" he asked, scaring me as the words bit into the silence.

"Yes, I'm here to help you get home, Dad," I said, expecting to find relief in his eyes.

"Well, then you've wasted your time because I'm not going anywhere."

CHAPTER FOURTEEN

Hunter's words haunted me, *What if he doesn't want to be turned?* I didn't want to consider it then, but my worst fear of how this whole plan could backfire was staring me in the face. But why would he want to stay? He was being held against his will, that much was obvious. When he addressed Nergal a moment ago, I sensed his distaste for him, or at least I thought I did. Was it possible I'd only assumed it? Was I projecting my own hateful prejudice onto him? Was it possible this whole damn thing was simply a trap, and my father was part of the conspiracy to reel me in? I prayed that wasn't the case.

"Dad, Mom needs you," I pleaded with him, hoping beyond hope my anxieties were unwarranted and his heartstrings could be pulled hard enough to listen to reason. I, however, had no idea what that reasoning would be. "Nergal has agreed to let you leave. You're free."

"Is that right?" he asked sarcastically. "Even if you are whom you say you are, which I doubt, Nergal doesn't do anything without gaining something in return." He peered over my shoulder to Nergal. "Isn't that right, *old friend*? C'mon Nergal, we've played this game too many times for me to fall for your old tricks. You've passed off your cronies as Cassandra enough times now that I've learned my lesson. You're going to have to find new material."

"Dad, it's really me." Instinctively, I grabbed hold of his hand, wanting him to somehow feel it was I, hoping our blood bond might be sealed from my touch. He snatched his hand away, and my heart dropped. His eyes burned with disdain toward me, and in that moment, I felt emptier than I'd ever felt in my entire life. First, Hunter turned his back on me, and now my father. Was I destined to live the rest of my days as lonely and deadened as my father appeared? Would I be bound to the Underworld, tortured by my own heart, longing for another life that could never be again? Is that what fate had in store for me?

I refused to go down like that. I knew fate could be changed because I'd changed it time and again for others. It was time I did it for myself. Nergal may have known all along my father would deny me. In fact, it sounded as if he'd prepped him for this very moment. But he didn't count on me pulling a magic trick from my own sleeve...or rather, my chest. I was about to cancel his best act.

"Here, I can prove it's me." I pulled at the chain around my neck, bringing the ring my father passed down to me as an heirloom so long ago. I held the ring between my fingers, stretching it toward him. The jewel caught the light just enough to reflect and shine his way.

He stared at it, as if inspecting every detail. I knew before his eyes even met mine that he believed me. I saw the love in them, but I also saw sadness.

"It's really you. Oh, Cassie." He put a hand to my face.

"Yes." I leaned into his palm. "Yes, it's really me."

"But your eyes...then it's true."

I lowered my eyes, almost ashamed at what he saw in them. Even though I was like him, I knew it wasn't something he'd be proud of. Our hatred for the dark fate we'd been dealt was something else we shared. But I also wanted him to know it hadn't consumed me, that I managed to keep my soul and still had control. I gazed back at him, hoping my eyes held the fortitude I wanted him to see in me. I wanted him to see that, like him, I could overcome my dark side.

"Now, Troy, if you would have only listened to me, this wouldn't have come as such a surprise to you," Nergal interjected.

My dad didn't pay Nergal any attention, but continued to hold my gaze.

"I refused to believe his stories of you," he told me. "I thought it was his way of tormenting me. When I left, you weren't showing any signs of becoming like me. I hoped you never would. Oh, God, I'm so sorry, Cassie."

"Dad," I took hold of his hand on my face, "it's okay. I can control it. The darkness hasn't taken over. I'm...different. I only let it through because I knew I had to get you out of here."

"You mean you're still a Guardian? But how can that be?" His eyebrows furrowed, and I noticed the lines between them were deep, as if they'd been etched into his skin too many times. I grew up thinking my world was so unfair at times, but those times were nothing compared to what he'd had to endure. And it was all to protect my mom and me.

"I'm not sure how. Maybe because Anael's blood mixed with Mom's was enough to shelter me from the evil. I don't know. All I know is that it hasn't consumed my soul, at least not yet."

"Then you have to get out of here, Cassie. Forget about me. I don't care what they do to me, it would hurt more if anything happened to you or your mom."

"Uh uh uh," Nergal sing-songed as he stepped forward to stand next to us. "No can do, Troy. Our deal has become null and void. You see, your darling daughter is much more valuable to me than you are, and she has agreed to a more profitable deal than you could ever offer."

My dad studied him, trying to decipher Nergal's cryptic message. When he got nowhere, he turned his questioning eyes to me.

"He wants to use me to lure more Guardians to the Underworld," I told my father, my lips drawing back at having to relay what might become my reality if I couldn't find a way out of this. "I'm his secret weapon because they would never suspect another Guardian. But he's also keeping me under watchful eye because of something else. It seems my blood can turn Seekers too."

My dad's eyes widened as he continued to stare at me. I almost thought I'd lost him to some permanent shock affliction, when he finally asked, "Back to what?"

There was silence for so long, I forgot what I last said to him, but even after I remembered, I didn't understand why he'd ask such a question. Wasn't it obvious?

When I only stared at him, he asked again, "What do you turn the Seekers back to?"

"They turn back to Guardians." But as I said the words, I realized I didn't really know for sure what I turned them into. My only lab rat happened to be a demon working closely with Nergal, even after he'd supposedly been turned. I assumed it was one of the reasons Nergal wanted to keep me in Hell, but how could I be sure of anything that happened now? In a voice now filled with doubt, I said, "At least, I think they do. Caleb has been the only one."

"Caleb?" he asked, mimicking my own disbelief. "Caleb? And you trust him? Please tell me you didn't come here thinking you would turn me based on an experiment with him? I can't believe your mother would let you do this."

I felt like a teenager being reprimanded for stupidly believing my parents couldn't smell alcohol on me if I only had one drink. Problem was, I had no defense. After seeing Caleb's green Guardian eyes that day, tunnel vision blinded me from reasonable thought. Even though I had a few suspicions Caleb may be faking, I was on a mission. In my mind, there were no obstacles I couldn't hurdle if it meant getting my dad back. But I never thought about the ten-foot brick wall that could obstruct my way. Even if I had thought about it, it wasn't like I could pluck a Seeker out from somewhere and do mad scientist experiments. Going into Hell was a one shot deal.

"Mom doesn't know," I said quietly.

My dad nodded, as if it didn't surprise him. "It's nice to know she hasn't changed. Your mother was always willing to protect you no matter the cost. If she'd known, she never would have let you come. But, of course, you knew that." He put his head down, shaking it sadly. Then he peered up at me again. I hated the pity I saw in his eyes. I could see he'd already written my plan off. I was still a child to him, trying to play grown-up and fix things that were far beyond my years. He doubted my ability to help him, and it killed me. But it also pissed me off. I didn't come all this way, putting me, as well as everyone else, in danger, to curl up in the fetal position because someone didn't believe I could do it. Even if that person *was* my dad.

There was only one way to prove I had control and the ability to pull this off, both to my dad *and* myself. I looked him in the eyes and said, "Dad..."

Spinning around, I snatched the dagger from the leather holster Nergal had on his belt. Before he had the chance to grab me, I sliced open my hand, threw the dagger behind me, and crashed into my dad. We both fell to the ground from the force, me landing on top of him, just as I hoped. I heard Nergal scrambling back to retrieve his weapon, so I knew I only had seconds to spare.

"Cassie, what are you—"

It was a rash decision, and one I trusted I wouldn't regret. With my father's mouth still gaping in surprise, I forced my bloody fingers into it, making sure to smear the blood onto his tongue. I gagged, but held back the bitter acid that was rising in my throat. Force-feeding blood to my dad wasn't something high on my bucket list. Then again, neither was being in Hell with the Devil, or seeing Hunter in love with another woman, so I guess I shouldn't have expected a tea party and crumpets.

Nergal had me in his clutches within seconds. I let him hold me prisoner within his arms, my back against his chest, as I watched my dad. He was lying on his side and attempting to spit my blood from his mouth. I didn't know how much I'd gotten into him, but if Caleb's transition were true, it shouldn't take a lot.

"Cassie, what did you do?" my dad yelled.

"I'm sorry, Dad."

"I'd say our little spitfire here is eager to get this deal underway, isn't that right?" Nergal asked, his lips way too close to my ear.

I ignored him, wanting nothing more than to go to my dad, but I didn't dare struggle with Nergal. Dad sat up, wiping blood from his lips. He gazed up at me with anger and pain in his eyes. I knew I wouldn't be able to make him understand, he was too much like me. We were both willing to sacrifice our own lives for family. Our only difference was that I wasn't willing to give in to fate at the hands of Hell. I wouldn't stay a slave to the Underworld. Somehow, someway, I vowed to get out. I only wished he could know that.

My dad tried to stand, but faltered, and while my heart fell watching him struggle, a glimmer of hope picked it back up. Was it possible he was transitioning already? I had no idea what to expect, since I never had the chance to see the actual process. Caleb was the only one that went through it, and after Hunter had beaten the crap out of him back then, he was taken away to Hell. The only witness to the progression was Nergal.

The light dimmed from his blue eyes. He was fading fast. I broke free of Nergal's arms, watching my dad struggle to stay upright. Running to him, I stretched my arms out in an effort to catch him, just as he lost control and fell back. I caught his head right before it hit the floor.

Gently, I lowered him to the ground. "It's my turn to be your Guardian, Dad. We're all going to be okay. I promise."

His eyes were closed, so I had no idea if he heard my vow. It was hard to see him that way. For years, I wished I could remember putting my dad to rest, having the chance to say goodbye one last time even if he couldn't hear me. It felt that way now, as he lay still before me. Leaning over, I pressed my lips to his forehead, and then rested my cheek against his. "It's only goodbye for now. I'll see you soon on the other side," I whispered in his ear as I prayed it would be true.

"Now we wait," Nergal said behind me.

Still studying my dad's lifeless body, I asked, "How long?"

"Who knows? Could be months, could be years. Caleb was out at least a month. It seems to take much less time to fill the blood with evil than with good. Must be that awful human side where evil lies deep, just waiting to be set free. Don't worry, we'll keep a close eye on him and be sure to tell you the minute he's green again." He said the word green as if it left a horrible taste on his tongue.

My own eyes roamed over my dad's closed lids at the mention of them. I willed them to open, eager to get him cut. I never considered how long the transition would take. I scrambled to think of a way to get him out, wanting him safe with my mom as soon as possible. I didn't want him waking up in this place. He'd had enough dismal memories of it, I was sure. But I couldn't think of anything, my mind racing too fast to even hang onto an idea. I needed time to think...alone, without Dr. Doom hovering over me.

"You look tired, Cassandra. Seems you haven't fully come into your true nature yet. Why don't we get you to your quarters so you can rest?" Nergal held his hand out as if to help me up. I wanted to smack it, but he was right, I was exhausted. My body felt as drained of energy as my head. I put my hand in his, only because I didn't think I could stand on my own. It wasn't like I was going anywhere soon, I reasoned with myself. Refusing to look at him while he helped me up, I kept my eyes on my dad.

"Oh, don't worry," he said. "You'll be able to see him whenever you want for a long time to come."

Long time to come? I studied his face in an attempt to clear up my confusion, but he merely smiled back, as if we were having the friendliest of conversations.

"I don't expect the transition to go any longer than Caleb's," I said, testing the waters.

"Oh, no." He squeezed my hand tighter. "I meant before and after the transition."

I glared at him.

"Come now, you didn't actually think I'd let a Guardian out into the world only to turn around and thwart my demons, did you? That would be extremely destructive to our aim here. My business ethics wouldn't allow me to do something so damaging and feel good about myself after."

"And what about breaking our deal? Where does that fit into your business ethics?"

Nergal shook his head, demeaning me with his eyes as he did it. "I'm disappointed in you, Cassandra. Didn't you study your Guardian rulebook? I'm quite certain rule number one reads, *never make a deal with the Devil.* My deals are infamous for that fine print people always miss." He looked up at the ceiling and tapped his chin with his fingers, the epitome of the deranged thinker. "I'm pretty sure I coined that adage, now that I think of it."

"Get to the point. What do you plan to do with him?"

I held my breath during his dramatic pause, waiting for the final bomb to drop on my already foiled plan.

"Your insistence on making your father a Guardian has only managed to tighten the noose around your own neck. He will be more vulnerable to pain, as you well know. Unfortunately, for you, Guardians have that fatal flaw. It is my intention to use that flaw relentlessly on him if you do not follow my orders as directed. You are mine now, Cassandra, to do with what I want. If you do not obey, he will suffer greatly. And if you even attempt to help him escape, I'll bring Mom in on the deal. For real this time."

Vomit rose in my throat. I fought to keep it down by clenching my teeth and locking my jaw. Muscles stiffened as I wrestled against the power boiling beneath my skin. I wanted to rip him apart, tear off his head, and send it soaring across the room. I wanted to hold his heart in my hands, watch it pump slower and slower until it stilled, but I knew there was only a black void where his heart should be.

Oh, God. What have I done?

CHAPTER FIFTEEN

Not only was my dad still a prisoner of Hell, now he was a *defenseless* prisoner of Hell. He would feel greater pain than he had all those years being stuck in his cell, both physically and mentally. And it was my fault. I acted impulsively, taking it upon myself to decide his fate for him, and now we would both pay the price. I wanted to spit at the irony of my life. After all my years of thinking he was a Guardian and died, I'd been miraculously reunited with him, only to saddle him with a fate worse than death.

There had to be a way to get both of us out of this mess, but how? Hunter was off somewhere, rekindling the fires of his past, and who knew where the hell Eric was. That left me...on my own. There was no Plan B that starred me as the lone hero. Even if I managed to get my dad out of his padded room, I had no idea where to go. The Underworld was a labyrinth of corridors that all looked the same. I'd never find the way out on my own.

Exhausted and defeated, I hung my head as Nergal led me to the door. I heard it click, and glanced up to see Caleb entering as soon as we reached it. *Great, just what I needed.* I would have rather had a vat of salt poured onto a large, gaping wound on my skin than deal with him.

"Caleb will escort you to your quarters now, Cassandra. You would be wise to rest, since there is much work to be done later. I'll send someone to get you when I'm ready. Until then, sweet dreams." Nergal moved in, as if to kiss me on my forehead, like a father to his child, but I dodged away. Unfortunately, the move landed me right into Caleb's grubby paws. *Lovely.*

I twisted out of his arms, but there was nowhere to go. I was caged between them. Caleb grabbed my waist and pulled me back.

"I can walk on my own," I said, hatred seething from my pores. "Even if I wanted to run, I have no idea how to get out of here. I'd be lost after I got out of Nergal's chambers."

Caleb leaned his head near the side of my neck. "Oh, I know. I just like touching you." He took a deep breath and exhaled, his lips hovering closely over the bare skin at the base of my neck.

Holy hell. Was he sniffing me?

"Caleb." Nergal said the name with a warning tone. "I'm letting you take Cassandra to her quarters, but you are to leave her alone, so she can rest. You'll have plenty of time to play with her once she adapts to her new lifestyle with us. Do you understand?"

Caleb groaned close to my ear before he stepped aside. When he removed his arm from around my waist, I let out a sigh, but my irritation quickly returned when he grabbed my upper arm, squeezing it enough to make me wince. I glared at him, making sure he knew the death threat I gave him earlier was still a prominent thought in my head. His cocky leer gave the impression that it only amused him.

We left Nergal in his quarters, doing whatever kings of the Underworld do when they're not making evil plans and breaking deals. He wished me a cozy stay, as if he were the host of some bed and breakfast, instead of the Motel Hell it actually was. Left alone with Caleb, I clung to the fact that I knew I could kick his ass, in order to tolerate the walk with him to my quarters. It turned out to be quite stressful as he used every turn of a corner as an excuse to brush my breast with the backs of his fingers. Apparently, my poisonous glares and jabbing elbows didn't deter him. If we didn't get to my room quickly, I feared I would lose my control and go rabid on his ass.

We turned another corner, and of course, the perve copped another feel. I swung toward him, forcing his back against the corridor wall and put my hands against his chest to keep him pinned. "Look, are we almost there? Or are you taking me in circles to molest me? I'm tired, I'm pissed, and I really kind of hate you, so could you just take me to my quarters and poof away somewhere?"

The self-satisfied smile he'd worn while we were walking turned malicious, so I knew I'd gotten to him.

"What's the matter, Caleb? You don't like it when a girl manhandles you?"

He cocked his head to the side and locked his gaze on mine, peering intently. "You know, you are so much sexier with blue eyes. And for the record, I don't mind a little manhandling once in a while, but if you're going to handle me, do it right." His hand came up so fast, I had no time to react before he forced my palm onto the bulge between his thighs and held it there. I was about to squeeze his jewels as hard as I could, but he anticipated my move and tightened his grasp on my wrist so intensely I couldn't clench my fingers. I pushed at his chest with my other arm, forcing him to let me go as I jumped away.

I snarled. "Don't ever touch me like that again."

"I believe that was your hand on me, Cassie, but I'll let that little technicality go for now. We can have a session on who's touching whom later if you like, though. Right now, I have to show you to your suite."

I stepped back as he stretched his arm out in front of him and held it there, urging me ahead. I stared at it, then back at him with a *hell no* written all over my face.

Caleb rolled his eyes and nodded, directing my attention behind me. I turned and glimpsed a door from around another corner on the right.

Narrowing my eyes at his smirking face, I said, "You couldn't have told me we were already here?"

"And miss out on all that fun? No way."

***

My suite was far from a slave's quarters. The décor was similar to Nergal's, but not as extravagant. Everything had a pastel hue, including the fabric of the furniture, imbuing it with a much more feminine atmosphere. The walls were bare, unlike his, which gave the room an emptier impression, but a large fire burning in the fireplace brought the walls to life with dancing shadows.

A small table with two chairs on opposite sides occupied the middle of a dining area to the left. On the table, domed silver platters, a bottle of wine, and two wine glasses awaited me like a welcome basket.

"I brought some dinner for us. I'm sure you're probably starving by now," Caleb said, ever the gracious host. He uncovered the platters, revealing tantalizing dishes of meats, veggies, fruits and more.

His mention of *us* didn't escape my notice, and I wanted nothing more than to refuse the meal, but the delicious aromas hit my senses. My stomach churned, reminding me I was still human...*and* hungry. Apparently, my demon blood could not conquer my basic human necessities. So far, I still needed food and sleep. While it was nice to be reminded I wasn't completely soulless, I could definitely do without the vulnerabilities right now. I didn't want to reveal my weaknesses, but these were two that couldn't go unnoticed by my enemies.

I drifted closer to the food, trying not to eye the buffet with too much interest. I picked at a slice of ham as if I could take it or leave it, but I saw Caleb nod and smile, apparently seeing right through my charade. Since the pretense was useless, I grabbed at more of the food, with no consideration for table manners, like a cavewoman who'd been released from an iceberg of centuries past. The ravenous urges came from deep within, as if my body had a will of its own to refill its fuel tank.

Caleb pulled out one of the chairs and motioned for me to sit. I did, but only because I was dead on my feet. As I sampled a little bit of everything, I watched him pour me a glass of wine and set it in front of me.

He chuckled. "Here, you're going to need something to wash all that down."

I shook my head. "No way. I've developed a strong aversion to drinking red liquids. I'm sure you understand."

He took the glass and sat down opposite me at the table. Keeping his eyes on me while he took a long swallow, I felt uncomfortable at the coziness of the situation and forced myself to stop eating.

"You need to relax, Cassie."

"Excuse me?"

"Embrace what you are. Stop trying to fight it. No blood can change you. You're already one of us, and there's nothing you can do about it. The sooner you accept that, the sooner you can enjoy all our world has to offer."

"Forgive me for not being overly enthusiastic about ripping souls from innocent people and handing them over to pieces of shit like you."

Caleb leaned over the table, his eyes narrowed, pinning me in place. "Don't pretend you've never had a wicked thought in your head that you've desperately wanted to act on, but didn't because of the petty human morals you're forced to live by. All humans have them, some more than others. And being a Guardian doesn't make you immune to them, does it?"

I leaned back from the table, my appetite diminishing as I gazed into the depths of his eyes. I don't know how I ever saw any good in him. He was pure evil down to the very core. That kind of evil could never be masked...not if you looked hard enough.

"I never want to be like you. Even if I were stuck in this hellhole for the rest of eternity, I wouldn't let myself drop as low as you. I despise you, Caleb, and it makes my skin crawl to even be near you, so if you think we're going to become some kind of demented couple down here, then you're mistaken." I rested my forearms on the table, boldly leaning forward until our faces were only inches apart. "If you ever touch me again, I will rip you apart, piece by piece. You know I can do it."

He laughed, deep and loud, as he sat back and stretched his arms to rest behind his head. "You actually believe you can overpower me? That's funny. No, that's hilarious." He continued laughing at his one-sided joke. "Don't you get it? I *let* you overpower me all those times. I thought you'd already figured that out."

I eyed him suspiciously. Several times when we fought, I easily gained control over him. He was trying to trick me.

"You're a liar."

"No, it's true," he said, standing and moving around the table. He picked a grape from a vine in a bowl and casually plopped it into his mouth. I continued to regard him as he moved toward the settee in front of the fire. Leaning his back against it, his body seemed larger than ever before, silhouetted in the glow of the fireplace behind him. His shoulders were broad and muscular, tapering to a narrow waist. My eyes wandered to his strong thighs as he crossed one leg over the other. His movements were slow and deliberate while he stretched his arms over his chest, and when I peered up into his face the self-satisfied smile he gave me told me I'd been caught checking him out.

I stood and masked my features with indifference, trying to convince him he had no effect on me. Knowing the size of his ego, I would have been better off trying to convince a pig it could fly.

"I'm supposed to believe you? After you've done nothing but lie to me since the day I met you? Give me some credit, Caleb. I think I've learned a thing or two about you and your kind in the last year. But I'm curious, what's your reason for *letting* me overpower you?"

"It's really simple—I didn't want to hurt you."

I snorted. "Oh, please tell me you have something better than that? I was going to snap your neck the first time we fought, and you were willing to let that happen because, *what*...you cared for me?" I laughed. He was ridiculous.

"I wouldn't go so far as attaching any emotion to it. I don't care for you, but I do *want* you." His gaze devoured my body. I crossed my arms over my chest when he seemed intent on staring at my breasts. "More importantly, I need you, Cassie. I couldn't risk killing you, so I restrained myself from retaliating against you. If it had come down to it, there's no doubt I could've easily killed you."

His confession, real or delusional, unnerved me. It was easier to think I only had one obstacle—Nergal—standing in the way of getting my dad out. After I survived all the times I came up against Caleb, I wrote him off as nothing but a pesky rat in this war. Now, I wasn't so sure. *And that sucked.*

"I see I have your attention now. Is it because I told you I want you? Did you remember how my touch made you burn for me? Or was it because I said I needed you?" He moved toward me. His eyes were glowing, and I knew he was more than willing to demonstrate his first argument. I wasn't ready to find out if he really could overpower me. I was too exhausted to fight.

I warned him off with my hands. "Just get to the point, Caleb. I don't ever want to relive those vile memories of you touching me, much less, make any new ones. So, how do you *need* me if it's not too pornographic?"

He stopped inches from my hands. "Awww, that's too bad. You and pornography, now that would be fun. We'll come back to that."

I rolled my eyes and crossed my arms over my chest again. I was seriously considering putting the theory of whether I could kill him or not to the test, even if it took my last gram of energy.

"Here's the deal. Nergal wants you to lure in the Guardians. *I* want you to lure in Nergal."

It took me a minute to process what he said, and when I did, I thought I heard him wrong.

"What the hell are you talking about?"

"What I'm talking about is your only chance of getting dear old dad out, without him being wrapped up in a body bag. You see, I don't really care if he's out in the world. One fucking Guardian out there isn't going to break up the order of things. Well, unless it's you, of course, but you're special. Him…not so much anymore. You help me, Mom and Dad live the rest of their lives *Cleaver family style* until they bore themselves to death, just like you always wanted."

"Wow. Really? What a great trick. I'd *love* to fall for that again." My words dripped with sarcasm. Maybe it was a good thing he thought I was so naïve. I might be able to take advantage of it at some point.

"Think about it, Cassie. What do you have to lose by striking a deal with me? You're already here." He motioned his arms out, indicating the surroundings. "And you've already been promised to me. I can do whatever I want with you." He stepped closer, catching me off guard. "You knew that was part of Nergal's deal, and you accepted it. What you didn't anticipate was Nergal not carrying out his end of it. And that's where I can help you."

Caleb was a snake, coiled and ready to strike, and I was being charmed by the hypnotic tune he was playing. I knew I shouldn't listen, but he was right. *What did I have to lose?* There was no one left to help me, I had no idea how to get out of Sheol, and I wasn't leaving without my dad. With no real options, it didn't hurt to hear him out, but I reserved the right to laugh in his face afterward.

"So what is it you want from me? What do you mean by luring Nergal in?"

A big, cheesy smile formed his lips. I had to knock it down some before it blinded me.

"I'm only asking. I haven't agreed to anything yet."

"Of course," he said, his smile fading into a smug smirk. "Why don't we sit and talk by the fire?" He motioned me toward the settee, while his other hand lightly cupped my elbow. I peered down at it, and then back up at him, expecting him to catch the meaning of my deliberate glare, but he challenged me with his gaze while his hand remained where it was.

I let out a sigh and allowed him to lead me. As I heard the click of the doors closing behind us, I fixed my eyes on the flames in the hearth. I had the feeling I was once again being led into Hell, destined to make another deal with a devil. But this time, I vowed it would be on my terms.

The settee didn't allow for the distance I would have liked between us when we sat down. I would have given anything for a wrap-around sofa. The thought of our knees accidentally touching gave me chills so deep in my bones the heat of the fire couldn't keep me warm. I angled myself awkwardly away from him, but only so much that I could still read his face for any signs of deception. He seemed to be enjoying the intimacy of the situation. In fact, I was sure he kept inching closer.

"Let's get this over with, Caleb, so I can get some rest. My patience is wearing way past thin."

"Straight to business, then," he said. "That's good, because I'm a businessman."

I stifled a laugh. I couldn't help it. I was mentally prepared to hear just about anything, but I sure didn't expect that. He was a demon, plain and simple. Did he think he was helping me buy stock options?

"Can I continue?" he asked, his expression scolding me.

I nodded for him to go on.

"As you know, I'm what you would call *middle management* here in Sheol. The only one between Nergal and me is Hunter." Hunter's name stung me like a slap in the face. I managed to force thoughts of him to the back of my mind in order to continue with my plans to get my dad out. I knew I'd have to deal with the hole he left in my heart eventually, but I couldn't think about that now. There wasn't time. Caleb's reminder hurt like hell, but I refused to let him see my pain by maintaining a deadpan expression.

"For a long time," he continued, "I thought once I got Hunter out of the way, I'd be right where I wanted to be, standing beside Nergal, a major player in the governing of Sheol. But with Hunter no longer a factor, I realized how wrong I was to seek Nergal's right-hand position. I'd never be satisfied with second place."

One by one, his words sank in, pooling into my brain and helping me form a cohesive conclusion as to what Caleb was intending to do. I gasped at the realization of it. My reaction clearly told him I'd put it all together, and he seemed to take great pleasure in knowing how much he'd blown me away.

"Yes, Cassie, I want to overthrow our King. I *will* be the new ruler of Sheol. And you're going to help me do it."

CHAPTER SIXTEEN

"Are you fucking crazy?" I asked. I didn't throw the *f bomb* around much, but the occasion warranted it. I was quite certain Hell was where the word originated anyway.

"Actually, yes," Caleb said with a dismissive wave. "I imagine I'd have to be at least a bit insane to kill the most powerful force in Sheol. However, I find my mind works best when letting a little crazy loose. It's gotten me this far, no reason to stop now."

That confirmed it. He'd completely lost his mind.

"You can't kill Nergal," I whispered, glancing around. "It's...not possible."

"It's as possible as killing any other demon in Hell, Cassie, only a tad more complicated. And that's why I need you."

I still couldn't believe he planned to go through with it, but if anyone could mastermind a plot against the Devil, it would be Caleb. He was a slippery, amoral, and devious demon. I'd already experienced how demented he could be. He was power-hungry with an ego bigger than a WWF personality, and that combination was a powder keg waiting for a spark. Apparently, he saw me as the spark.

My first instinct was to stay as far away from the conspiracy as possible, but then a little seed of my own started to grow in my head. Maybe, just maybe, Caleb would be so focused on his own greed that I could somehow use it to my advantage. Suddenly, there was a new light at the end of this tunnel. I just had to figure out a way to get to it.

"Okay, you captured my interest. What would I have to do?"

"Before I let you in on my dirty little secret, you must vow your loyalty to me. I can't have you going double agent on me and ruining everything I've set to accomplish. That would be a very bad career move on my part."

"So...what? You want me to sign my name in blood or something?"

"Hmmm," he said, tapping his finger against his cheek as he peered at the ceiling.

I rolled my eyes.

"Why don't we seal it with a kiss?" he asked, as if the thought of it didn't gnaw at my intestines.

"Is there a door number two?"

"Well, I could stay at your side every second until Nergal is dead." He grinned. "And before you ask, there is no door number three."

"Really? How does kissing you prove my loyalty to you? This is just another one of your schemes to act out your perversions."

"Satisfying my perversions is merely an added bonus. Nergal must see that you are willing to work with me. We'll need to practice on you being close to me without doing that upper lip thing you do." He wagged his finger toward my face, and I realized my lip was doing exactly what he was describing.

"Fine. Let's get it over with then." I figured after enduring his touch so many times before, what did once more matter? I swear, sometime in my life I must have picked the short straw.

Caleb scooted closer to me. His hand came up to my face, and I recoiled.

"Relax, I won't bite unless you want me to." His hand cupped my jaw while his thumb brushed my bottom lip.

"Can we skip the foreplay before I lose my nerve?"

He pressed his lips together and shook his head as he gazed into my eyes. "Cassie, it doesn't have to be this way, you know. If you work with me, I'll never hurt you. I know I said earlier I didn't care for you, but the truth is, I do. Very much, in fact."

He was right about one thing—it didn't have to be this way. If I was going to pull this off in order to escape, I had to work with him. That meant I had to suck it up and cap my gag reflex when it came to him. It was probably going to be the hardest thing I ever did, but if it helped me get my dad out safely, it was worth it.

I gave a small nod, and he smiled as he leaned toward me. Forcing myself to concentrate on his lips seemed to help quench the queasies. If I looked into his eyes, there was a chance I'd see desire, which I didn't think I could stomach. I had to admit, his lips felt very nice, soft and succulent. On any other guy, they could have been lips to fantasize about. As it was, I told myself to do exactly that—pretend he was someone else. Problem was, all I could picture was Hunter, which only managed to depress me further.

I tried to make it a chaste kiss by keeping my lips closed, but his tongue slipped between my lips. He was persistent, although surprisingly tender. I expected a much more forceful intrusion. His hand shifted to the back of my head, weaving his fingers in my hair. Tingles ran throughout my body, shaming me with their sensual reaction to his touch.

The pretense felt too real for me. Maybe demons had some kind of autopilot for seduction. I could only hope mine was working on him too. Caleb wasn't stupid enough to think I'd lose myself in his kiss, but maybe I could convince him I was willing to give our partnership an honest go of it.

The kiss seemed to last forever. When he finally pulled away, his luminescent eyes penetrated mine, as if trying to read my inner thoughts. I expected to see a self-satisfied expression, as well as overt cockiness at my involuntary reaction to him, but there was none, only thoughtful contemplation. For some reason, that unnerved me more than his normal tastelessness. I decided I didn't like him being quiet.

"So, did I pass?" I asked, attempting to break his unsettling stare.

"Deliciously," he said, continuing to stare at me with the same staid expression.

I fidgeted under the intensity of his gaze. I couldn't read him and it scared me.

"Okay, sooo...are you going to tell me what you want me to do?"

"Didn't you feel anything, Cassie?"

"What?"

"The kiss. Did you not feel anything when we kissed?"

Crap. He *did* sense my body's reaction to him. Was this a test? If I lied and said no, would he assume I was disloyal? I was more afraid of saying yes, not only because of how he might react to my admission, but also how it would make me feel by saying it out loud. Hearing it come out of my mouth might make it more real, not a pleasant thought. I didn't know what to say. In my eyes, it was a no-win situation, so I went with the only thing I was good at—sarcasm.

"Yeah, Caleb, I did. I felt your tongue in my mouth. Now, I've done what you asked me to do. Can we please move on with your plan? I'm still pretty exhausted here."

He sat straighter, putting more distance between us, and his chin raised the tiniest bit, so small, if I were not watching his every move, I would never have noticed. I should have been able to breathe easier from the space he gave me, but he seemed more strained now, and I was pretty sure a tense demon was not a good thing.

"Cassie, I'm going to be blunt here."

"Are you ever not?"

"I want you," he said, ignoring my barb. "I want you bad, have so from the beginning. I thought maybe you'd come around after you found out you were more like me, and, of course, after I got Hunter out of the way. I still have faith you will come to appreciate what I have to offer you, but if you don't, and you get in my way, I will hurt you in ways you could never imagine. I'll take out everyone you've ever loved and leave you with no one and nothing *but* me. So, as I was saying, I want you, but I want my power more. Keep an open mind, Cassie. Power can be pretty irresistible. You may find yourself unable to keep your hands off me."

"Look, I'm not going to promise you true love, but I will help you kill Nergal, if it means setting my dad free. But what guarantee do I have you will let him go after I help you? I made that mistake with Nergal. And let's not forget you haven't exactly been Honest Abe since we met. I'm sure you see the predicament I'm in, right? I need some kind of insurance."

He seemed to ponder my request as if it never entered his mind I might question his oath to me. In my eyes, I doubted whether Caleb was ever *capable* of performing good deeds, even as a Guardian. I couldn't picture him as anything other than the poster child for the Fiery Down Under.

Finally, after feeling like he was either undressing me telepathically or trying to figure out what material my T-shirt was made of, he got up from the settee and stood in front of me. "I would do just about anything to ensure my queen's happiness."

I started to nod my acknowledgement until his meaning flashed through my thick head. Oh my God, he was serious. He stood statue-still, without any hint of humor or sarcasm, while I felt like my jaw just dropped below my knees and my eyes were about to pop out of my skull. I imagined myself in a red wedding gown, walking down a long aisle flanked by flames, with the masked Phantom of the Opera playing a dirge on a grand organ, while Caleb waited for me at the altar next to a hideous creature with horns and a forked tail. A shiver ran up my spine, and I couldn't stop my upper body from shaking, as if it were trying to purge the tortuous visions.

"You're joking, right?" I asked with a small smile on my face, hoping he'd suddenly laugh and put my mind at ease. When he didn't reply, I pleaded my case. "You can't be serious, Caleb. I'm not royalty material, really. Hell, I was dethroned as class president back in high school. Queen? No way."

"You've certainly matured since your high school years, Cassie." Caleb eyed up my crossed legs. "You'll grow into it, especially if it means your dad has a chance to live out the rest of his glory days with Mommy Dearest."

"Fine, whatever you want." I was tired of hearing the new rules that kept getting applied. There was no way I would go along with all of this in the end anyway. Once Nergal was dead, I'd get my dad out and test my skills against Caleb. By then, there would be nothing else to lose. "Just tell me the plan. How do you intend to kill Nergal?"

He seemed satisfied as he sat next to me again. With a smirk on his face, he took my hands in his. "No, Cassie, the correct question is—how are *you* going to kill Nergal?"

It amazed me how much shock my psyche could bear without going into a state of catatonic paralysis. I almost wished it would. To be cocooned in my own little world seemed like paradise. I felt like I could go to sleep for a good ten years to recuperate from all the twists and turns my life had taken. If I ever got out of Hell alive, I vowed to find an island in the middle of nowhere, where I could take up residence all alone and live off coconuts and plantains. Even though I'd probably have to learn how to fish and leery of the ocean, it had to be much safer than swimming in the shark tank I found myself in lately.

After overcoming my initial reaction of *hell no*, which seemed to be my motto of late, I let Caleb explain his entire plan. Apparently, Nergal actually *did* have tougher skin than the rest of the Underworld demons. Normally, stabbing a demon with the Sword of Final Death was a demon's guaranteed demise. With Nergal, however, it had to be at the hands of an angel. The only angel I knew who had even been in Hell was Anael. I wondered if she ever realized all the power she held during that time. When I first met her, she insisted her relationship with Nergal had been on the rocks for quite awhile. Either she didn't know she had the power to kill him, or she simply didn't take the opportunity.

There was also the possibility Anael simply couldn't bring herself to do it. I knew nothing of how she felt for him. All she'd told me was she was in love at one time. How long and how deep that love extended was a question only she could answer. I couldn't imagine anybody falling madly in love with the Devil, especially someone who shared my blood. I mean, he wasn't bad to look at, but he was gruesome and hideous on the inside. I had to guess he wasn't always like that. I hoped someday I'd get the chance to ask her about it.

Caleb also explained how Nergal kept the Sword in a vault only he could open. No doubt, it had to be through the mind lock thing he did.

Was it possible to mind-pick a lock?

"So, how am I supposed to get the Sword if he keeps it in a vault?" I asked. "I don't even know how to open my own doors, much less Nergal's keyless vaults."

He got up from the settee to explain his scheme. Standing in front of the fireplace, he stared into the dying fire as if their rhythmic flames wove the grand design for the plan's success.

"You won't have to." He used the poker to stoke the logs in the fireplace. The flames spread in power and heat with each prod. I had no idea how he could stand so close to them, as my legs were starting to burn, and I was, at least, five feet away. I stood and moved behind the sofa, using it as a barrier against the intense heat. Caleb turned when he heard me get up and watched me. I eyed him expectantly, waiting for him to go on.

"You're going to tell Nergal I plan to kill him."

"What? Wh—" The proverbial light bulb turned on before I could even finish my question. "Oh...that's how we get him to bring the Sword out," I said, thinking out loud. Caleb nodded and a slow smile spread over his lips. He was looking at me like a mentor does his protégé after having a breakthrough. "That's all well and good, but how am I supposed to get it from him before he offs your head?"

"And all this time, I didn't think you cared, Cassie." He placed his hand over his heart, or where it would be if he actually had one. "There's hope for us yet."

"Don't hold your breath."

"I'll be ready for him. I've planned this for some time and gained quite a following. My supporters and I will be waiting for him."

Supporters. As if this were some political race in which he were a mere candidate. *God*, he really did think of himself as a businessman. I still thought he was delusional. There were too many loose ends.

"Still great," I said, raising my finger in the air, "but *he* is the one with the weapon that can kill every single one of you...I mean, us. Plus, I'm sure he has his own *supporters*."

He came around the sofa, and I spun to face him as he stood before me. "See? You're underestimating me again, Cassie."

He was less than a spit away from me, and I instinctively backed into the sofa, latching onto the back of it with my hands. *Mistake*. His eyes fixated on my chest, which pushed forward from my movement. I let go of the settee and crossed my arms over my breasts, bringing his eyes back to mine. Of course, he'd already gotten an eyeful out of the deal, which he made clear with the lecherous look on his face.

"Can we cut to the chase? I'm too tired to solve your cryptic puzzles."

"Let's just say, even the most powerful men have been rendered utterly defenseless by those whom they least suspect."

"You mean me?" I asked.

"No, Cassie. He knows you hate him, and I'm quite sure he expects you will try to kill him at the first opportunity you have. I mean those whom *he* is closest to—his guards."

Now, I was surprised. "You have his guards in your back pocket? How can you be so sure of their loyalty to you? What if they're only pretending to be on your side and have been reporting your plan to Nergal this whole time?"

"If that were the case, I'd be dead already." His hand came up to caress my face. I shied away from it as much as I could, but there was nowhere to go. "The plan is solid, Cassie. You have nothing to worry about. And before you come up with any more misgivings, ponder this—what do you really have to lose? As it stands, you are trapped down here for the rest of eternity...you *and* your dad. You will be an administrator of the King's dirty work, while your dad suffers who knows what kind of torture in his newly humanized form. Weigh your odds carefully. As I see it, Lady Luck is on our side. It's really a no-brainer."

Although our eyes locked as we stood there, I wasn't really seeing him. I was running everything over in my head, mentally gauging my risk and opportunity with his plan. On the one hand, Nergal could kill us all if we failed to get the Sword from him. But *without* killing him, I didn't see any other way of getting my dad and me out. Sure, somewhere down the line, I might be able to gain his trust and blindside him in the same way Caleb intended to use his guards against him, but how long would that take? And would my dad survive that long? With Caleb's plan, the Sword of Final Death was literally being placed in my hands. The ultimate weapon against all evil. Having it in my possession would give me the ability to kill the most powerful force in Hell. And Nergal wasn't the only demon I could kill with it. *That* was the thought to seal the deal.

"So when do we start?" I asked.

A genuine smile came over Caleb's face, and I returned it. Mine wasn't so much directed at him, but the result of my covert plan to kill two birds with one Sword.

CHAPTER SEVENTEEN

I was finally alone in my quarters and ready to pass out the instant I touched the luxurious expanse of pillows that decorated my enormous bed. They went to extremes in Hell. If I weren't being forced to spend an eternity stealing souls for the Devil, I might have felt like a celebrity staying in the best hotel money could buy. Nergal went all out for my comfort, which was really confusing, but I was too tired to wonder why. Unless he filled the bed with poisonous creepy-crawlies, I intended to sink in and surrender to a deep sleep.

Caleb and I agreed to obey Nergal's wishes for the next few days, which meant training in what I called, *the demon arts.* Caleb was my coach and trainer, which gave us the opportunity to solidify our plans right down to the dirtiest detail. I had to keep up appearances with Nergal, showing no more than robotic cooperation, but cooperation just the same. If I pretended to show any excitement about my new lifestyle, he'd know in a second it was all a farce. I also needed time to keep up the pretense of gaining Caleb's trust, so he would confide his traitorous plan.

My training basically encompassed how to lure the Guardians in and get them to drink Seeker blood, with which I would be supplied. I still wasn't sure how I'd get the blood, or which Seekers planned to donate. I secretly hoped I was given the chance to obtain Caleb's with a sharp object. I would also be trained to tap into my Seeker senses in order to track the Guardians. Personally, I didn't think I'd be capable of it because I'd been living with Nora the past few years without one *extra-spidey* sensation. But who knows? I wasn't able to fling a one-

hundred-and-eighty-five-pound man across the room before
either.

Caleb already taught me how to open doors with my mind,
thankfully. Every room in my suite was sealed and locked,
including my bedroom and bathroom. My little bathroom joke to
Nergal became a reality once I realized I couldn't find it. Luckily,
I noticed just as Caleb was leaving.

Apparently, each demon was mentally attuned to the doors
they could open. It was as easy as imagining the door unlocking,
and so it was—*ta da*! Unfortunately, only certain doors were
attune-able. So much for me sneaking into my dad's cell and
attempting the Great Escape. I was quite certain I was restricted
to my quarters, but I definitely planned to see how far my
abilities extended as I toured the place for the next few days.
Before Caleb left, we made sure I'd gotten the hang of it and
wouldn't end up locking myself in the bathroom.

I took off my shoes and climbed into bed, fully clothed in
my jeans and T-shirt. Expecting sleep to hit me within seconds, I
dropped onto the pillows. But the minute I closed my eyes, I was
inundated with apprehension and worry about everything that
had already happened and what was to come. *Where was Hunter
now? Was he still with Alison? Would I be able to go through
with this plan? Would Nergal see through it and kill us all?
Would I eventually have to kill Hunter and Alison if I succeeded
with Caleb and Nergal? Could I do it?*

Foreboding thoughts whirled around in my head, refusing
to listen to my body's need for sleep. I tossed around, trying to
find a comfortable enough position so my exhaustion would take
over, but I only managed to sweat from the effort. It became
unbearably hot all of a sudden and I wanted nothing more than
to take off all my clothes and feel the smallest draft of cool air
over my skin. I glanced at the door and mentally checked the
lock before pulling my jeans off. It was as far as I would go, not
comfortable enough with who could or could not get in to take

off anything else. As more of a precaution, I pulled back the quilt on the bed and slipped between the sheets. They were cool over my damp legs, and I felt the first urges of sleep filtering in as I sank back.

I wasn't far into unconsciousness when someone knocked on the door. I almost pawned it off on my overactive brainwaves until another one came through loud and clear. I clutched the sheet.

"Cassie?" Caleb called from the other side of the door.

I groaned into my pillow. There was no way I was opening the door for him. For one, I'd had all the Caleb I could take for one day, but worse, I was half-naked. Even the thought of a sheet being the only barrier between my underwear and his eyes caused me to shudder, and made me reconsider the quilt I'd pulled back. I held my breath, in case extra-sensitive eardrums were another of the demon perks I wasn't aware of yet. In case it *was*, I concentrated hard on them, trying to listen for the sound of his footsteps walking away. I heard nothing...until the door clicked open.

Shit. Did I accidentally unlock the door while trying to zone in on listening for Caleb?

Quickly sitting up, I grabbed the edge of the quilt and threw it over me. Caleb had just stepped into the room, but I could tell he caught my frantic movements by the way his eyes scanned the length of my body, despite the quilt. I clenched the covers tighter, feeling as if I didn't have a stitch of clothing underneath by the way he was drinking me in.

"What do you want, Caleb?" I asked, the irritation evident in my tone. It didn't stop him from approaching the bed, however. I felt like a trapped animal, but I was prepared to bare everything to defend myself if it came down to it. Sitting up straighter, I kept the blankets around my waist so he wouldn't be able to tell I had no pants on underneath. Thank God I kept my T-shirt on.

"I wanted to make sure you were comfortable. I know how it is to sleep in strange places. Some people find comfort by having others with them."

"No, thank you." I said. "I've never been the cuddly type. I was doing fine until you came in. By the way, how'd you get in? I didn't unlock the door."

"Let's just say I have an extra set of keys, in case yours don't work."

Splendid. I wondered if there was a way to change the locks on these things. All I needed was Caleb with free access to my bedroom. Another thing to worry about. Now, I'd never sleep.

The door closed behind him when he stepped further into the room, so I took the opportunity to prove I had no problem with this particular skill. I turned my attention to the door and smiled when I heard it unlock and slowly open. Caleb glanced over his shoulder at it, before peering back at me. I eyed him expectantly, assuming the open door would be enough of a hint, but he didn't get it.

"Well, it seems my keys work fine. Feel free to leave your set on the table on your way out."

He chuckled. "I think I'll hold onto them for a while...just in case." He winked.

"I figured you'd say that." When he still made no move to leave, I said, "Okay then...thanks for checking in on me. I'd like to get some sleep now, if you don't mind." He gave me a nod. "*Alone.*" If that didn't get him out of my bedroom, the next step would definitely involve pain...his.

"Alright, well, if you're sure you wouldn't like any company, I'll let you sleep. Goodnight, Cassie. I'll come for you in the morning."

"Goodnight, Caleb," I said when he looked back at me from the open door. I mentally closed the door as soon as he turned away.

I let out a loud sigh and dropped back into the pillows, on edge now that I knew Caleb had free rein to come and go as he pleased. After contemplating several ways of making him suffer if he dared to come near me when I slept, my eyes closed of their own exhausted will. As I drifted off, I said a little prayer that the only intruder to my room would be a beautiful dream taking me away from all the evil and darkness that existed around me.

***

Wide-awake in the darkened room, I was unsure what jolted me from a dead sleep. I couldn't remember any dreams, but maybe there was one so frightening my conscious mind forced me up. The quilt and sheet were entangled around my calves, and I was chilled beneath the sweat-drenched T-shirt that clung to me.

Sitting up, I started to straighten out the blankets from my legs in order to pull them over me, when a loud knock sounded on the door. If I weren't so wound up in the blankets, I might have jumped right off the bed from the scare it gave me. It took me a moment to catch my breath, and when I did, I wasn't sure whether I wanted to respond. If it was Caleb again, he'd probably come in anyway, and I certainly didn't want that to happen considering the predicament I was in at the moment.

Better to head him off.

"Caleb, I told you, I'm not the snuggling type. I don't want to play any more games with you tonight. Go. Away." Unfortunately, my voice didn't sound half as convincing as I wanted to convey. My legs fought with the quilt, frantically trying to escape, while listening for the click of the lock I knew was coming.

"Open the door, Cassandra," a voice growled. Definitely not Caleb's. There was only one voice that could send every nerve in my body into a state of turmoil.

"Hunter?"

"Mmm...hmm," he grumbled.

As much as I wanted to race to the door, fling it open, and throw myself into his arms, I didn't get the vibe he was in the same frame of mind. My hands shook as I finally released the tangled mess of blankets and jumped out of bed.

"Cassandra?" It was a warning, not a question.

"Okay, okay. I'm coming." Halfway to the door, I realized I couldn't physically open it. Hearing the sound of Hunter's voice got me so disoriented I couldn't think straight. Calming myself, I concentrated on unlocking the door. Standing back, I allowed it to open, which was a good thing because it slammed open so hard, if there were hinges, they would have popped right out of the wall. I silenced a small scream of surprise, covering my mouth with my hand.

Hunter stood in the open doorway, a huge man, seething with determination. He appeared bigger to me for some reason, or maybe it was the way he was examining me that made me feel so much smaller.

"H...how did you get in my quarters?" I asked, after catching my breath.

"I can get into anyone's quarters. One of the perks of being number two on the totem pole of Hell."

"Then why couldn't you open this door?"

"I don't know. I guess they're starting to clamp down with security on Seekers who go AWOL."

I wasn't sure if he was joking or serious. His grim expression didn't falter when he said it.

Standing in my damp T-shirt and panties, I suddenly felt nervous under his gaze. I pulled at the bottom of my shirt in an effort to stretch it over as much of my lower body as the material would allow. His eyes moved with my hands, and then slowly down my legs, heat spreading through the parts where his gaze lingered. I couldn't seem to breathe. He took his eyes off my body and looked toward the floor behind me. Turning, I saw my jeans lying on the floor beside my bed.

"I...I got too hot," I blubbered out, sounding like a complete idiot.

"Was Caleb inside or outside of the room?" he asked.

"Outside, of cour—" I stopped, remembering the last time I saw Hunter. My blood boiled. "You have a lot of nerve accusing me of anything. Shouldn't you be with Alison?"

I was in his arms the second I said it, crushed to his chest so hard I could barely breathe. "The only place I should be is with you." His lips pressed to the side of my head.

My heart burst open, accepting him as if his words released it from the darkness that previously consumed it. Closing my eyes, I inhaled him, wanting all of my senses to tell me he was real and we were together again. I relished feeling every inch of contact with him, until my dignity returned, and I replayed the image of Hunter's reunion with Alison in my head.

Struggling to push away from him, I pressed at his chest until he finally released me, but remained at arm's length. He gaze was curious, as if surprised his flowery words hadn't resolved everything between us. I admit, it worked for a few minutes, but I still had some pride. And he had some 'splainin' to do.

"Why aren't you with Alison?"

"Because I don't belong with her."

I waited for more, but it never came. He was going to make this painful. Well, I was ready to dish out a bit of pain myself.

"Wow, really? It sure *looked* like you belonged with her when you walked off into the sunset together without a word, abandoning me to the two most frightening monsters in Hell."

I pulled out of his grasp, turned my back on him, and snatched my jeans off the floor. Sitting on the bed, I pulled them over my legs. Hunter came over and sat next to me. I stood to pull my pants up the rest of the way. When I finished, he reached out and gently tugged at my wrist, turning me to face him. He continued to sit on the bed as he held both my hands in his.

"I'm so sorry, Cassandra," he said, his blue eyes searching mine for absolution. "When I got my memories back and saw Alison, I lost my head. I wasn't supposed to see her again. *Ever.* Saving her soul is the reason I am who I am. She's the reason I became a Seeker."

"What are you talking about? You can only become a Seeker by drinking the blood of another Seeker. You told me yourself, it's a choice you make."

"And it *was* a choice I made, but I made it to save Alison."

I didn't know what to say. *I'm sorry* seemed to fit the moment. I mean, if he hadn't done it, he wouldn't have lost his soul. Up until the day before, he never even knew what he did to get here. He simply...was. And if he weren't the Seeker he came to be, I would have never met him. I would have never loved him. Guilt washed over me. *How could I be happy someone had given up his soul to this Hell?*

He let the silence linger for a moment, searching my face. My feelings about what he told me were so convoluted I wasn't even sure what my expression revealed.

When I didn't say anything, he continued. "When I was a Guardian, a Seeker tried to seduce me into drinking blood, but I wouldn't do it. I was dedicated to Alison." It hurt me to hear that, but I couldn't blame him for loving someone in another life. If anything, I should have praised him for his fidelity. Most people nowadays give in so easily to temptation. I remembered what he told me about how Caleb went after family and friends to lure a Guardian in. I knew it was true because I *lived* it. No one should have to go through that, and my heart went out to him then, as I realized this was probably what happened to him. And now he had to relive it.

Pulling my hands from his, I sat down next to him on the bed. When our eyes met again, I reached up and cupped the side of his face, brushing my thumb across his cheek. "They went after her, didn't they?"

Hunter nodded. "She was hit by a bus two days later. He guaranteed she'd recover if I cooperated. I didn't think twice about it."

"I'm so sorry. I can't imagine how hard it is for you to see her here after all you did to prevent it. It's obvious how much you loved her."

God, my heart felt like a stone in my chest. He died for this woman and now she was back. It was as if fate were telling us we should never have been together to begin with. Maybe if I'd listened to my own head and never loved him before, I wouldn't be hurting so bad now. I felt guilty even thinking how his love for me compared to his love for Alison.

I didn't even notice my hand had dropped from his face until he brought it back up with his own, drawing my eyes back to his as he leaned into it.

"Alison and I shared a life back then."

"I know." I averted my eyes from his. I couldn't look at him. It was killing me. This was it, the final blow, and I hated it. *Fate freaking sucked.*

He tipped my chin up, forcing me back to his eyes. They were so tender, but I braced myself for the final words that would shatter the giant lump in my chest and break it into a thousand shards.

"You didn't let me finish. We shared a life then, but that was a different life. So many things have changed. I've changed. And the only woman I want in *this* life is you."

CHAPTER EIGHTEEN

Hunter's lips were on mine before I had the chance to comprehend what his words meant. They were urgent, and I savored his taste as I opened my mouth to his tongue. It slid against mine, sending shockwaves throughout my body, rekindling a fire I thought was lost forever.

He pulled back, but only enough to lock his eyes onto mine as he held my face in his hands. "It will always be you, Cassandra," he whispered against my lips. Then he kissed me again, much softer this time, as if gently transferring every ounce of love he had for me onto my lips. I didn't need any words; this was all I ever needed to know he loved me.

Everything around me faded. All my worries, all my fears, disappeared when he touched me. We weren't stuck in this hell, we weren't even in its realm. We were in our own world, no one around to save, or to slay. God, if only we could stay here. I didn't want to face reality, not when I had him with me, not after thinking I'd lost him.

Alison's name crept into my head, and suddenly what we were doing was wrong. I was like a mistress who'd stolen someone's husband for a few hours of passion. But it felt so right being in his arms again. Still, having her memories back, if she had as much love for Hunter as he had for her, it would kill her to see us together. I knew it would kill me...it *had* killed me.

Damn it, I hated having a conscience.

I gently pushed Hunter away. His face was flushed, and I knew mine probably looked the same. There was no denying I wanted him. Even if I refused, he wouldn't take no for an answer. But I had to find out what was going on with Alison.

After a few seconds of trying to catch my breath, he moved toward me again, but I held my hands against his chest.

"What about Alison?"

His exasperated look inferred he didn't care much for my conscience either.

"Where is she right now?" I prodded.

"I told her I had to attend to some business."

"So, what are you going to do? You have to tell her something, Hunter. She probably expects you to pick up where you left off, even if she is a demon now."

"You're assuming."

Gazing at his beautiful face, I tried to picture what he looked like as a Guardian. His eyes would be different, but he had the kind of face not many women could resist. It was hard for me to imagine him without a soul, even though that's exactly what it meant to be who he was. I always thought the heart could not function without a soul, but both Hunter and my dad had proven that was merely a myth. They had both loved with everything they possessed, at least, that's what it felt like to be on the receiving end of Hunter's love. Could it have been even stronger before he lost his soul? If it were, Alison must have gotten the pleasure of experiencing it firsthand, and there would be no way she'd let him go now.

"She didn't ask for this either," I said. "As much as I want to throw her across the room for coming anywhere near you, I have to remember she's merely a pawn in their sick game...same as me."

"I know. She had a life, and I want her to live it. That's why I want you to turn her back."

His words came from left field, and I wasn't prepared for them. He wanted her to go back? It shouldn't have surprised me. He already sacrificed himself for her happiness, why wouldn't he want that?

"Have you talked to her about this?"

"No."

"So...what? You just want me to walk up to her and make her drink my blood? I'm pretty sure she's not going to want me near her. She seemed content to be here with you now."

"I don't care. Alison shouldn't be here, and it's my fault. I wouldn't ask you to do this if you weren't my only hope. I'll get her to drink it, you only need to give me some of your blood."

I noticed something different about his eyes since he first came into my room, and now I realized what it was—guilt. Guilt *and* pain. I wanted to pull him into my arms and make it all go away, but I wasn't sure if I would be enough. The guilt he felt wasn't his to bear. Alison was here not because of him, but because of me. Ultimately, I was the target and she was one of the many casualties of my war. So was Hunter.

I held my breath, delaying what I was about to propose because the words would cut so deep I'd be permanently scarred.

"I could turn you both." I was barely able to get it out as I held his gaze.

"What?" His eyebrows furrowed as he glared at me.

I was taken aback for a moment. I expected his surprise, but *anger*?

Grabbing his hands, I held them in mine. "You could be together again, as you were before. I could give your life back to you, Hunter, your former life with Alison."

He snatched his hands from mine and stood. "Have you not heard anything I've said to you?"

"I only thou—"

"You thought what?" he yelled. "That you'd be saving my life by sending me back to her? Is that what you thought?"

I was confused. My offer was a gift, but he made it seem like I'd insulted him.

Before I knew what was happening, I was being hoisted up from the bed, his fingers digging into my upper arms as he

pulled me against him. His eyes glared into mine, searching
them fiercely for something.

"Tell me, if you send us off together, what would you do
then? Live happily ever after here with Caleb? Is that what you
want?"

"No," I said, disgusted.

"Do you love me?"

"What? Yes. You know I do."

"Then why do you want to send me away? I told you,
you're all I want. You wouldn't be saving me, Cassandra. You'd
be killing me all over again."

My heart melted. As mad as he seemed to be, as much as
he was glaring at me, a smile lit up my face, reaching beyond
what he could even see.

"Are you laughing at me?"

I bent my arms up to resist his hold, and he released them.
Putting both hands on either side of his face, I gazed into his
eyes, still beaming at him. "No, I'm smiling because, even
trapped in Hell, with the Devil promising a torturous eternity,
you make my future seem bright. I don't ever want you to leave
me, Hunter. I only suggested it because I want you to be happy.
You've given up everythi—"

Hunter's finger came over my mouth, halting my words.
He watched his own finger slowly brush over my lips, a whisper-
light touch, back and forth, circling my mouth, as my breathing
grew heavier. His eyes lazily found mine again, and I saw all the
passion I felt for him mirrored in them.

"I won't give you up, not for anything. I warned you, once
you were with me, you would always be with me. That won't ever
change."

"I don't want to be anywhere else."

"So you'll do it? You'll give me your blood?"

I nodded, unsure of how I really felt about it, but if it was what he wanted, I'd do it. "But it has to be after I kill Nergal. If I do it before, the plan will never work."

"What are you talking about...killing Nergal? That was never part of our plan."

"Not *our* plan. Our plan was blown out of the water when Alison entered the mix. And now my dad is in some kind of transitional phase, with Nergal threatening to torture him once we know he's been turned. Caleb wants me to kill Nergal—'

"Whoa, slow down, Cassandra." He shook his head. "Did you say Caleb wants you to kill Nergal?"

I realized I was rambling, but there was so much to tell him, I couldn't get it out fast enough. It was as if we'd been apart for days already, what with everything that transpired. I stood, took a deep breath, and paced while I recounted everything that happened since he left with Alison. I tried to go through it all slowly, and with as much detail as I could recall, but there were a few minor things I left out, like kissing Caleb, mainly for the sake of time and self-preservation.

Hunter continued to sit on the bed, listening intently, as I went over the details of Caleb's plan. His face showed nothing of how he felt. Unfortunately, I didn't think silence was golden in this case. In fact, I could almost picture a bomb being carefully crafted in that mind of his, waiting for the right moment to start ticking away to the lethal explosion that would take me out. I braced myself for the impact.

He closed his eyes when I was done. *Was he counting to ten? And when had he gotten so close to me?* I stepped back, the backs of my thighs hitting a nightstand next to the bed. I lost my balance and almost fell, but caught myself and rose up as tall as I could, which was ludicrous since he towered over me.

"No."

Wait for it.

"No, what?" I asked.

"No, I will not allow you to go along with this moronic scheme, Cassandra. Are you fucking crazy?"

Boom.

His eyes were blazing as he glared at me.

"You will not *allow* me?" Okay, I could take having him pissed off. I could even take his strong disapproval of the whole thing, but *allowing* me? I drew a line when it came to who called the shots in my life. "You know, I don't really remember asking for your permission."

"*Damn it.* I leave you alone for a couple of hours, and you wind up planning to kill the King of the Underworld. This isn't some lowlife, *piece of shit* demon like Caleb. And need I remind you that Caleb, whom you're putting your trust in, already deceived you twice. Are you really so naive?"

Now *I* was counting to ten. My jaw hurt from clenching my teeth, and I could feel half-moons indenting the skin of my palms where my fingernails dug in.

Hunter moved closer and somehow reined in his anger, which pissed me off even more since I was all jacked up. Standing before me was the familiar, calm, cool, and collected Hunter, whom I wanted to kick in the head for it. How could he blow up one minute and look like we were out on a summer stroll the next?

"I can't let you do this. You understand that, right?" He rubbed his hands up and down my arms. "There's another way to get your dad out and we'll find it, I promise."

"But there is no other way," I argued. "An angel has to do it...me."

He shook his head, even as I spoke, refusing to hear me out. "The battle of good and evil has been going on longer than you and I have existed. The angels have built armies for the sole purpose of taking him down someday. Armies, Cassandra, not one angel. What makes you think you can accomplish by yourself what they have already spent a millennia training soldiers for?"

"But how many angels have been able to get as close to him as I have? He thinks I'm going to be working for him. I can get even closer. This is a chance to kill Nergal, Hunter."

"Or a chance for you to die. I'm not willing to play the odds. And what if you do manage to kill him? What then? You think Caleb is going to let you walk out of here with your father and me? Caleb is a sadistic monster. With Nergal no longer keeping him under wraps, he'll assume it's a free-for-all. There's no telling what else he has planned."

I looked away too quickly and knew immediately the mistake I made. I tried to squeeze out of the small space that seemed to have become a vacuum all of a sudden, sucking all the breath out of me. I didn't get far before Hunter's hand held me back.

"What are you not telling me right now?" he asked with deadly calm.

"Look, it doesn't matter what Caleb has planned, he's not getting out alive either. The Sword will be through his heart before Nergal's body hits the floor."

With that, I was pretty sure I hit the big *delete* button on his last shred of sanity. The way he rubbed his hand over his face and hair was a good indication. He would never let me do this. He thought I was completely insane, and I couldn't blame him. I seemingly evolved from Naive College Girl to Fearless Devil Hunter in a matter of months, except I wasn't fearless. I was scared to death. But what choice did I really have?

"You're not strong enough," he said softly.

I gazed up at him, burying my doubts in a vault so he couldn't see them in my eyes. After knowing everything he'd done for Alison, not to mention for me, I didn't want him to see me as a helpless victim anymore. I wanted him to look at me and be proud of the woman I'd become.

"I don't need strength to do this. All I need is determination and a big sword."

Hunter's eyes penetrated mine, as if trying to break down my walls of resolution from the inside out. He wasn't convinced, but he didn't refuse to listen either. Maybe I gained some leeway. If I did, I had to seal the deal.

Standing on my toes, I brought my hands up to the back of his neck and pulled him down to my lips. "And I need you, Hunter." Ever so gently, I pressed my lips against his and held them there. We stood, relishing the feel of each other, as if nothing else mattered. I was playing on his feelings for me to get what I needed, but I loved him. Being with him like this was bliss, despite the hows and whys of it. I opened my eyes and saw his were closed. *Was he thinking the same thing?*

His arms went around my waist and he drew me tightly against him. Angling his head, he deepened the kiss when I opened my mouth, absorbing the taste of him. My body heated in all the places I knew he would bring to a state of ecstasy if I let him, but I had to know he trusted me enough to take on my mission. I pulled back to look him in the eyes. "I can do this."

He was battling within himself, the strain on his face evident. "I can't lose you."

"Believe me, I'm going to do everything I can to make sure you don't."

"So am I."

I was so afraid to ask what he meant by that, but decided to use it to my advantage. "I'm going to need you to get my dad out for me."

"We'll get him out together after we kill Nergal."

I slipped away from him, knowing what I was about to say would put him over the edge. I needed his promise, or I would blow away this whole conspiracy if he refused. I didn't know what the alternative would be, but there was no way I could go forward without his help. He turned to watch me pace the room, but...*Wait. Did he say* we*?* I stopped before him, grabbing his arm.

"There's no *we* when it comes to killing Nergal. You can't be there. There's no way I can take him off guard with you there. Besides, I need you to concentrate on my dad. I want you ready to get him out as soon as this is done...one way or another."

His eyes narrowed, instantly realizing the gravity of my request. Calm and cool instantly turned into furious and about to explode, with me holding the pin in place.

Before he could respond, I added, "You promised me you'd do whatever you could to get my dad out. I'm calling you on that now."

Pin pulled, now it was time to run for cover.

CHAPTER NINETEEN

I took a step back. Hunter took a step forward. It was a classic case of predator versus prey, and I didn't stand a chance.

"You've put me in an impossible position," he yelled, cutting the distance between us as he prowled toward me.

"Shhh," I warned. If Caleb found out he was in my room, I could kiss the whole plan goodbye.

I felt the wall against my back as he caged me between his arms. He was breathing heavy, but I could only tell by the fast rise and fall of his chest. His mouth was closed, his lips thin and tight, and the muscles of his jaw were visibly clenching and unclenching in a steady rhythm. He glared at me with such intensity, if my dad's life weren't on the line, I probably would have relented from the sheer intimidation of it.

My heart raced, not only because of the anger emanating from him, but from my own paranoia of being caught with him in my room. I didn't dare say another word for fear of provoking another outburst, so I simply stared back at him, hoping he'd calm down.

"Maybe you didn't hear me right," he said, low and close. "I can't lose you."

"I heard you, I on—"

"Shhh," he threw back at me, his finger hard against my lips. "Now you listen to me. I will not stand by somewhere, waiting to find out whether you're dead or not. If you think that's the kind of man I am, then you don't know me at all. You are my one and only priority. I know *you*, and I know no matter what I say, you are going to do this with or without my permission. Unfortunately, down here, I have less power to stop you without putting your father in danger. But know this—I will be watching every move they make, and if they so much as nick your arm with their fingernails, I won't stay hidden, and I can't promise you what will happen. Only after I've been assured you are safe, will I help get your father out."

What could I say? He was as pig-headed as I, so I couldn't argue with him. And I had to admit, knowing he'd be close made me feel less alone. Since the day he walked into my life, he always made me feel safe. But now, because of the feelings I had for him, he also made me scared. Not scared for myself, but scared to lose him. There was a part of me that wished he accepted my offer to turn him, so he wouldn't be involved in any of this, and I'd know he was safe. Yet again, fate had its own agenda, which apparently included Hunter remaining a part of my world, no matter how much I tried to forge new paths.

"Okay." I put my hands on his face, sealing our pact with my eyes locked on his. "Okay."

We came together, as if the idea of kissing developed from the space between us, drawing us to each other. There was a desperation to it that came from both of us. Would it be our last chance to taste one another? I pulled at the short strands of his hair as he weaved his fingers through mine, searching for the back of my head, cupping it in his palm, and angling me even closer when he found it.

The knock on the door was like an explosion in my head, and I shoved Hunter away.

"Cassie?" I heard Caleb call from the other side.

Oh, shit. Shit. What the hell would we do now?

I glanced at Hunter in a panic, hoping he had something in mind, but seeing the look on his face, I knew he was fully prepared to confront Caleb. Pushing him toward my bathroom, I mouthed for him to hide in there. Caleb wouldn't check there. *Would he?*

God, Hunter wasn't moving fast enough. He was barely to the bathroom when I heard the door to my room unlock. Caleb was coming in. My body froze against the wall, but my eyes darted back and forth between Hunter and the door. I realized I had to open the bathroom door for him because of that mind unlock thingy, but it was too late, the other door was already opening. Even if I had been able to concentrate enough to unlock it, Hunter would never have made it in without being seen.

Caleb opened the door and opened his mouth to call out to me again, until he saw me at the wall. His brows furrowed at the sight of me, most likely because I had a deer-in-headlights expression as I stood plastered against the wall.

"Cassie?" He opened the door further.

I held my breath and glanced over at Hunter, only to see he was gone. *Where the hell did he go?* My confusion was mixed with relief, but all I could worry about was Caleb, who was staring at me as if I developed a case of the crazies.

Peeling myself from the wall, I internally grasped for some reasonable explanation. Unable to think of anything, I opted for nonchalance.

"What's up, Caleb?" I asked, seemingly bored by his appearance.

"I thought I heard something. What were you doing?"

Think, Cassie. "Jesus, can't a girl have some privacy? How close is your room to mine anyway? Or were you lurking outside my door again?" *When all else fails, take the offense.*

"I have very good hearing. It sounded like someone yelling. Was someone in here?"

No dice, he wasn't letting this go. Persistent bastard.

I let out an irritated groan as I moved to the bed. "No, just me. What'd you think? I was hosting a little slumber party in here with all my new demon friends?"

He rolled his eyes, obviously not amused. "What were you yelling about?"

"Seriously, do you have to know everything? I woke up and forgot where I was, walked into the damn table, stubbed my

freaking toe, and when I tried to open the door to go out there"—
I motioned beyond the door he was standing in—"I couldn't get
the damn thing open because I was disoriented. What do you
guys have against doorknobs anyway?" For appearances sake, I
rubbed my toe.

"So why were you up against the wall when I came in?"

"Because you scared the shit out of me."

Caleb nodded. Whether he believed me or not, I had no
idea.

"Are you okay?"

"Well, I'd prefer to be in my own bedroom at home,
dreaming of ponies and rainbows, but since I'm stuck here, I
guess I'm as good as can be." That got me another eye-roll. I
sighed. "I'm fine, Caleb. I just need to get some sleep."

He studied me for a minute, making me nervous. I
continued the toe rub to avoid fidgeting under his steely gaze.

"Okay, I'll let you get back to sleep. If you need anything,
call me, okay?"

"You mean call out to you?"

"Yes."

"You never answered my question. Are your quarters that
close? Or are you continually lurking around mine?"

"I'm not far away."

"Great," I said, with a tad too much sarcasm.

"Someday you won't see that as a bad thing, Cassie."

He stood in the doorway as though he expected something
more from me. Did he think I'd actually agree or say *thank you*?
This place would freeze twice over before he'd ever get that from
me.

"Goodnight, Caleb."

"Goodnight," he said, turning and walking out.

The door shut behind him, and I listened for the outer
doors to close to make sure he was completely out of my
quarters. When I didn't hear anything, I opened the door and

checked around. The living room was empty. Satisfied I was alone, I ran to the bathroom to check on Hunter, baffled as to how he made it in there. I peeked in, but couldn't see him anywhere. The bathroom was a generous size, but it wasn't so big I wouldn't be able to spot a hulk of a man standing somewhere in it. The stand-up shower stall was sealed with a transparent glass door, so there was no use checking there either. He was simply gone. But how? Did he transport himself out of there? I wasn't aware it worked that way, but I still had a lot to learn.

Deep in thought, I drifted back into my bedroom, and right into something big and solid. Arms embraced me. Scared out of my wits, I opened my mouth to scream, but once I peered up and realized the arms were attached to Hunter, my fears vanished.

"Where the hell did you go?" I asked him.

"What do you mean? I didn't go anywhere." He turned, glanced at the door, and looked back at me, confused. "Where's Caleb?"

"I don't know. Probably back in his quarters, wherever that is. He just left, but I didn't bother asking him where he was headed. Sorry." I couldn't understand why he was staring at me as if he had no clue what was going on.

"He was in here?"

"*Yes*," I said, frustrated. The problem was Hunter seemed legitimately confused. What was going on? "He came in, and the next thing I knew, you were gone. I thought you made it into the bathroom somehow. He said he heard noises and came to see if everything was okay. He just left."

Hunter gaped as if I'd grown another head. His fingers tightened on my arm, and I winced from the pressure. He must have noticed, because he let go, turned, and paced the room. I waited for him to bring me in on whatever internal conversation he was having with himself while he trod a hole in the carpet.

"Hunter?" No response. I grabbed his arm and spun him around to face me when he was near enough to catch him. "Hunter, tell me what's going on. Please. You're scaring me."

He finally focused on me, and I held his gaze, silently urging him to tell me something...*anything*.

"I'm sorry, it's...I don't know how it's even possible...but I think you made me fade."

"Fade?"

"Yes. I think you made me disappear while Caleb was here."

I remembered seeing the ability from Caleb. He'd managed to make an entire room full of people disappear at a restaurant.

"You mean like at Celestino's?"

"Yes."

"So, you're telling me I just earned another patch on my Girl Scouts of Hell sash? I didn't know that worked on demons too."

"It doesn't."

My eyes grew twice their normal size. My mouth hung open, but no words came out, and any that might have been forming were lost forever. There had to be a reasonable explanation.

"I don't understand."

"I'm not sure I do either. Tell me, what were you thinking before I disappeared?"

"Uh...I don't know." My head was spinning. Trying to recall what I was thinking *two* minutes ago felt like a huge feat, much less twenty minutes ago. I sat down on the bed in an effort to calm myself enough to think straight. "Caleb was coming in the room...and I was thinking you wouldn't make it in time. He didn't come all the way in right away, and I remember praying you'd be gone by the time he did."

He nodded as if it all made sense to him. *How could it possibly make sense?*

"*Really?* That's all you have to do to make someone go away? Like, *poof*, they're just...gone? Christ, had I known that, I'd have gotten rid of a lot of people by now. You're actually pretty lucky I didn't have this nifty gift back when we first met."

His demeanor remained calm while his eyes narrowed with invisible daggers shooting my way. "First of all, Cassandra, you have to *want* the person gone in order for it to work, and we both know that was far from what you wanted to do with me. Second, it's *not* that easy. It takes focused concentration to accomplish it, but it's something that gets easier to do with practice. I simply can't figure out how you did it, or how you could use it on me. Last of all, don't ever do that to me again without my permission."

"Well, while I'd love to abide by your wishes, Your Majesty, I obviously don't really know how to control it yet. And what's the big deal? It worked out to our advantage. Caleb didn't see you."

"It worked out to *your* advantage. I really don't care if Caleb sees me in your room. In fact, I welcome it. Maybe then he'll finally accept that you belong to me." He paused when he saw my reaction, and quickly added, "...with me. You belong *with* me."

I waved him off, less concerned about his testosterone-fueled pride than what my new ability meant in the whole scheme of things. "This could change everything." I said it not so much to Hunter, but more to myself. I had more power over the situation than I thought. But how much? "If I can use this on Nergal—"

Hunter knelt in front of me, his expression devoid of all my excitement. He had that *I'm going to burst your happy bubble* look on his face, and I prepared myself for the crash.

"As much as I want you to forget all about the ridiculous partnership you made with Caleb, I'm not sure I feel safer with you going rogue because you have a new toy to try out. We have no idea how it actually works. You said yourself, you didn't ever know what you were doing. We could be completely off on this, and I'm not willing to let you experiment with it on Nergal. More than likely, even if you do learn to control it, it won't work on him. He's too powerful."

"But—"

His finger came up between us, stopping my protest midstream.

"I'm not saying we don't want to pursue your new ability or whatever it is you might have. In fact, I think it would be a great idea for you to practice using it in the next few days during your training with Caleb. Feel free to *poof him away*, as you so eloquently term it, for longer periods of time. Maybe even see how long you can make it last. But let's make sure you can control it before we decide to use it against Nergal."

"You still want me to train with Caleb?"

"Do I want you to? No. I don't want you anywhere near him, but I don't really have a choice until I find a way to get your father out. Just don't do anything stupid until then, okay? Try to put off your suicide mission for as long as you can. I'm sure I can find a way to get your father out without you having to go through with it. Do we have an agreement?"

His eyes bore into mine, demanding compliance to his terms. But he was thinking short-term and I had the long haul in mind. Chances were, if I didn't kill Nergal now, when I had the chance, he'd come after my family and me again. He wouldn't stop until he had me. I was the main pawn in his ultimate victory over Heaven and Earth. His thirst for power would not end, and that left me running for the rest of my life unless I changed the game now. I realized Hunter would never go along with it. If I told him I still planned to kill Nergal, one way or another, he would stay close to me and none of this could work. I hated lying to him, but maybe I wouldn't have to. For now, I could agree to his terms, while still sticking with my plan.

"Cassandra?" he asked with a warning tone. His fingers gently tilted my chin up. He searched my face, silently gauging my intentions.

"Yes," I answered quickly, afraid I'd become too transparent, and he would know exactly what I resolved to do. "I'll be careful."

"And you'll wait for me?"

"Yes." Waiting for him didn't mean I couldn't ultimately kill Nergal. So technically, I wasn't lying.

Hunter continued to study me, until his gaze finally softened. My heart dropped, because as much as I justified my answers, I knew I was deceiving him on some deep, soulful level that we shared. I only hoped in the end he'd understand.

His thumb caressed my cheek. "You should get some sleep. Nergal and Caleb will be coming for you soon enough, and you look exhausted."

I knew he was right, but I didn't want him to leave...*ever*. I put my hand over his and leaned into his palm. "Where will you go?"

"I have to get back to Alison."

His words cut like a knife in my chest. The thought of him going to another woman was enough to make me want to forget the whole plan and run away with him, only him and me forever. But I knew what I had to do was far too important, to too many people, for me to be selfish about it. Someday, if we ever made it out of this Hell, I planned to be selfish with him...over and over again.

"What will you tell her?"

"The truth. What we plan to do. What you plan to do to her when we get out of here."

"She's going to want to be with you then, you know that right? I mean, she'll expect me to turn you too."

"Maybe. Maybe not. I don't really know what her life was like after I left. She may have a new life, a new family to go back to. But if she does expect us to be together again, I'll be honest with her. There's nothing that will come between us, Cassandra. Not now, not ever."

I was sad for Alison in a way. None of this was her fault either. But all I could do was wish she had someone else to go back to.

"Promise me," I said, grabbing both of his hands in mine and holding them against my heart.

He leaned up and pressed his lips to mine. "I promise."

"I don't want you to go," I said. "Not yet. Will you stay with me for a little longer? Just until I fall asleep?" My heart felt as if it were ripping inside, knowing he'd be leaving me soon. I didn't know what the future held for either of us after he walked out that door. The plan was so incredibly full of holes it would be a miracle if either of us actually came out of it alive.

Putting an arm under my knees, while the other went around my back, he stood and carried me to the bed. After setting me down gently in the middle of it, he positioned the pillows under my head and lay down next to me. He didn't say a word. He didn't need to. I could feel his heart reaching out to mine without any words to explain. I placed my arm across his stomach and rested my head on his chest, but I didn't dare close my eyes. Not yet. I wanted to savor the feel of having his body next to mine. I moved my hand underneath his T-shirt, longing to feel his skin. As I traced the solid planes of his chest, I felt his heartbeat quicken beneath my head. He let out a long hiss when I continued my delicate path down the waves of muscles at his stomach.

"If you continue this sweet torture, I won't be able to stop myself from taking you here and now."

Coming up on an elbow, I lifted his shirt, exposing his beautiful body to my lips. I kissed him lightly, anxious to sample a taste of his succulent skin with my tongue. Looking up from his stomach, I whispered, "Maybe I don't want you to stop."

CHAPTER TWENTY

I barely finished my sentence before Hunter had me on my back, underneath him, in a graceful flash of movement. As I caught my breath, he tenderly swept the stray curls that blocked me from looking into his eyes. My gaze locked with his for only a second before it was drawn to the succulent lips I longed to feel pressed against my own, tasting and exploring my body, claiming every inch of me as his. Somehow sensing my inner thoughts, he slowly lowered his head and lightly brushed his lips across mine. As he trailed his tongue across my bottom lip, I drew in a heavy breath, and he used the opportunity to suckle it into his mouth. It was the most erotic feeling I'd ever experienced from a kiss.

My body went on autopilot, undulating against his, as much as his weight on me allowed. His legs sank between mine, his arousal pressed between my thighs perfectly, sending waves of pleasure exploding through my body every time he met my pulsing rhythm. I knew we didn't have much time, and Caleb could drop in at any minute, but my mind would not listen to reason while my body luxuriated in the ecstatic sensations Hunter was creating. Promising eternal bliss, his lips slid down my neck, as he swirled his tongue in tiny circles over the sensitive spots only he would know. He hovered over the places he knew would set my body over the edge. There was no way I could stop or resist. Logic was overthrown like an unpopular dictator by its emotionally charged civilians, as sexually heightened hormones seized the throne.

I couldn't take much more. I needed to feel his skin against mine. Reaching between our bodies, I grappled with the buttons of his jeans, while he pulled his T-shirt over his head. It was as if we were in sync with one another, knowing exactly what we needed to do next. His pants came down, and all of my clothing came off. I couldn't say who took off what, as our hands were in constant motion over each other. Our urgency no longer had anything to do with being caught, it was all about a raw yearning to experience each other in every way possible.

His fists sunk into the bed on either side of me as he leaned over, and his biceps corded around his arms when he held himself up. I couldn't take my eyes off his dark, steely features, while his gaze touched every part of my body, leaving tremors in its wake. I felt his hard, hot shaft burning my skin, teasing me with its intimacy. I arched to meet it, and he rewarded my effort, sliding heat against the sensitive, slick nub between my legs.

I moaned, feeling the vibration from deep inside my throat. The sweet torture of longing to feel him inside me made me think of drowning. I was so desperate for the air that waited at the surface above me, yet it seemed much too far away. His smooth, warm skin trembled under my palms as I slid my hands around his waist and over the solid planes of his back, making my way to his strong, toned buttocks. He let out a long, ragged breath, which only fueled my craving for him. Finally, I reached for the one prize I knew was sure to sate my hunger and release the immense pressure currently threatening to drive me mad with pent-up desire. My fingertips barely grasped the silky skin of his shaft, when he caught my hand and pulled it up over my head. Capturing my other hand in his vise-like grip, he caged them both with one hand, watching as I silently pleaded for their release.

He slowly shook his head. "No distractions."

I had no clue what he meant until his free hand cupped my breasts, shaping and squeezing them. His fingers tugged at my nipples, pinching them, bringing them to small peaks, first one, then the other. He sent jolts of electricity straight to my core. I arched my back, lifting my hips closer, aching for more. His arm supported my back, holding me up, as if my body were his personal offering. After releasing my wrists, he said, "Be good." But I needed no chiding. No way would I move when his other hand took its turn at my breasts, holding them for his lips to suckle, while his teeth gently nibbled my tender nipples. My body blazed with need, becoming almost intolerable, but he relentlessly indulged his hungry ministrations.

Devouring my breasts, his hand slid down my side and over my hips and thighs before slowly exploring between my legs. He lingered just beyond my most sensitive area, teasing me with his slow, deliberate hesitation. My lids felt like lead shutters, weighed down by my passion when I gazed into his eyes. His reflected my own, aglow with obsession, lust, and fervor.

"Hunter, please," I breathed.

Two of his fingers plunged into me, sending me nearly over the edge. I cried out, forgetting the danger of being heard. I didn't care, I couldn't think anymore. He took me to another world where no one else existed except the two of us. There were no complications, only blissful emanations from our bodies exploring each other, fulfilling our hearts' desires. It was ironic that we were in Hell because this was Paradise.

Our mouths merged together, his tongue thrusting around mine, matching the rhythm of his fingers inside me. My muscles contracted with every wave of pleasure and every minuscule movement I felt inside me. I was on the brink of exploding into total oblivion, but dared not let it end. I wanted to prolong the moment, if not forever, then for long enough to last forever in my memory.

Our kiss ended and his lips were gone. Wanting to cry out for their return, the complaint died in my throat when I felt their whispered kisses climbing the insides of my thighs. I was unaware his body no longer covered mine, having become far too entranced by the magic he could conjure. His two fingers turned into three, as he prepared my body to receive all of him. The pressure building between my legs mounted until it was almost too painful for me to bear any longer. I had to have him inside of me, to release me. I begged him to do so, but my words came out as moans of pleasure, which only encouraged him to continue his sweet torture. His tongue lapped the tender spot at the center of my femininity, beginning slowly and languidly, then quickly flickering over it, sending me to heights of uncharted delight, releasing all the built up tension created by him in a flood of ecstasy. My pleasure soared high enough to cross eternal dimensions, riding the swells of elation before finally abating to small tremors. He continued placing tender kisses on me, as if sealing our connection. I think he wanted to make sure my body knew he was the one who brought it to such a blissful state.

He came back on top of me. His smoky, passion-filled eyes connected with mine, revealing his obvious hunger. I knew what he needed, and it wasn't only his eyes that told me. His whole body seemed electrified against mine, pulsing with lust. It made me want him all over again, but this time, I wanted *him*, deep inside of me.

Hunter's hard shaft taunted me, remaining at the threshold of where I needed him. How could he stand it? One orgasm, and I could barely breathe, my desire for him was so demanding. I rocked my hips, inviting him in, urging him to push past the brink of my longing. His features froze when he peered down at me. "Cassandra," he whispered, before sliding inside my walls. His ample size was no issue, because I was so wet for him. He pushed himself deeper, as deep as he could go, eyes closed, as if savoring the pleasure of a good meal after starving. Our connection felt so spiritual I imagined our souls entwining, neither angel nor demon, but some other entity that was completely immune to outside forces.

His lids slowly opened and revealed eyes that glowed, an indicator of his emotional intensity. I reveled knowing I was on the same emotional level. I loved him with my entire being, and I knew he loved me.

He rocked steadily against me, pulling out slowly before plunging back in. Then he went deeper and faster with every thrust. A storm began to brew inside of me, a small rumble at first, but quickly becoming a full-blown eruption of focused energy. His mouth crashed down on mine with a bruising impact. His tongued lashed out, desperately seeking mine. I mirrored his frenzy, reaching for the same peak I knew he was fast approaching.

Pulling back abruptly, Hunter gazed into my eyes. "I love you," he said, before plunging himself deeper. His whole body stiffened above and inside me. The release triggered explosions throughout my body. Subsequent aftershocks rattled my entire being. Neither of us let out a sound. There was no residual breath left inside me to free the cheers of joy inside my head. Peering at Hunter, I could tell he was experiencing the same blissful moment. Finally, he fell against me, and we both inhaled mouthfuls of air.

Breathing heavily near his ear as he rested his head next to mine, I whispered, "I wish we could stay this way forever."

"You only need to say the word, and I would take you away from all of this. We could make love for eternity. I can be very creative, Cassandra."

I sighed, fantasizing of another life I knew he'd make sure fell nothing short of what he described.

"If it weren't for my dad—"

"If it weren't for your dad, I'd give you no choice."

I let him have his alpha male thoughts, as there was no point in arguing about a fantasy that wasn't possible anyway. Our world didn't include the luxury of a happily married couple.

There was only one reality. My dad was in Hell. And I was going to kill the Devil.

We lay in each other's arms for quite some time. The quiet rhythm of Hunter's breath, coupled with the heat of his body and my exhaustion, finally conquered my restless mind. I fell in and out of consciousness. I tried to fight it at first, to avoid missing any moments I had left with him, but when he leaned over and kissed my temple, before insisting I to go to sleep, I let go. The blackness overcame me within seconds.

I had no idea how much time passed, but at some point, I felt his caress on my cheek and the soft pressure of his kiss upon my lips, right before there was a shift of weight beside me. I knew he was leaving me, but the overbearing veil of sleep was so thick, I couldn't wake up to stop him. From a distance, he asked me to unlock the door. Instantly, my thoughts jumped to the mental mechanism. If I did actually manage to open it, it was purely through my subconscious. I had no will to make it happen.

I fell back into the darkness, but not for long.

Something pulled me out, something inside of me. It was as if a siren went off in my head, issuing a warning of some impending catastrophe. I felt the urge to wake up and search for the source.

Jumping out of bed, I almost lost my balance from my body reacting faster than my mind could process. Mentally swatting away the cobwebs of sleep, I glanced around the room. It was empty. As I sprinted toward the door, it opened instantaneously, and somehow I knew it was because of me. It seemed I was quickly assimilating my newfound powers. I promised to congratulate myself later after I identified what was making my skin crawl into hypersensitive mode.

It only took me a second more to figure it out. Hunter and Caleb were standing in the middle of my living room, face-off style. No words were exchanged, and the room was deathly quiet, aside from the crackling tension in the air. Apparently, I walked right into some kind of testosterone-driven dogfight just as they were baring their teeth. It gave me déjà vu. I'd already witnessed their pissing matches one too many times. This time, they were on my turf, and I wasn't about to stand by and let it happen. I made my way further into the room toward them. Caleb glanced my way, causing Hunter to look as well.

"Caleb," I said in casual acknowledgement.

"What's he doing here, Cassie?"

"I could ask you the same thing," Hunter retorted before I could answer.

I opened my mouth to take control, but was shot down again when Caleb interjected. "Apparently, Nergal underestimated Alison's power to lure you back." His eyes cut over to mine, dripping with accusation. "And, I guess I underestimated Hunter's power over you."

I needed to recoup, and fast. "He was only here to check in on me, Caleb. And to explain about Alison."

"I can speak for myself, Cassandra," Hunter said, calm, but deadly. "If I choose to." With deliberate silence that spoke volumes, he stared Caleb down.

"It must be difficult to choose between the woman you gave up your soul for and the one you gave your black heart to," Caleb goaded him. "But let me make it easier for you. You're in my world now, the one where *I* outrank *you*. And in this world, Cassie is mine."

"Cale—"

"*The hell she is.*" Hunter took a step toward him, his body poised, fists balled up at his sides, ready to pounce. I couldn't see his eyes, but I didn't need to. I knew they were glowing brightly.

"Hunt—"

"You know as well as I do, I'm the only one that can give her what she needs now," Caleb said with a mocking grin.

"Maybe I'll have you barred from entering her suite." He nodded as if it solidified this light bulb of an idea.

It outraged me. I couldn't live without Hunter. I had no idea how long our plan would take. I needed to know we could share another night like the one we had in order to get me through it, and now I felt helpless.

Hunter went for Caleb. It was so fast I had no time to react. My feet didn't even get the message to move before he had Caleb up in the air by the throat, about to crash him against the wall. I ran toward them, ready to test my power to break them up, but I only got halfway there when Nergal entered the room.

"Well, here they all are," he said as he moved closer, revealing Alison, who was standing behind him. He coaxed her in further. When she came forward, it was as if he raised the curtains and a spotlight caught her on stage. Hunter and Caleb both stopped to watch, as if drawn to her. She was a few inches shorter than I, but her fitted tank top and combat-style pants revealed a toned, strong body, ready for battle. And the way her eyes drilled into mine, it appeared I was the one she wanted to do battle with. I could only wonder if she was this way before being turned, or if Hunter had intended to marry GI Jane. Sure she had long, luxuriant black hair, but shave it all off and I was looking at a woman who knew her way around an armored tank. I didn't notice how lethal she looked when I first saw her. Maybe they used steroids in Hell, or perhaps it was an accelerated boot camp program.

"I'm disappointed, Cassandra. We didn't get an invitation to your party," Nergal said, making me break eye contact with Alison. It was just as well, she was creeping me out.

"Yeah, well, we were already over-capacity, in my opinion," I said. "One too many."

"Interesting," Nergal said. "Tell me, which is the *one,* and which is the *too many*?" He eyed me through narrowed lids, daring me to say the wrong answer.

It was my turn to stand in the spotlight. I only hoped my performance would be convincing.

"Actually, Hunter was just leaving." I caught Hunter's reaction from the corner of my eye as I kept my gaze fixed on Nergal. The way his head jerked toward me, I knew he was more than surprised I'd called him out. *Please, Hunter, just go with it.*

"I think that's a good idea," Nergal replied. "It was quite rude of you to leave your fiancée all alone on her very first night with us anyway, Hunter. I suggest you take her out and show her a good time to make it up to her...or stay in, if you prefer."

"Yes, Hunter," Alison chimed in with an icy edge to her tone. "I'm feeling a bit neglected."

Her tone was so unexpected all I could do was watch as she glared at Hunter. I'd thought she was a small, helpless victim, up until she walked in full of attitude. It completely threw me off. The confused expression Hunter gave her told me he was as surprised as I. She had become the demon, only too much, and too fast. I had an incredible urge to knock her on her ass, take her down a few notches. Turning her just got higher on the priority scale. That's if I didn't kill her first.

"Well, it sounds as if you have your hands full here," Caleb chimed in with a smirk. "Don't worry, Cassie will be well taken care of."

Hunter stiffened once again, pinning Caleb with a toxic stare. He was primed and ready to go at him, regardless of who witnessed it. I wanted him to let it go. They had to believe we were done. It was the only way to move forward with the plan and get closer to them. Close enough to kill them.

I went over and pitted myself between Hunter and Caleb. Placing my hand on Hunter's arm, I said, "You need to go. We both have responsibilities now that we need to fulfill." I prayed he caught my double meaning. "I can take care of myself. You do what you need to."

Our eyes locked, and I hoped he saw the reassurance I was trying to send him. I gave his arm a small squeeze. If only my new powers included telepathy to ensure he got it. For now, it was all I could do. His eyes went to my lips, and reflexively, I licked them. When he met my gaze again and nodded, I knew he understood.

"Okay, run along now," Nergal said, breaking our mental connection. "Cassandra has a big day ahead of her. Lots of new things to see and do." He said it in such an uplifting manner it sounded more like my first day at school, rather than my first day in Hell.

Now, I merely had to figure out how to become teacher's pet long enough to get to the Sword of Final Death.

CHAPTER TWENTY-ONE

We must have been walking in circles again. Corridor after corridor passed without change, or color. It was dismal, but I guess that's how Hell was supposed to be. I almost laughed out loud when thoughts of *Dead Girl Walking* and *The Green Mile* crossed my mind. But dead was exactly what I felt like inside, knowing what the day had in store for me, as well as trying to keep up appearances by training to be a good little demon. All I really wanted to do was put a hole straight into where Nergal's heart should have been.

Every once in a while, I'd peek into one of the cells. They were all empty. Only a faint pattern of light passing through the bars on the door lit up the floor to interrupt the chilling darkness within. In a small way, that relieved me, knowing no prisoners were being held, the way Hunter had been, the way my father still was. I wondered where all those lost souls were, though. I knew they were trapped in Hell for all eternity and forced to service the Underworld, but where? Would I ever see them? It might have helped to know what I was actually looking for.

"I'm keeping them away from you," Nergal said, interrupting my thoughts.

"Keeping who away from me?" I wasn't sure if he read my mind, or if my actions were that obvious. I hoped for the latter. Nergal's mind reading could be extremely harmful to my health.

"Our servants," he said nonchalantly, his pace not slowing as he continued the conversation. They were no more than pesky flies to him, deserving nothing more than a swat of his hand. "We can't have them tempting you now, can we?"

"My blood works on them?" I blurted out, regretting it only seconds after.

Nergal spun around and tightened his grip on my arm. I winced from the pain.

"You would be wise not to find out, Cassandra." His voice was low, menacing, warning me there really was no other option. He relaxed his grip and lightened his tone. "Maybe someday you won't feel so alone down here."

What the hell did that mean? Would I get playmates if I was a good little demon?

He dropped my arm and continued walking. I followed in silence. My skin prickled, alerting me Caleb still lurked behind.

"I do like to keep a few of my favorites around though," Nergal said, almost as an afterthought.

The words were no sooner spoken when the sight of someone sitting in a chair, in the middle of a cell we passed, caught my eye. We didn't stop walking, so the image was fleeting and still being processed in my mind's eye. The curly blond hair, the body frame, the long, lean legs. They all started coming into focus, like looking through a camera lens, and zooming in to capture the features of someone you knew your whole life. And I did know her. The girl in the cell was Tiffany, my childhood friend, and the first soul I ever lost.

My skin ran cold, and I stopped dead in my tracks. Tiffany was the reason I accepted my fate as a Guardian. I vowed to never lose another soul after her. It had been a long time, seemingly centuries, but her memory never faded from my heart. I was frozen, compelled to run back and prove what my eyes saw, but dreading the sight of her at the same time. If she were here, I would have to relive her death. I didn't know if I could handle that.

Nergal watched me, and I knew right then she was here. He was gauging my reaction. My eyes, burning with hatred, were riveted on his, while his challenged me. My glare didn't faze him in the least. I turned toward the cell, barely aware Caleb was staring at me in confusion, before he followed my gaze. My legs felt like lead, weighing me down, warning me to go no further. I caught Caleb exchanging a glance with Nergal before he stepped aside, out of my way. As if in a dream, I lumbered forward until I was standing before the cell door. I kept my eyes closed, prolonging the heartache I knew sat only a few feet away.

When I opened my eyes, I stared at the empty cell with mixed emotions—relief, denial, anger, and misery. She wasn't there, but a part of me wanted to see her again so badly, regardless of what state I'd find her in. God, I was reliving her death all over again, blaming myself again for losing her. Would she still be in that cell if I didn't hesitate before coming back to her? How could I want to see my best friend soulless and suffering in Hell? What kind of person had I become?

Deep down, I knew it was another illusion created by Nergal, his way of torturing me, forcing me to comply, but I couldn't help how it made me feel. I wanted to be young again, free from all the responsibilities expected of me. Nergal wanted to prove to me he knew my deepest, darkest fears and regrets, and was eager to use them against me. I hated him. I loathed his very existence. He conjured up dark things in my mind I didn't think I was capable of. He kindled my desire to inflict pain, torturous, relentless pain. He made me look forward to killing him.

"Anything wrong?" Nergal asked, the concern in his voice so intentionally forged, it might have been humorous in any other situation.

I turned stoically to face him. "Not at all," I said, my jaw clenched, while defiantly staring at him. I was ready to explode inside, but resisted, knowing it would only add to Nergal's amusement. I prayed Caleb wouldn't spout his mouth. I was right on the verge of inflicting violence, and he'd be an easy target. He must have gotten the vibe, because he stood as still as I did, watching me.

After several deep breaths, I moved back to Nergal, talking myself down to calm my over-wrought nerves.

"Good, let's move on then."

"Where are we going?" I'd had it with the rat maze.

"You'll see. It's not far now."

We walked down a few more corridors before we stopped in front of a solid door, similar to the one that locked my dad in his cell. I held my breath. This didn't look good.

"Here we are," Nergal said happily, as if we'd reached the end of the Yellow Brick Road, and all of my questions would be answered beyond the closed door.

"What is this? I thought I was supposed to be training?"

"Every good training discipline has its lessons and rules, Cassandra. This is where you learn that, before you move on to your...on-the-job training, if you will." With that, the door inched open.

I stood to one side, afraid to find what awaited me in the room. Nergal's cryptic speeches never prefaced rainbows or a pot of gold. Surely, this was no exception.

"After you, dear," he said, motioning me forward.

I braced myself for the inevitable and walked into the room. What I saw before me was familiar, but so unexpected it made me gasp. A large, naked man stood in the middle of the room, chained to columns that flanked either side of him. His short, blond hair was wet and matted to his head, with sweat dripping down the entire length of his body. Beyond him, at the far wall, a huge fire blazed. I could only catch glimpses of the flames, as his body blocked most of it, but I could feel the fire's heat even from where I was standing. I could only imagine how painfully scorching it must have felt to him, being so much closer.

Flashbacks of Hunter being tortured in the same way haunted me. I studied the man's body before me, and while he was built similarly to Hunter, I instinctively knew it wasn't him.

This man was shorter, but only by a hair, and his physique was slightly leaner. I decided not to waste any time contemplating all the twisted methods Nergal had to get his jollies off, and bravely stood before him.

I was right. The fire's intensity was so hot near him I could barely breathe. I quickly turned my back to it so my retinas wouldn't burn right through to my brain, and peered up. Eric stared back at me. His face was a mass of cuts and bruises, his eyes revealing defeat and regret. As he slowly closed and reopened them, I knew he was silently apologizing. He got caught, leaving Nora and my mom without protection. I only hoped that was all he wanted to apologize for.

"Are they okay?" I asked.

"Yes," Eric managed. His voice sounded harsh and strangled, as if he'd been screaming or yelling for hours.

The fire blazed hotter behind me, as though a blast of fresh oxygen made it explode. But there was no wind in the cell.

"That's enough," Nergal said from beside the door.

I came back around, marching right up to him.

"Why?"

"I'm certain you're not that naive, but I'm only too happy to answer you. After all, this is your first lesson. It's very simple—Eric broke the rules, and I will not tolerate any renegades, as you well know. Perhaps my Seekers are beginning to fall prey to their own ploys of seduction. I'm going to have to nip this in the bud somehow, maybe re-wire all of them. I don't know, I'm still deciding. And until I do..." He waved his hand in Eric's direction. Over his shoulder I saw Caleb's eyes widening.

"You've already ended the relationship between Hunter and me with Alison, so why is this a lesson for me?"

"Oh, I was just getting to that. I wanted you to see that Eric is no more than a speed bump compared to whom I could have down here if *you* ever break the rules again. As I said before, I will not tolerate renegades."

Panicking with thoughts Nergal knew of our plan, I glanced over Nergal's shoulder at Caleb again. He appeared as confused and scared as I felt.

"What are you talking about? I've done noth—"

"Do not lie to me, Cassandra," he yelled.

I jumped back. His anger was abrupt and so contrary to his usual, calm demeanor.

Trembling, I shook my head, afraid to say anything. Power radiated from him, so strong I could almost feel the walls vibrating.

"Let me make this lesson as easy for you as possible. If you rendezvous with Hunter again, the way you did last night, the people whom Eric was *supposed* to be protecting will occupy the empty cells we just passed. Is that clear enough for you?"

A bomb could have gone off, but it wouldn't have been as disastrous as my impression of things. My mom and Nora were sitting ducks, framed in Nergal's crosshairs, and only my actions from here on out determined their fates. Actions such as...*oh, I don't know*...planning to kill Nergal.

I was terrified. If he knew what happened between Hunter and me last night, there was a good chance he knew about our plan to kill him. I searched his face for any sign this was the case, but he was a stone. Surely, if he knew, there would have been much more punishment than capturing Eric. Not to diminish his pain, but Nergal was capable of much more horrible torture that exceeded anyone's imagination. If he didn't intend to kill us, he still had the means to inflict unbearable suffering. I could feel myself sinking into some kind of crazy trap he was designing. If, by some tiny chance, he didn't know about our plan, I sure as hell wouldn't volunteer any information. For now, I needed to play along. Or maybe I just kept telling myself that because I didn't know what else to do.

"Yes, it's clear. I'll do as you say. But, please, let Eric go, or at least, put out the fire and unchain him. I promise I won't make any more mistakes."

Trying to make myself appear as convincing as possible, I did my damnedest to clear any thoughts about our scheme, in case he could read my mind.

He studied me for a moment or two, making me feel as if he were probing beneath my skin with his eyes. "You know, I think I'll let him hang around for a little while longer. At least, until you prove you've adjusted to your new career path."

I was afraid to ask, but I had to know. "How do I prove that?"

"By being one of us. Tomorrow. Caleb will train you on how to lure in your first victim until you need to rest. When you wake up, you and he will go out and retrieve a new Seeker for me. So far, there are two you owe me. I suspect it will take you much less time than my current Seekers, since you can use your Guardian qualities to bait them. Once your first Guardian is turned by Caleb, I will make Eric a little more comfortable."

My stomach dropped, and I felt the blood drain from my face. My worst nightmare was suddenly upon me. It was all happening too fast. I completely blocked out what I might have to do in order to pull it off. I was naïve to think I could fly under Nergal's radar until the moment I stabbed him in the heart. Preparing myself for it didn't matter anymore, the time had come. I was going to have to think quickly, or find out exactly how it felt to steal someone's soul.

I wanted him gone. I couldn't think with him around me. It probably wasn't even safe to think around him. Hunter was right, even if I could control my ability to fade, it wouldn't work on Nergal. I felt sure of that now.

With eyes downcast, I nodded, accepting his terms as if I had a choice.

"Don't look so sad, Cassandra. You may actually find you like it. Caleb," Nergal said, turning to face him as he lingered in the doorway.

"Yes, sir?" Caleb said. *What a good little soldier.*

"I suggest you make this a success. I'm not opposed to re-wiring you either. Report back to me after your training."

"Yes, sir."

Nergal faced me. "Say your goodbyes now. You won't be seeing Eric for a while. But make it quick, time's a tickin'."

As I approached Eric, the fire diminished to a mere flame. I slowed my pace, wanting to give Eric as much of a reprieve as I could. I was shocked Nergal had eased up at all, but I certainly wasn't about to thank him. Eric's eyes were closed. I knew he wasn't sleeping. Seekers needed no sleep. Maybe he was savoring a break from his torture, or simply praying to a god that was lost to him for eternity. I didn't know, but I spoke to him anyway. "Eric, I'm so sorry." I reached up and lightly touched a spot on his face that wasn't injured. "I'm going to get you out of this, I promise."

He opened his eyes to meet mine and I saw such sorrow that I struggled to hold back my tears. "Save them," he rasped. "Your mom...Nora..." His voice broke. "Don't let them get her."

"Time's up," Nergal yelled.

"I promise," I whispered before tearing myself away.

Nergal led me out of the room. Somehow, I managed to bear the weight of my heavy heart as I went. It felt like whatever was left of my soul was being torn away, piece by piece. Is this what death felt like? Having every bit of your life ripped away from you until there is nothing left? I wasn't sure how much more I could take before I shut down and succumbed to the darkness. I could feel it lingering nearby, waiting for when I became so empty it could enter and fill me up.

After Nergal left us, Caleb leaned against the wall of the corridor, glaring at me. The bug up his ass was the last thing I wanted to deal with.

"What?" I asked sharply.

"You were with *him* last night?"

"Oh, for God's sake, Caleb, get over it. I don't have the patience for your ego right now."

He came at me so fast, I wasn't expecting it. His body rammed into mine like a bulldozer, pinning me easily to the wall. A rush of air shot out of me as our bodies collided. He pressed his face so close, his nose crushed into mine. "You better learn whose ego to worry about real quick, babe. I could just as easily make you my slave as my queen when I become King."

There was no build-up. I didn't even need to think about it. The power surged from me and straight into Caleb. He flew back in the air, smashing high into the wall across the corridor, and then sliding down into a heap on the floor. He sat so still, for so long, I thought I must have knocked him out, until he slowly moved his head. Before he had the chance to get up, I ran over, pulled him up, and straight-armed his shoulders against the wall. My strength was so enhanced his weight felt like nothing as I held him up. My confidence was soaring. I was a different person in that moment—mind, body, and soul—and it felt good. *Really* good.

"I think you have a few lessons to learn too, Caleb. It seems you may have met your match, maybe more than you can handle. You need me as much as I need you. In fact, I'm almost starting to think I don't need you at all. So, watch yourself, or *you* may become the slave. Oh, wait, you already are." I pressed my finger against the tip of his nose, smashing it the same way he did mine. He glared back at me. "Don't push me again, or I promise, you'll regret it. Now let's stop playing *who's got the bigger dick* and get this shit over with."

I shoved him into the wall, before letting him go and walking away, unmindful whether he followed or not.

"And don't call me babe," I added without looking back.

CHAPTER TWENTY-TWO

Caleb eventually managed to peel his pride off the floor and catch up to me. Thankfully, he kept his mouth shut, aside from directing me through the maze to get to his quarters. I was starting to get a sense of the layout as we passed some of the same hallways when coming from my suite. From what I could make out, all of the rooms were in the general vicinity of each other, but I wouldn't call them close together. Several twisting corridors and empty cells threaded between them, putting them far enough away that borrowing a cup of sugar might be a bit time-consuming.

After advising me we would be training in his quarters, I initially balked at the idea, but soon realized I didn't care where we did it. Caleb didn't scare me anymore. I'd already seen what I could do to him. I knew if it came down to it, I'd at least be able to defend myself against him. Plus, I fed him enough humble pie back in the corridor that I didn't need to worry about him doing anything stupid for a while. Then again, it *was* Caleb.

In the time it took us to get there, I managed to cool off. At least, I simmered down enough so I wasn't on the verge of murdering the first member of Team Evil to look at me. I didn't think I could ever let my guard down fully anymore. There comes a time when the little picket fence you once used to ward off potential threats while you were young and innocent grows as thick and impenetrable as the fortified walls of a medieval castle. After everything that happened during the last year, my walls were fortified about ten layers thick.

I expected the whole training business to go pretty fast. How much could Caleb really teach me about getting close enough to someone to make him or her drink a little blood? I imagined it was more of a *fly by the seat of your pants* situation anyway. I remembered Hunter telling me the Guardian had to drink it of their own free will, so maybe there was some protocol I had to follow in that regard. Whatever. I just wanted to get it over with, so I could return to my room and decide what to do now that Nergal had thrown an industrial-strength wrench into our plan. Obviously, I couldn't talk to Caleb about it anymore, since Nergal had eyes and ears everywhere. Caleb's plan had been good enough, workable. Now, however, I had to start from scratch and whip up something all on my own. It was just as well, since I planned to kill them both. But I still had no idea how to get away with it.

Caleb's quarters were laid out exactly as mine, the only difference being the color scheme. His was a little more Goth, which didn't surprise me. I half expected to see large, marble statues depicting devils or other horrendous creatures displayed everywhere. Luckily, there weren't any. The fireplace was burning bright, of course. I could see that the whole hellfire concept wasn't merely a crazy notion mothers used to scare their children in order to keep them from telling lies. Every room I entered had one, roaring away as if it stayed lit eternally. Perhaps the goal was to make everything appear eerie. I preferred to think of them that way, rather than as pits of torture, accessible throughout the Underworld. Getting chilled while walking through the corridors, I took a seat on the sofa in front of Caleb's fire. Caleb came around soon after and offered me a wineglass filled with an off-white liquid.

"Its only wine. I know you're put off by the red." When I started to decline, he sat down next to me and pushed it into my hands. "Take it. It'll calm your nerves."

A peace offering? Who was he kidding?

"I'm fine."

"Cassie, you and me are not so different. And I know I sure need it." He took a sip from his own glass.

"You're wrong. I'm nothing like you."

"Maybe we employ different methods, I'll give you that much, but we are both willing to do just about anything to get what we want. I want to be King, and you want to save your friends and family. Both very different end goals, but the means to them are the same. Nergal has to die."

"Shhh," I said, instinctively covering his mouth with my fingers. It was a stupid gesture, since the damage was already done.

Our eyes locked. His surprised expression changed into something I couldn't quite make sense of at first. Longing possibly? He gently took my hand and held it against his lips for a moment longer than I would have liked. Yep, definitely longing. I quickly pulled it away and took a gulp of my wine.

"He doesn't know," he said, reaching behind the sofa and setting his glass down.

"Of course he does. Obviously, he knows everything that goes on down here. The jig is up, Caleb."

He shook his head slowly, as though I were a stubborn child. "No, it's not. Nergal only watches over those he doesn't trust. He can zoom in on them telepathically, but he has to do so on an individual basis. Besides, he only does it when he has reason. It's not some complex security system. He doesn't trust Hunter. That's whom he was watching. He told me so before I even brought you to your suite. He didn't want me to worry about Hunter showing up and trying something stupid. Nergal has no reason to doubt my allegiance, so we have nothing to worry about."

"But he has every reason not to trust me."

"That's true, but you're with me. Right now, he's confident I can handle you."

"Does he know I overpowered you several times already?'

That hit a nerve. "It was a few times. And only under special circum—"

"So, he doesn't. Well, I guess that's good, if what you're saying is true. But what if it's not? What if he does know?"

"Cassie, if he knew, do you think I'd be here? If he knew, my head would be displayed on his wall."

"He does that?" I asked, horrified. "Like in a...trophy room or something?"

Again, I got the *I'm with stupid* look.

"Okay, okay. So, if the plan is still a go, can we speed this up? Say, like, tomorrow? Before I have to go out and scout for prey?" I still wasn't totally convinced Nergal was clueless about our conspiracy, but I *really* didn't want to go out and sport my Seeker hat. I'd have to devise Plan B, or C, or whatever letter I was on, tonight. I only prayed they would let me sleep in to give me enough time. Improvisation seemed to be my M.O. lately anyway. It got me this far, which wasn't saying much, but at least my family and friends were still alive. Then again, I also had Hunter by my side, up until now.

"No, we're still not ready yet. I have a few loose ends to tie up. You're going to have to go through with tomorrow. It'll be good practice for when you're my queen anyway."

I narrowed my eyes at him. "That's still up for debate."

"A deal's, a deal."

"Yeah, well, deal-breaking seems to be pretty rampant here. Ugh...we'll work that out later."

His lips tightened, and I could tell he was clenching his teeth by the way his jaw throbbed at the sides. He wasn't going to let it go. Stupid, stubborn, pride. Why couldn't I keep it in check around him? I needed to get out of there to give myself time to think on my own. The longer I stayed to argue about our relationship status, after the fact, the less time I had. "Look, I'll still be your...partner, but that doesn't mean we're going to be some Bonnie and Clyde team. I'm still part Guardian. You have to give me a little room here."

"Fine. But you still have to follow through with tomorrow. I need a few more days to make sure everything is perfect."

"I guess I really don't have much of a choice then. Okay, tell me what I have to do."

I finished my wine off and set the glass down next to his, none too softly. I would have liked to drink a whole bottle to get through Caleb's excited instructions of how to seduce a Guardian, but I had to stay clear headed for what lay ahead. One thing was for sure, Caleb *really* enjoyed his job. He became the most animated I'd ever seen him, aside from the few occasions he felt me up. It made me sick, giving me all the more reason to avoid becoming a Seeker at all costs. Heaven help me if my eyes lit up like his when talking about stealing someone's soul.

I was so done with Hell.

***

Caleb and I finally finished our training session, and I was thankful it was over. My head was spinning with thoughts of what they expected of me, as well as ways to get out of it. *Would the plan to kill Nergal really work? What was I going to do about getting my dad out? Would I ever see Hunter again?* Then other nightmarish thoughts crept in to mingle and stress me out even more. I worried if my mom and Nora would be all right without someone to watch over them. It was way too much, and all I wanted was be alone to sort it all out. Most of it was probably beyond my control, but I had to do something. I couldn't abandon everyone I loved to some hellish fate.

I was ready to let Caleb know I wanted to head back to my room for a while, when a small knock came on his door. At first, I thought it might be Nergal checking on us, but quickly remembered he wouldn't bother knocking. The door opened after Caleb got up and stood beside it. I wasn't sure I could ever get used to not groping for a handle or knob to open a door down here. I hoped I wouldn't be here long enough to worry about it.

As if preparing for a dramatic entrance, Alison didn't walk through the door until it was fully open. She came through like some regal princess turned military soldier—small, lithe, and beautiful, but very deadly. Her skin appeared more radiant, and her long, black hair more vivid and rich. Even her demeanor seemed more...adjusted. She almost looked like she belonged here.

Her eyes fell immediately on me, and they didn't seem to be saying they were happy to see me. *Yeah, honey, the feeling's mutual.* What the hell was she doing here without Hunter? I thought he was supposed to be her *escort*, yet here she was, all alone, searching for Caleb. Why?

"Alison," Caleb said, all cheery and gracious. "What a pleasant surprise. Was there something that you needed, sweetheart? Or are you bored with your old beau already, and looking for a little excitement in your new life?"

She didn't even glance his way. I almost wondered if she heard his little diatribe since she continued to stare me down. I had no problem keeping the connection. It was difficult to hold on to the former sympathy I felt for her, especially while dodging the virtual daggers from her eyes, which threatened to impale me. I began to have really bad thoughts of my own, visualizing a certain blade being plunged into her heart. I was also beginning to doubt whether I really wanted to turn her back. Maybe she did belong in Hell.

"I was hoping to speak with you." I almost thought she meant me until I saw her turn her head to Caleb and add, "Alone."

I felt like the nerdy girl showing up at a party full of jocks and cheerleaders, all the music stopping with the scratch of a needle against vinyl, followed by a deafening silence. I could feel Caleb's gaze in my peripheral vision, while I proceeded to glare at her. He feigned a scratchy throat, trying to interrupt the awkward silence. As much as I wanted to stay and find out what she was all about, I knew she wouldn't say another word with me present.

"I was just leaving," I said, working my way toward the door. Alison watched me, her penetrating eyes washing over my skin, raising the hair on it in their wake. Had the fire been stoked since she walked in? I suddenly couldn't wait to leave. My power tingled within me, and I was afraid if I didn't get out of there soon, it would erupt beyond my control. This woman seemed to push buttons in me that no one, not even Nergal, could touch. Was it merely the jealousy I felt over what she once had with Hunter?

She blocked the door and didn't seem to be in the mood to step aside and allow me to leave. If that were the case, our egos were about to play a game of chicken, because there was no way I would go around her. I moved directly in front of her. Standing a few inches taller, it felt good to look down on her. Our eyes battled, blue on blue.

"Didn't you want to talk to Caleb?" I asked.

"Yes."

"Then talk, or move."

She stood her ground for seconds more, before finally stepping aside. I gave her a cocky grin and moved toward the doorway. Without the slightest glance at her, I peered over at Caleb, who seemed to be enjoying the show. "I can find my own way back to my room."

"I'll see you later then," he said as I walked out. "You'll do fine tomorrow, Cassie. Just remember what we talked about."

I didn't bother telling him I hoped tomorrow never came.

Arriving back at my room without turning any wrong corners, I used the time it took to get there to calm my ragged nerves, which was no easy feat. My mind kept flashing back to Alison's hostility toward me, and every time it did, my power surged back up. It was obvious she hated me. No, hatred was probably not strong enough for what she felt toward me. She appeared as though she would have liked to see my name etched in blood on a cement slab, after burying me alive beneath it. I could only hope Hunter would keep us apart until this was over, or inevitably, blood would be shed, be it hers or mine.

Sandwiches were already on the dining table when I got back in my suite. I scanned the place for whoever might have brought them in, but there was no one around. My stomach grumbled at the sight, and I surrendered to it. While eating, I mulled over what the hell I was going to do. As it stood, my only options were to place my fate in the hands of Caleb or Nergal. Unfortunately, neither one looked promising. Both demanded I serve someone whom I despised, and spend my eternity in Hell. I couldn't do it. They weren't options at all, but death sentences. I *wouldn't* do it. I had to find a way out of this. The powers I was born with precluded me from giving up and letting someone steal my soul. I intended to fight for my life, as well as the lives of the people I loved, or die trying.

I had the biggest urge to see my dad. I wanted him there, awake, telling me I could do anything I set my mind to, like normal dads say to their normal children during times when they need a boost of confidence in their normal lives. What I wouldn't give for that to be the case. As it was, I still wanted to see my dad, if only to be in the presence of someone I knew loved me.

Nergal promised I could visit with him, and I intended to take him up on that. *Now.*

CHAPTER TWENTY-THREE

I stood outside Nergal's door, questioning my determined will, which I carried with me all the way to his quarters. Was I showing weakness by asking to see my dad? Would I look like a little girl crying for her daddy? Well I was, I couldn't deny that, but I sure didn't want Nergal to see me that way. I would demand to see him. *Yeah, right.* He'd laugh in my face. And I'd let him as long as I got to see my dad. For nearly twenty years, I believed he was dead. Now that I knew he was alive, I'd be damned if I let Nergal keep me from him.

I ratcheted my spine straight and tilted my chin up, oozing determination. *That's it, Cassie, lay it on thick, because he'll probably rip a few layers off before giving in.* I knocked on the door, two quick, hard raps. Even my knock oozed purpose.

Nothing happened. The door didn't magically open, or mysteriously invite me in. I knocked again, but no answer. *Great*, all my ooze was for nothing. I turned to go back to my room when a crazy thought hit me. It was a long shot, but I figured now was the time to give it a try. Back at the door, I closed my eyes and imagined the door's internal locking system, while picturing myself springing the mechanism free, and opening the door. I heard a loud click, as if a metal deadbolt turned, and opened my eyes. The door slowly opened inward. I stood outside, eyes wide, mouth gaping, amazed it actually worked. Either I was more powerful than I thought, or Nergal's security system sucked.

Well, I was in, but now what? I was paralyzed. I'd illegally unlocked the Devil's lair and was about to voluntarily enter it. I pictured stepping through the threshold and immediately being fried by some flame-throwing device. The risk was beyond all sense of sanity, never mind survival, but if I could open this door, there was a good chance I could open the door to my dad's prison. I had to go in. *Ooze, don't fail me now.*

I decided to simply walk in as if it were the most natural thing in the world to do. *Hey, Nergal. I was walking by and saw your door open, so I thought I'd come in to see what you were up to.* I was pretty sure he wouldn't welcome my intrusion or offer me a beer, but I rehearsed my reply anyway.

The room was deathly quiet, which didn't calm my nerves any. My eyes darted back and forth, expecting someone to jump out at any minute, but there was no one there, at least, as far as I could see. Unfortunately, that didn't mean someone *wasn't* there, maybe in one of the other rooms that were closed off...or crouched behind the sofa, lurking, watching me. I rubbed my hands up and down my arms, trying to remove the chill that had soaked into my skin.

"Nergal?" I called out hesitantly. I was torn between wanting a response to end this cat-burglar impression and hoping to hear nothing, so I wouldn't have to face the death squad. Receiving only silence, I hightailed it down the hallway, toward my dad's cell. I made sure to glance over my shoulder and check the inconspicuous spot behind the sofa. No lurker.

The hallway wasn't very long, but I was breathing heavily by the time I got to the door at the end. Without a moment to waste, I said a little prayer before mentally repeating what I did earlier. It didn't work. My heart raced and, I swear, I could feel blood thrumming through my veins. I needed to calm down. My paranoia made it too difficult to concentrate. I took a few deep breaths and shook out my hands, willing myself to relax, before trying again. Shocking me no less than the first time, the door opened right in front of me.

My heart rate quickened again. If it kept up, I was sure I'd end up with some kind of irregular heart ailment. No human heart should have to handle so much emotional wavering. Then again, I wasn't completely human.

Holding my breath, I went in. The room appeared no different than before, with bright lights around me that faded into darkness at the other end. I had no plan. There was obviously no way I could get my dad out on my own if he were still unconscious. Even if I could, and he could walk on his own, there was no way we would make it out without being caught. I wasn't that stupid. But if he were awake, I'd, at least, have a chance to talk to him without anyone watching over us or listening. Maybe he knew a way out. Having lived in the Underworld for decades, he had to know a lot of its secrets.

I ran toward the darkness, but was stopped by the sound of a loud click that echoed throughout the room. The blood drained from my face, and an icy chill swept down my arms and legs. I stood motionless in the middle of the room, my body refusing to turn around and face the judge who would, no doubt, order my death sentence.

"You didn't really think it was that easy, did you, Cassandra?" Nergal's voice penetrated the silent void I cocooned myself in. "I must say, I'm very disappointed. I had such high hopes for you...for us. Wielding power is like a drug, is it not? Once you see what it can do, you crave it. You imagine what more you can do, and let it obsess you, making you desperate to have it. And desperation leads to carelessness." He moved to stand in front of me as he talked, his final words coinciding with the fire in his eyes. Somehow, I had the feeling we weren't talking about opening doors.

I needed to tread carefully. "I wanted to see my dad. So, I tried to open a few doors." I shrugged. "Why'd you let me? Where is he, by the way?" I noticed while standing there that my dad was no longer in the room. If Nergal knew I couldn't get in, why did he move my dad?

"Oh, he's around. No need to worry. I let you in as a lesson. While you may think you possess greater power than I, you will never possess enough to overthrow me, Cassandra. Every being in this place carries my blood, including you. That means you only have a portion of my power, but can never have more. Anyone that tries to deceive me will fail. You would be wise never to ally yourself with someone who would try, for the punishment is the same, whether it was your idea or his."

His. He said *his.*

"And what do you suggest, if I should be put in such a situation?" I asked, sidestepping a confession.

The sides of his lips pulled up in a knowing grin. "I suggest you prove your allegiance before it's too late."

"What would I need to do?"

"That's easy. Kill the deceiver."

"Me?"

"Yes."

"But how?"

"With this." He patted a scabbard that hung at his side from the belt at his waist. I was so focused on reading his facial expressions I hadn't noticed he was wearing it. If I had glanced down, I wouldn't have missed it. It was huge. It had to be the Sword of Final Death. "Yes, it is," he said, reading my thoughts. "And I'm willing to lend it to you to prove your loyalty to me one last time. You must kill Caleb with it, or I will consider you a lost cause."

A lost cause? It was only fitting since I was no more than a pawn in his mission to rule the world. I'd already seen what happened to defectors of the Underworld. It terrified me to think what might happen to lost causes. I eyed the Sword again, contemplating my own mission. The stipulation didn't seem that horrible really. Killing Caleb was part of my agenda anyway. I simply hadn't expected to kill him before Nergal. *Who was I kidding?* My agenda was nothing more than an improvisation, and killing either of them was tantamount to a wish for a miracle. I was wondering how to get my hands on the Sword, and now the Sword was being handed to me. The more I thought about it, the more it looked like a free pass.

"Fine," I told him. "When do I start?"

"Well, it seems our guest of honor has arrived. How does *now* work for you?"

Oh shit. I wasn't ready. Despite my intention to kill Caleb and convincing myself that a big, fat bonus was being handed to me, I wasn't prepared. I needed to psyche myself up to kill. At least, I thought I did. It wasn't like I had a lot of practice. When I'd led a normal life, I saved lives, I didn't take them. But Nergal didn't care. For him, it was now or never. He made it all too clear when he moved to leave the room while I stood trying to catch my breath and muster up the nerve to go through with it.

Nergal stepped into the room ahead of me, so Caleb didn't see me right away. I thought Seekers could sense others, but the surprised expression on his face told me a different story. Either it was for show, or perhaps something in Nergal's quarters nullified any powers he might have. It really didn't matter. It all had to go down whether he was shocked at seeing me or not.

"Ahhh, Caleb. We were just talking about you," Nergal said.

Caleb stopped where he was, but not too abruptly. I could tell by the way his gaze darted between us that he was leery of what he walked in on. "Oh yeah? What about?" he asked casually, but the fear in his eyes deceived his calm demeanor. He was questioning me with his eyes, as if trying to read the situation.

"Cassie was telling me all about your plan."

"Is that so?"

I held my breath. I was paralyzed, waiting for things to play out, but not prepared to go through with it yet. I was so tense, I didn't think my muscles could get any stiffer. God, it felt like I was in one of those horrible nightmares you have as a kid, when you freeze up the moment something monstrous starts after you.

"Yes, and I must admit, that while I'm shocked by it, I think it's a brilliant idea. I never expected you would persuade her to prove her loyalty to us in such a way, but I'm very pleased by it. I really didn't want to keep Eric around, he was more of a toy for me, and I have plenty of those. Watching her kill him would be much more entertaining for me anyway."

Nergal moved toward the table behind the settee. I stayed where I was, unable to move. I was so confused by what was going on. *Kill Eric?* I wanted to believe he was only luring Caleb in, but I knew trusting Nergal was a mistake. There was no way I could kill Eric. If this was some kind of twisted scheme by Nergal, I had to think fast.

"You certainly impressed me, Caleb," he continued as he picked up a canister of brownish liquid and poured some of it into a glass. "Your devotion will not go unrewarded. Come, let's have a drink before we begin."

Caleb gave me a brief, questioning look before he started toward Nergal. The blank stare I had on my face couldn't have revealed anything. Hell, I didn't even *know* what was going on.

As Nergal handed Caleb the glass, he asked me to join them. I had to force my legs to move, and even then, it was a slow go. My mind raced with scenarios of what to do, but not knowing Nergal's next move, kept them merely scrambled brainwaves. I kept trying to establish a small semblance of word order, but failed miserably.

I was handed a glass, which I robotically accepted. After we all had glasses in our hands, Nergal said some kind of triumphant toast that never registered, and I watched them both swig the liquid back. When they finished, they both turned to me as I stood lamely with my glass still in hand.

"Go ahead, Cassandra," Nergal said. "It will help take the edge off your task."

I stared into the glass, watching the brown liquid ripple from my trembling hand. I knew they saw it too, but I couldn't help it. Slowly, I raised the glass to my lips, concentrating on steadying my hand. With the rim on my lips, I peered up at them. They were staring at me, waiting. I could prolong it no longer. My last thought before pouring the burning liquid down my throat was that I'd probably need it anyway. As it seared through my chest and cascaded heavily into my belly, I almost wanted to laugh. I expected it to be some kind of deadly poison that would corrupt the rest of my soul, but it ended up being something as unremarkable as whiskey.

Nergal took the glass from me and set it back on the table. My body felt the alcohol within seconds, slightly numbing my frazzled nerves, while surprisingly, clearing my head.

"Well then, shall we get started?"

There was a loud whooshing noise as Nergal unsheathed the Sword. I instinctively took a step back, as did Caleb. Nergal chuckled as he held it up in front of his face. "It's beautiful, isn't it?" He studied the gleaming silver from tip to hilt, gazing at it more like an old flame than the deadly weapon it was.

My eyes were instantly drawn to it, not only its glossy, steel blade and intricately detailed hilt, but also the power it generated, as if it were alive and pulsing. It was hard to grasp how much power the Sword held, or more importantly, how much power it gave to the person holding it.

After we all stared at it for a while, Nergal placed it in his hands, palms up, and offered it to me. My fingers itched to grab it, but my mind warned me not to, as if one touch would permanently scorch my soul. An inner conflict played out in my mind that no one else could see. It represented life itself. Right in front of me laid the one element that could tip the scales of good versus evil. In my hands, it could eradicate the evil that paralyzed the mortal world, but would it also bring out the demon in me? The weapon defined the Devil's power. I was terrified of what it might do to me. Did the Guardian in me stand a chance trying to resist the omnipotent control that befell its possessor, as it did Nergal? As it would Caleb? My heart suddenly became a voice of wisdom, ending the battle, and convincing me that regardless of the mixed blood that ran through my body, only the dictator could prevail. And the dictator in me, without question, was good.

"It's time, Cassandra," Nergal said.

Yes, it was. I gently took the Sword and thrust it through Nergal's black heart.

CHAPTER TWENTY-FOUR

Nergal fell back against the table, the Sword still protruding from his chest. I let go and stepped back, shocked by what came to me so instinctively, feeling triumph, horror, and trepidation, all at once. Caleb yelled something as he moved backward, but I was deaf to everything except my own crazed thoughts.

Nergal's eyes were wide as he collapsed to the floor. *I did it.* I killed him. It seemed too easy. One would think assassinating the King of the Underworld would be much more grueling, not merely an impulsive action from a fledgling half-demon. I watched in fascination as he went down. I should have run, but I was too entranced by the scene unfolding in front of me—world-changing history in the making.

There was no blood. Shouldn't there have been blood? *Shit,* what was the Devil supposed to look like dying? I gazed into his eyes. I couldn't figure out if it was pain or shock staring back at me. Then he reached for me. I backed up further and glanced in a panic toward Caleb, who somehow had already made his way to the door. He motioned his hands at Nergal, but I was oblivious.

A glass shattered, and I spun my head to see Nergal reaching up to the table, trying to gain some leverage on it. *Why didn't he die already?* The jewels in the hilt of the Sword caught the firelight, and seemed to wink at me. Then I realized what Caleb was trying to tell me. *I had to get the Sword.* Nergal lost his edge on the table and fell again. His eyes no longer held their powerful gaze. They were dimming slowly as he blinked more readily. It was working. I couldn't believe it was really working. Now, would be the time to grab the Sword. If I waited too long,

Caleb might try and take it himself. I couldn't let that happen. I wasn't finished yet.

Slowly, I inched toward Nergal, bending as I got closer. My hands shook uncontrollably, my mind racing with images from too many horror movies where the monster never died after one blow. My fingers were a hair's breadth away from the hilt, and I began to feel a surge of energy. It started in my upper arms and extended down to my hands, steadying my trembling fingers. It moved out from my fingertips toward the hilt of the Sword, as if magnetically drawing it into my hands. It wanted the Sword. It *needed* the Sword, and that scared the hell out of me. I started to pull back, but before I could, Nergal grabbed me with much more strength than someone whose energy should have been nearly drained. *Good God*, I'd turned into one of those blond bimbos from the horror flicks.

Nergal pulled me down with such force my legs couldn't stand the pressure and collapsed under me. I fell into him. His grip dug into my forearms, holding me in place, with the hilt of the Sword poking into my chest. He brought his face close to mine, so close I could feel the glow of his eyes burning mine.

"You've failed your last test, Cassandra," he snarled, his hot breath washing over my face. "I will enjoy your punishment."

"*No*," I screamed. My thoughts automatically went to my dad. "Please, don't hurt my dad. Take me, punish me."

"Oh, you're definitely the pleasure I had in mind, don't you worry." He ran his slimy tongue up my cheek, and I jerked my head as far away as I could until he stopped. His laughter was more terrifying than any threats he could have made. His sinister plan would soon be my destiny.

He stood with no effort at all, lifting me, the Sword still stuck in his chest, with him. In one movement, he pulled the Sword out and spun me around in his arms, putting my back against him. The Sword now rested across my chest.

"Well, well, well. It seems your co-conspirator has taken the coward's way out and left you to suffer alone." I glanced around the room, desperate for Caleb or any means of escape, but Nergal was right, Caleb really had left me to the wolves. "Too bad," he continued, "I would've had fun with him too. Another time, perhaps."

I saw a flash of movement pass the doorway, but I doubted it was Caleb sticking around for a rescue. *Fucking coward.* I regretted not killing him when I had the chance.

"Why don't you join us, Hunter?" Nergal called out. "There's no sense hanging out in the shadows when I know you're there."

I sucked in a breath, praying he was wrong, but feeling in my heart it had to be Hunter. He warned me he'd be watching out for me. *Damn it.* This was his chance to get away. Take Alison and run. Get my dad out of there. Nergal might be content solely with my imprisonment and torture. He might have forgotten about them.

Hunter's frame filled the doorway, ominous and dark, aside from his glowing eyes. I saw the outline of his jaw, set in a grim, tight position. I could almost feel the heat of his anger emanating from his body. He was prepared to fight. I wouldn't let that happen.

"Just let him go, Nergal," I begged. "I'll go without a fight."

"*You* have no favors left, my dear," he said against my ear as he pulled me closer. I was pretty sure it was as much to egg Hunter on, as it was to put me in my place. He succeeded at one of his endeavors—Hunter stealthily moved toward us.

"Hunter, no," I yelled. "Stop. I'll be okay. Please, don't do this. It'll only make it harder on me."

Hunter stopped moving, but continued to glare at Nergal.

"Please, Hunter," I choked, tears clouding my vision. Through them, I saw Hunter slowly close his eyes, pain softening the hard lines on his face as he struggled with my request. When he reopened them, they locked onto mine, and I forced my tears back. I didn't want him to see how scared I was. I wanted him to know my love for him would get me through this. It was all I had left. He couldn't defeat Nergal, we both knew that. If he died trying to save me, there would be nothing left for me to stay strong for. Without him, all hope was lost. He was my only chance of survival, not only for myself, but also for those I loved. I hoped my eyes conveyed everything I wanted him to know.

"What an endearing moment," Nergal said, interrupting our bond. "If I were anyone else, I might actually feel bad about this, but alas, I'm not. However, I do have a special place in my heart for you, Hunter, since you served me well for so long. So, here's what I'm going to do. I'm going to give you a chance to relieve your precious piece of ass here from her torture. All you have to do is bring Caleb back to me."

I couldn't believe what I was hearing. It had to be a trick. He'd never let me go after what I did.

"Oh, you're right, Cassandra, I'd never let you go for trying to kill me. I said relieve, not release." His mind-reading abilities really pissed me off. "So, how about it, old friend? Will you help make Cassandra's stay here less...painful?"

Hunter glared. "No torture and I'll bring Caleb back to you."

"This is *not* a negotiation. The deal remains as I said, or there is no deal. She will be tortured like all the other traitors, as you well know, until you bring Caleb. That should be enough incentive for you to find him quickly, should it not? C'mon, Hunter, what other options do you have? Will you wage battle with me for her freedom? We both know you could never win that battle. Ask Cassandra here." He crushed me against his chest. "Neither of you are capable of killing me. You don't have the *wings* to do it." He was the only one who laughed at his crude reminder.

Seeing Hunter stand so rigidly, aside from the rapid rise and fall of his chest, was like watching the lit fuse of a cannon slowly burn its way to the inevitable explosion. He was going to blow at the slightest spark, and I was the only one who could defuse him.

"Hunter, he's right. None of us can stop it. I'll get through this, just go." In my mind, I wasn't telling him to go find Caleb, I was telling him to leave and never come back.

Hunter closed his eyes again and nodded. I regarded him closely for any signs he was trying to mislead Nergal into thinking he would go along with it, but he remained committed.

"Wonderful," Nergal said happily. "Why don't we get this party started then?" A heavy weight came off my chest when he lifted the Sword from across it, only to be replaced by a clenching pain in the pit of my stomach. I braced myself for each nauseous wave that tried to climb up to surface. If I lost it now, Hunter would go off the deep end. I stepped forward, straight and strong, defying my nerves, and ready to face my fate.

"Hunter, why don't you lead the way to the cell you formerly called home not too long ago," Nergal continued. "Maybe Cassandra will find some spiritual solace knowing you shared the same accommodations when she endures her trying times."

Hunter stayed in place for a minute more as I mentally urged him to move. Finally, he stoically turned and started out of the room. I felt the tip of the Sword at my back and took it as my cue to follow.

***

"Ah, home sweet home," Nergal said. His Walmart welcome was expected, but unappreciated by Hunter or me. "Hunter, why don't you take Cassandra in? Show her around before we get her situated and say our farewells...or, your farewell anyway."

Hunter shook his head and took a deep breath before coming toward me and wrapping one arm around my waist, while his other hand lightly claimed my elbow. He didn't need to prod, I willed my body to do what it was vehemently opposed to—entering the cell. I kept my eyes and face forward even though I could feel Hunter watching my features closely. I couldn't look into his eyes, not yet. I had to get control of my nerves. If I looked at him, I'd break.

The fire pit appeared wide and deep, mocking me with its dust and grime from myriad conflagrations. Flashbacks of seeing Hunter's and Eric's pain in its relentless heat and suffocating smoke, kept crossing my mind, but I forcefully ignored them. I refused to let my last moments of freedom be inundated by anguished memories. I turned my head away and glanced at Hunter, but the agony I saw in his face was even worse.

"Don't," I whispered, bringing my hands to his face, and trying to iron the lines of worry away with my fingertips.

He dropped his eyes from mine. "I'm so sorry, Cassandra," he said in a hoarse voice. "I should have tried hard—"

"Shhh," I soothed, pushing his chin up so he'd look at me. "There's nothing you could have done differently. This is our fate. And having the chance to be with you those few precious times we had together, I'd do it all over again."

"We're not done," he said, with determination in his eyes and tone. It was the same expression that won my heart in the first place, and I knew he would never give up on me, or us. I nodded to show him I still had faith in him. "I mean it, Cassandra. I'm going to get you out of here. Or die trying."

"I know." I tilted his face toward mine and reached up to his lips for a soft, heartfelt kiss. Our lips faintly touching, we gazed into each other's eyes, conveying much more than the kiss could express. As we parted, I told him, "Help my family first. I'm much stronger than I used to be. I can get through anything as long as I know you're out there for them. Promise me, Hunter."

"Enough," Nergal yelled. He was so quiet up until that moment I almost forgot he was still in the room with us. "Hunter, chain her up."

Hunter's head jerked up to peer over my shoulder at Nergal. His eyes glowed, and I could feel his body tensing close to mine. "*No*," he yelled back.

"Do it now or I'll have you chained up beside her to watch her suffer, with no chance of any deal."

The air from Hunter's nostrils as he rapidly breathed in and out caused the wisps of hair that fell out of my ponytail to tickle my face. I placed my hand on his chest, mentally trying to slow it down. We had to get this over with fast or Hunter would never make it. I didn't think I could pacify him much longer. Nergal was relentless with his tests.

"I'm ready." I moved away from him and braced myself between the two pillars in the middle of the floor.

"Good girl," Nergal said in a patronizing tone.

I ignored him and hoped Hunter would do the same. Reaching one arm up toward the chain, I realized it was too high for me. It was last adjusted to fit Hunter's height. I wondered how many times these chains had to be adjusted and readjusted. The thought of it made me queasy again, thinking of how much pain had been inflicted in this horrible room, with me as the latest victim in its sinister history.

"You'll have to adjust these," I told Hunter, indicating the chains. "I can't reach them."

He came over like a robot and went to remove a large, metallic pin used to keep the clamp holding the chain in place. Once he took the pin out, he slid the clamp down the pillar until it was parallel to my hips before replacing it.

"I'm allowing you to do that," Nergal said in warning. "You *do* know that, don't you Hunter? Do not think for one moment that I am not scrutinizing every detail."

By setting the pin lower on the chains, it allowed my arms to hang more naturally at my sides rather than being pulled overhead, which, as Hunter well knew, was extremely painful. I didn't even breathe for fear Nergal would change his mind and make Hunter raise them up.

"You'll be more comfortable like this," Hunter said softly, which was ironic, considering comfort was the last thing Nergal intended for me. He locked the manacle in place on my wrist, making sure it was loose enough not to chafe my skin, but tight enough that it wouldn't slip off.

"I know."

We stared at each other for another long moment, misery and love intertwined between us, before he turned to secure the other chain.

"Wait," Nergal called out. "Release her."

Hope sprang from my heart immediately, but soon turned to confusion. Hunter looked over my shoulder with narrowed eyes as I tried to twist my head to see Nergal, until he came around to face me.

"I said, release her."

"Why?" Hunter asked.

"Just do it."

Hunter gazed at me with as much uncertainty as I felt, but I nodded, urging him to do whatever Nergal said. He released the manacle from my wrist. I shook my hand, as if I'd been shackled for too long already. It was as much of a reflex as breathing.

"Now strip her."

"What?" I screamed.

At the same time, I heard Hunter shout a resounding, "No."

"Strip her," Nergal yelled.

Hunter moved to stand directly in front of Nergal, and I feared he had already reached his final straw.

"Hunter," I cried out.

Bowing his head to Nergal, he said in the most desperate and humble voice I ever heard from him, "I beg of you, King, please do not make me do this. At least, let her keep her clothes on."

"I've already explained the rules to you. You can relieve her when you bring Caleb to me. Now, strip her, or I'll do it for you. I guarantee you will not want me to. I'll do it very slowly, taking my time to enjoy every titillating detail."

Hunter let out a growl that sounded so loud in the chamber I had to cover my ears. Nergal reacted by aiming the Sword in the direction of Hunter's neck.

"No," I yelled. "I'll do it. Just...let me...do it." I pulled my T-shirt over my head. My fear of losing Hunter overpowered any modesty I might have retained. After popping off my tennis shoes with my feet, I proceeded to push down my jeans.

I couldn't look at the two men standing before me, but I could feel Nergal's eyes poring over my skin without having to see them. The idea sent chills over my body. When I stood, wearing only a bra and panties, my chin was held high. My gaze remained on Hunter. His jaw was clenched so tight I wondered how his teeth didn't fracture under the pressure. His eyes were glowing bright, blinking rapidly, as though he were trying to rein control over them.

I reached for one of the chains again, but Nergal didn't let me get far. "Ah ah ah," he sing-songed, making my heart drop into my stomach while the acid rose in my throat. I knew what was coming. "Finish."

Slowly, I closed my eyes. A feeling of hopelessness and despair washed over me, consuming me. There would be nothing for me to hide behind. My naked flesh was symbolic of my exposure to the evil I'd soon be facing. The realization of my sordid situation dropped on me like a bucket of ice. I would be tortured beyond anything imaginable. Only those who had experienced it knew its devastating effects. For that very reason, I couldn't look at Hunter. He knew what to expect, and I worried if I looked at him, I'd see it in his eyes. I didn't want to know. The mere anticipation could drive me mad before Nergal's sadism even began. Maybe it would be better—to become so delusional I wouldn't know what was happening anyway.

There was no sense in prolonging it. I was past the point of needing to be done with it. I anxiously wanted Hunter to find Caleb and put me out of my misery. Of course, that was only if Nergal kept his word, which I didn't put much faith in. I peeled away my bra and panties, letting them drop to the floor. Blood rushed to my face before radiating all over my skin. But as hot as my embarrassment made me feel, it couldn't warm me enough to get rid of the tremors that were taking over my body.

My eyes locked onto the fireplace straight ahead. I couldn't see Nergal or Hunter, but I could feel their eyes on me. *God*, it felt like there were eyes coming from every angle in the room.

"Very nice," Nergal commented.

I stopped myself from cringing although it was all I wanted to do. I wouldn't allow him to see how he affected me. It would only feed his hunger for my submission. Instead, I spread my arms out and prepared to be chained.

Hunter sucked in his breath before chaining me up. His fingers were hot on my wrists, and I knew he was peering at my face as he worked, but I refused to meet his gaze. He moved quickly, almost as if he understood my need to get it over with. When he was finished, and my shackles were secured, he stood in front of me, blocking Nergal's view. I had no choice but to look directly at him. I expected to see his hard features again, complete with glowing eyes and flexing jaw, but they were soft and full of love. Tears welled in my eyes.

"You have one minute. I suggest you make it last," Nergal said before walking away.

Hunter's hand cupped my face, his thumb gently caressing right below my eye, as if ready to swipe away any tears that might fall. "Cassandra, it's killing me to leave you like this."

"You have to go. Please, just kiss me goodbye and make sure everyone is okay. You have to do this for me."

"I know." His hand came around to the back of my neck as he pressed his forehead against mine. "I know," he repeated dejectedly.

I tilted my face toward his, trying to reach his lips with mine. His other hand came up and he braced my face with both hands, angling it perfectly to meet his kiss. It was light and gentle, and so full of emotion, my tears escaped and slid down my cheeks, only to puddle between our lips. We tasted the salty drops at the same time, and Hunter pulled away to wipe the streams from my cheeks.

"Be strong for me, baby," he said. "This is only goodbye for now. I'll be back for you soon, I promise. I love you, Cassandra."

"I love you too, Hunter," I whispered, kissing him one last time. "I'll be waiting."

CHAPTER TWENTY-FIVE

I could feel a change in the atmosphere as soon as Hunter left. The room was icy cold, darker, lonelier. Like my heart. I truly believed Hunter would do everything in his power to find Caleb as quickly as he could, but a shadow lingered over that small ray of hope. It took the form of the most deceptive being in existence. There was nothing left to stop Nergal from making this my permanent home. I, however, wanted to live, *really* live, so I had to hold onto something.

I let out a small scream when the clamps attached to the chains suddenly rose, dragging my arms with them. I was slowly being stretched, and when they finally stopped, my toes could barely graze the cold, stone floor beneath me. Fear had its grip on me until Nergal appeared.

"Don't worry, Cassandra, the chill will soon be gone," he said, staring at my hardened nipples.

"Fuck you."

"That might not be such a far-fetched event in your near future, my dear."

I ignored his repulsive insinuation and motioned toward the chains with my head. "Not even five minutes into the deal, and already you're breaching the contract?"

"We had no contract. I was merely making your boyfriend feel better. You should thank me."

"For stringing me up like a puppet?"

"For easing Hunter's anxiety. I truly believe if I refused to let him ease your discomfort, he'd have done something stupid. Then where would you both be?"

"You told him to strip me, Nergal," I said, my resentment dripping on my words. "I hardly think that eased his anxiety. He's much stronger than you think."

"Not when it comes to you, I'm afraid. We both know that." He ogled my body, making my skin crawl. Thank God, I couldn't read *his* thoughts. "I hope it takes him a long time to find Caleb. I just know I'm going to enjoy our time together. But there's a reason Hunter was my chief Seeker. His persistence and determination allowed him to excel at everything, and he always got anyone he set out to get. Much to my dismay, I'm certain he'll raise the bar even higher for you."

As much as I hated hearing about Hunter's evil accomplishments, it did manage to give me hope this would soon be over, at least, the worst of it.

My brief respite of free thought was quickly dissolved when Nergal moved in on me. He was standing so close I could almost feel a static charge in the little space between his clothing and my naked skin. I held my breath as he slid one finger down my cheek, his eyes following it as it continued over my jaw and down my neck. When he reached my collarbone, he leered up at me.

"Maybe I'll kill them both when they return, after a little torture, of course. Yes, that would be perfect, now that I think of it. You've got them both drooling over you like dogs, so maybe I'll use that. It'll drive them nuts watching me mount you over and over again. Well, maybe not Caleb so much, he's a bit more into himself, but we could give it a shot anyway." He smiled, appearing very pleased with himself.

I returned his smile. "If you think your little scenario shocks me, I'm sorry to disappoint you. I fully expected you to live up to your reputation. Anything less than putrid would be beneath you, Nergal." I kept my tone calm. I couldn't let on how terrified I was that he would do exactly what he described.

"Well, I *am* the Devil. Now with that being said..." he spun with a flourish as I let my breath out. "Let the fun begin." As he waved his hands toward the fire's embers, they erupted into dancing flames.

When he moved to the side, a wave of heat blasted me, forcing me to suck in a breath once again. The flames shot out sparks that flew toward me like forked tongues—sensing, reaching, burning. I tried dropping my chin down in an attempt to breathe fresher air, but to no avail. The blistering heat scorched my body, and I instinctively withdrew until the shackles seared my wrists. The pain of them cutting into my flesh was nothing compared to the sweltering agony of the fire singing my bare skin.

I forced my head up, squinting toward my arms, half expecting to find my skin charred and blistered, even melting off my body, but it was perfectly intact. Nergal laughed, and I turned toward him as he stood at the fireside. His eyes sparkled with glee as he watched my primal reaction. He was enjoying my anguish. When I saw his devilish smile, I glared back at him, but it only made him laugh harder.

"Oh, Cassandra. I knew you wouldn't disappoint me. And we've only just begun."

In defiance, I tried to remain strong, but my wrists kept slipping against the shackles from the sweat that was pouring down my body. The white-hot metal felt like a branding iron. My skin acted like a pressure cooker, boiling my insides, instilling excruciating agony like nothing I'd ever experienced. With my mind, I fought to resist it, trying to transport myself to another location and time. But it was too powerful, and I was too helpless to ignore it. Nergal's laughter continued, or maybe I imagined it. His laughter and my pain were the only things I knew. My strength was quickly fading with every new blast of heat that enveloped me. Blackness billowed in and out against the fiery backdrop of my closed lids, trying to overtake me, rescuing me from my unendurable reality. My pride fell like a wounded warrior to its knees, straining to hold its ground until the bitter end. I bellowed out a war cry I wasn't sure even passed through my lips. Finally, unconsciousness triumphed and its sweet blackness swallowed my pain.

***

Something was slithering down the back of my arms and woke me. The minute my eyes opened, the fire rekindled in front of me, as if the lifting of my lids was the only accelerant needed to spark it. The front of my body felt badly sunburned, so the heat only intensified the stinging under my skin. I twisted my face away from it, closing my eyes in hopes of fooling it back into submission. But it knew better, or rather, Nergal did, I imagined.

The pain from the fire distracted me from what woke me in the first place. Then I felt the grasping creature slide down my shoulder blades and across my lower back, inching slowly around my waist. I shook, and tried to throw it off, but it persisted toward my belly. I looked down, expecting to see a scaly, monstrous pair of hands touching my skin, but nothing was there. Making their way up my rib cage, I squeezed my eyes closed while shaking my head. When I opened them again, there was still nothing. But I knew they were there, I could feel them pressing and sliding over my skin.

They were on my breasts, and no longer sliding lightly over the surface. I squirmed, wrenching my body left and right, trying desperately to shake them off. It was no use. Invisible hands lifted, pulled, and mashed my breasts. Tiny puncture holes appeared, as though unseen claws were piercing my skin. Blood trickled down my chest and stomach. I screamed and thrashed my body as far as the chains would allow. My skin was slick with sweat from the fire, which seemed to grow hotter. My sweat, now mixed with blood, ran the length of my body, dripping off my feet. A large puddle was accumulating beneath me. I watched helplessly as droplets formed at the ends of my hair before diving into the pool below.

For a brief moment, I got a reprieve from the violation. I tried to take a deep breath, but it was cut short by the intense heat of the fire and little oxygen. My chest was heaving as I held my breath and saw the hideous hands appear in the flesh from out of nowhere. They were exactly as I imagined them—green, rough, scaly fingers and long, talon-like nails that curled into sharp points. I screamed again at seeing the arms materialize, stretching from the hands that grappled my breasts, before they disappeared around my waist. Hot breath on the back of my neck made me cringe as I realized the thing whose arms embraced me was now behind me, in full body, and holding me against it.

I closed my eyes as a slimy tongue licked the sensitive spot at the base of my neck, right above my collarbone. I was so outraged and delusional, if I weren't shackled to the pillars, I might have flung myself right into the fire. A burning, fiery death would have been a much better fate than enduring the paws of an abomination. I looked deep inside myself, urging any residual power I still had to help me get away, but the atrocity held onto me tightly, not allowing me a fraction of an inch.

"You taste even better than I thought you would. I can't wait to get to the good stuff." It was Nergal's voice in my ear. I opened my eyes in surprise at seeing the monster claws were transformed into human hands...Nergal's hands.

"You're pathetic," I spat out wearily in a hoarse voice. "What's the matter, Nergal? Can't get a date without chains?"

Nergal laughed. "Oh, come now, Cassandra," he said in a husky voice. He squeezed my breasts so tightly I could not mask the pain that shot through them. "I'm the Devil. I like it rough."

I winced.

One of his hands skimmed down my belly. I knew where it was heading so I put everything I had into flailing against him. I grabbed onto the chains above the shackles at my wrists and pulled myself up as much as I could, kicking him squarely. After the first hit, I was left kicking air. All at once, the fire went out, and Nergal stood before me. I found my legs suddenly outstretched, shackled at the ankles and chained to the pillars.

"There, that's better," he said. When he started toward me, as parched as my mouth was, I managed to spit in his face. He stopped. I glared. He wiped the wet mess from his cheek while licking his fingers provocatively. I spat again. He came at me quickly, grabbing my hair as he pulled my head back sharply. "I can take care of that too." His mouth was on mine, and as soon as his tongue forced its way inside, I clamped down on it with my teeth. He withdrew with a yelp and an expletive, giving me cause to smile over my small victory.

When I eyed him again, his glib expression was gone. I'd finally managed to make him angry. I knew he'd make me pay for it, but I still felt somewhat vindicated.

"I can see you need more training," he said. "No matter. I'm a patient teacher."

He stepped aside, allowing the fire to blast me again. There was no crescendo of pain from it this time. There was instantaneous agony. It didn't take long to fall back into the comfort of blackness once again.

***

"I'll kill him."

Hunter's voice penetrated the haze of my exhaustion. Dried sweat and tears crusted my lids, making it an enormous effort to open my eyes. My body felt like it was used as a punching bag in a heavyweight training facility. I couldn't remember being beaten physically, but I felt bruised and scarred internally. My body hung limp from my outstretched arms, the blood long drained from them. The fire no longer blazed, leaving me with an icy chill, but too weak to tremble anymore.

Blinking lazily, I tried to lift my head, but only managed a weak bob. I caught glimpses of Hunter's form standing before me, but my vision was so blurry in what little I did see that I doubted whether he was really there.

"Hunter?" The words formed in my mind, but that was as far as they got. My throat was so parched it felt like my voice dried up from the lack of moisture. I could only manage to move my lips and breathe, which didn't offer much relief.

Hands were pressing against my cheeks and gently lifting my head. I forced my eyes open as my vision cleared and settled my gaze on Hunter's beautiful face. Even seeing the torment in his eyes was like a rainbow after a long, devastating storm. Tears ran down my face as my heart ballooned with relief. He came back for me, and I was still alive to see him. I attempted to speak again, but only managed a scratchy groan as searing pain ripped across my throat.

Hunter caressed the tears away with the pads of his thumbs before placing one of them against my lips. "Shhh, baby, don't talk. You're safe now. I'm going to get you out of here."

I was ashamed by my vulnerability. Nergal had broken me. I tried so hard to stay strong, but my body couldn't handle my determination. Eventually, I gave in to what I thought was my ultimate demise. Although my body was still weak, one glance at my savior refreshed my will to live, to be strong. I gazed longingly into the depths of his eyes, trying to convey my love for him, but there was no way to show how my heart beat only for him. He wasn't my soul *mate*, he was my *soul*.

"I'm going to release you now," he told me. "I want you to lean on me when I unshackle you. Do you understand?"

I managed a slight nod, only because his hands were bracing me.

"Okay, here we go."

He gently let my head fall back down. I knew he was working on the clamps of one of my shackles because I could hear the chains clinking. My lifeless arms felt nothing. At some point, I lifted my head to see the progress he was making, and my heart stopped when I saw Nergal standing behind him. Adrenaline coursed through me like liquid fire. My eyes widened with panic and I opened my mouth wide to scream, splitting open my cracked lips with the effort, but my voice refused to work.

I was helpless to warn Hunter when I saw Nergal raise the Sword of Final Death before driving it through his back. Hunter froze and his back arched against the intrusion, as he let out a deafening howl of pain. The scream died on his lips, and his eyes locked on mine. I watched as their illumination dimmed, rendering them lifeless. Nergal pulled the Sword out and Hunter fell to the ground with a loud thump, in harmony with the ripping noise of my heart being torn into pieces.

With my eyes closed, I welcomed the blackness if only to eliminate the sound of Nergal's laughter. Maybe I'd be lucky, and my heart would never recover from this final blow, abandoning me to the blackness for good.

***

It was bright. Daylight, filtering from the windows in my mom's living room, burned my eyes, making me squint. When my pupils adjusted, I glanced around the empty room. Everything appeared normal, peaceful, as it always was at Mom's house. The television was on and there were two goblets of wine sitting on the table in front of the sofa.

What the hell is going on? How did I get here?

I started toward the kitchen, but stopped as my mom walked in from it, carrying a bowl of popcorn in her hands.

"Mom," I cried out in surprise.

"Don't forget the napkins," she yelled over her shoulder, as if she didn't hear me.

"Mom," I yelled again, moving toward her.

She ignored me as she approached the sofa and sat down, placing the bowl on the table between the two glasses of wine. I stared at her as she grabbed a handful of popcorn and then shoved some in her mouth.

"Mom?" I tried again, confused.

As I moved to sit down beside her in an effort to get her attention, my dad came out from the kitchen.

"Got 'em," he said, bypassing me without a glance, and sitting down next to her.

I was so blown away I almost buckled at the knees from seeing both of them. Here we all were, at my mom's house, as if it were a family movie night. As if we all hadn't just been to Hell and back. What's worse, they acted as if I weren't even there, standing in the middle of the living room like someone who'd lost her mind.

Holy shit. Am I dead?

"I can't believe we're watching this again. How many times have we seen this movie?" my mom asked.

Really? This was death? Watching my parents have date night? I mean, it was great to see them together again, but *really*? Maybe this was my life passing before my eyes. That would make more sense, at least.

"Does it matter?" my dad asked, placing his hand on her cheek. "Did you ever imagine we'd get the chance to do this again? I dreamt of it all those years I was chained up, but I never thought I'd see you again."

Okay, the last theory took a nosedive. *Shit, shit, shit.* I *was* dead. I was dead and watching my parents live on, happily ever after.

But that meant...

Tears welled in my eyes as I realized the implications of what was playing out before me. Hunter must have somehow freed my dad. Obviously, I didn't make it, but he kept his promise. My dad was here, very much alive, and they were back together. Sadness came over me, knowing I'd never be with Hunter again, and we'd never have *our* time, but my heart swelled with love for what he did for me. This was his parting gift to me.

I smiled through tears as I watched my parents giving each other a passionate kiss. My dad leaned back and grabbed both glasses of wine, handing one to my mom.

"Let's toast," he said, and she nodded. "To Cassandra."

"To Cassandra," my mom repeated.

They both took a long sip and replaced the goblets on the table. Then they comfortably sat back, snuggling together, watching the television.

My mom coughed. When the cough became more persistent, she sat up. My dad leaned back, and I watched as my mom's eyes widened in horror.

"What have you done, Troy?" she choked out.

My dad sneered at her. "Your turn."

My mom's green eyes turned black before rolling back in her head. It was the last thing I saw before my knees gave out, and I collapsed.

CHAPTER TWENTY-SIX

"Stay with me, Cassandra. Don't give up," Hunter's words echoed through my head. "I'm not done fighting for you yet."

I could have sworn I felt his breath against my ear, but I knew better. He wasn't really there. It didn't matter. My heartbeat surged at the hallucination of him being so near. I was surprised my heart could still beat at all.

I didn't bother to look, didn't even know if I could, but I heard the chains clanging above me. Shortly after, a dead weight fell against my side as my entire body shifted down with it. A steely arm wrapped around my waist.

"Shit, Cassandra, I'm so sorry," Hallucination Hunter said. "Here, lean on me as best you can while I get the others off." I was positioned against his hard body, my arm placed over his shoulder, as tiny pins and needles attacked it.

Would Nergal never let up? As if the last session weren't enough to put me over the edge.

"You're losing originality points," I whispered, my voice grating on my throat.

Nergal chuckled in the background.

"This is real, baby," Hunter said. "I'm here. We're getting out."

My other arm dropped, and I fell onto whoever was holding me. My legs were still spread wide and shackled, so I didn't have much of a choice. Even if they weren't, I wouldn't have the strength to stand on my own. My head was on his shoulder, my other arm hung limp at my side, tortured by the pain of blood circulating. He held me tight, and I managed to lift my head to peer over his shoulder. Nergal was standing a small distance away, taking great pleasure in the scene unfolding before him. The fire was out, with only a dwindling wave of smoke wafting from it as evidence of the sweltering inferno that blazed there not long ago. Obviously, Nergal kept it nice and toasty for me while I was out.

"Can you support yourself against the pillar?" Hunter asked before placing a kiss upon my cheek. "I need to free your legs, and there's no easy way to do this."

I was regaining feeling in my arms, so I slowly moved one arm around his waist.

Did I dare trust this reality? What did I have to lose? My sanity? That was already long gone.

With a nod of my head, I held onto him as he positioned me against the pillar and wrapped my arms around it. The awkward twist and stretch of my body should have hurt me, but other than my aching head and arms, I was numb. I held onto the pillar with every gram of energy I had left as he removed the last two restraints. My body gave way before he could stand, and I collapsed onto him. He pulled me onto his lap, holding me up with his arm across my back. His other hand cupped my head to keep it steady.

"I'm so sorry," he choked out, as if crying. Demons couldn't cry, but it sure sounded like that's what he was doing.

I forced my lids open to look at him as he pushed the sweat-drenched hair from my eyes. While there were no tears streaking down his face, his agony was plain to see. I imagined that if his tear ducts still functioned, they'd be flooded. I wanted to put his grief over my condition at ease, but my body refused to cooperate. There was still a nagging feeling this was all another trick to kill me all over again.

"How do I know you're real?" I asked.

He stared right through me for a moment, as if in deep thought. Then he leaned over and said, "Look at me."

"I am."

"No. *Look* at me," he demanded, placing my hand over his heart. "I love you, Cassandra. I told you once before that you made me into something I never thought was possible. It shouldn't have been possible. And I also promised you I'd fight Heaven and Hell to be with you. We're halfway there. This fight is almost over. I need you to trust me a little longer."

I focused on his eyes and locked onto them. I was falling into a world of blue that wiped the chills from my body and filled my heart with warmth. The depths I could see in his eyes were far more than any hallucination could create. I recognized them as the eyes I gave my heart and soul to. They were the same ones that gave me Hunter's whole being and never looked back. There was no doubt in my mind this was the man I fell in love with. I was doing it all over again in that very moment.

"I do," I said. I raised my hand to his face, desperately needing to touch his loving features as a final test that he was truly there.

"Then let's get you out of here, shall we?"

He carried me to the door but we didn't get far before Nergal moved toward us. I turned my head to face him with as much strength as I could muster.

"Cassandra, it's great to see you up and...well...up. I was afraid I lost you there for a bit. Leave it to Hunter to save the day again. I knew he'd find Caleb for me. And so quickly," He said it with a giddy smile on his face. Just as I reminded myself not to trust his joyous enthusiasm for one second, his smile turned into a grim scowl. He cast his gaze down, slowly shaking his head.

Molten lead filled my veins and headed toward my heart to weigh heavily upon it. This was it, his final act.

Exhaling an exasperated breath, Nergal said, "I seem to be in a bit of a quandary—do I put all of you in one cell to witness each other's purgatories? Or separate you so I have room for more...frolicking? Such decisions."

Hunter didn't miss a beat. "Neither. I'm taking her out of here."

"Oh, really? And how do you plan on doing that?" Nergal asked.

"By force, if necessary."

"Come now, Hunter, are we going to do this again? I'm getting tired of your smitten savior routine. Chain her up again and let's be done with it."

My body tensed. Fear of returning to my personal hell swept through me. Hunter peered down at me. I expected to see more pity, sympathy, pain, guilt—the same reactions as the first time he chained me, but I saw nothing but pure determination on his face. I'd seen the look before, and I knew whatever he intended to do, nothing could stop him. I lamely shook my head, realizing it didn't matter.

He turned and walked the few steps back to the pillars, my heart rate increasing with every single step, adrenaline coursing through my veins. I searched his eyes, trying to figure out what his plan was, but he was stone-faced.

"Good boy," Nergal said behind us.

Hunter set me down near the pillar, and steadied me with his arms around my waist so I could gain my footing. Before I knew it, one of his hands came up and cupped the back of my head. His arm tightened around my waist, pulling me into him before his mouth came over mine. His kiss was hard and fast, my lips crushed against his as his tongue demanded entry inside my mouth. Before I could even think about the sensations he was creating within me, his tongue retreated, but his lips remained. "I love you, Cassandra."

"I love you too." I didn't realize I was crying until I tasted the saltiness that slid onto my lips.

"I want you to run. Run as fast as you can to your portal and don't look back," he whispered. "Do you understand what I'm telling you?"

I shook my head. "No. I'm not leaving you," I whispered back. "What are you talking about?" My heart was racing while power grew inside of me, making my body tense, but stronger with every breath I took.

"She's not going anywhere," Nergal's voiced boomed as he came toward us.

"Go now, Cassandra. Trust me," Hunter demanded as he pushed me across the room, away from him.

I fell to the ground from the force of the shove, skinning my knees and palms on the stone flooring. It took me a minute to get my bearings and glance behind me in time to see Hunter blocking Nergal's path. He stood in a wide stance, his back made even broader as he rested his fists on his hips. I could see his biceps pulsating under the short sleeves of his T-shirt. I couldn't see his face, but I imagined it had the look of a bull—huffing, snorting, and cleverly waiting for its target to make the first move before it charged.

I stood, trying to balance myself on weakened legs, my adrenaline the only thing keeping me from collapsing. "Hunter," I cried out, not sure of what to do.

As if reading my mind, Hunter yelled, "Cassandra, get *out* of here."

His thundering voice jolted my legs into motion, and I ran for the door, fueled purely by instinct and fear. What the hell could I do? I couldn't leave him there. I wanted to run back in and stand beside him against Nergal. At the same time, I wanted to use any power left within me to pull his stubborn ass out of there so we could make a break for it.

I peeked around the doorframe, thinking of what to do. If I went back in there, I would only distract him with worry.

Damn it. Think, Cassie, think.

"You stupid piece of shit," Nergal spit out at Hunter. "You think you can stand up to *me*? You think you can defy *me*? I will rip out your black heart, shred it to pieces, and feed it to your precious whore."

Those were the last words spoken before an explosive battle erupted in the room while I watched, shell-shocked, from inside the doorframe.

I didn't want to watch, but I couldn't look away. There was no way I would leave Hunter to face Nergal alone. *What was he thinking?* We both knew Nergal couldn't be killed. It was a suicide mission. I had to help him, but I had no clue what to do, so I stood there, peeking around the doorway at them.

After Nergal's insult, Hunter's shoulders dropped, before he vaulted himself into Nergal's stomach, hurling him into the wall near the hearth. The wall caved from the force, cement crumbling around them. Ash and smoke billowed out in a gust from the fireplace.

It was Nergal's back that slammed into the stone wall, but he seemed to recover faster than Hunter from the blow. Nergal grabbed Hunter's head, forcing him up. He had him in a chokehold, with Hunter's back against Nergal's chest. I gasped as his other hand came up across his forehead. He was going to snap his neck. I wasn't aware of all the ways to kill a Seeker, besides the Sword of Final Death, but I assumed breaking the connection between their heads and bodies might do it. Hell, with Nergal's power, he could probably tear it clean off. I had to do something.

As I moved from around the doorway, I saw Hunter whip his head back into Nergal's face at the same time his elbows jabbed into his ribs. The sound of crunching bones echoed throughout the cell, making me cringe and shudder. Hunter threw Nergal's arm from around his neck and turned to face him. Blood ran from his nose, but quickly stopped, leaving only a long, red stain. Before Nergal could recover, Hunter grabbed the sides of his head and rammed it into the wall behind him...repeatedly.

I knew it wouldn't kill him, but at least it appeared to daze him. When he regained control, everything moved so fast, I couldn't keep up. It was like watching a movie on fast forward, when the picture changes so quickly, your mind doesn't have time to process what you're really seeing. Punches were thrown, knees were jabbed, bones were cracked, grunts were expelled, and the metallic smell of blood lingered in the air, even though it dried as quickly as it spilled. It was like a dance with each of them getting tired, and the other one taking advantage.

They had an infinite amount of energy, and I thought the bout would never end, until Hunter flew backwards through the air. He smashed directly into the pillar, a few feet up, splitting it down the middle, but not enough to break it apart. He slid onto the floor and landed with a hard thump. I stayed in the doorway, trying to get a look at his face, but his back was to me, and his head hung forward. He didn't appear conscious anymore.

I dragged my eyes away from his limp form as soon as I heard the metallic swish of the Sword. Nergal had completely unsheathed it and held it in front of him with a treacherous look. Hunter's name was ringing in my ears before I realized it was coming from my lips. Power filled my veins, vaulting my body into the room as if controlled by some force other than my own will. Nergal's eyes locked onto mine and we charged at each other like two animals fighting for territory. It wasn't too far off the mark. He intended to take something that was mine, and I was willing to do anything to keep that from happening.

I didn't expect the impact to be so explosive. He was much stronger than he appeared, which was like a brick skyscraper. Still, I wasn't prepared for it, but neither was he. I heard the Sword sliding across the floor while I sailed through the air. For a minute, I felt no floor beneath me until my back and head smacked into it. Hard. Air blew out from my lips as forcibly as it exited my lungs. It felt like every rib in my chest was broken, and I could barely breathe.

Trying to sit up, something drained into my throat, and I instinctively coughed up blood. I was back against the wall by the door. No, I was *in* the wall by the door. I had no idea what injuries I incurred, everything hurt. But there was no time to think about it, Nergal was in my face again. His hand came up and grabbed me by the throat. I struggled against him as he picked me up off the floor with his hand around my neck.

I gasped for air as he pressed into my windpipe. My fingernails tore at his arm in vain, but he held me in place against the wall. His eyes were maniacal, penetrating mine with their piercing glow. The pressure in my head was unbearable, scattering my thoughts. My body became heavy and I knew I would crumble if he let me go. I was losing consciousness, fighting for every last breath I could get into my lungs.

With my vision starting to fade, I blinked and Hunter appeared behind Nergal. The hilt of the Sword of Final Death was in his hands and poised above his head, with the steel targeted on Nergal's back. My heart leapt for only a moment at his valiant effort to save me, but I knew all it would do, if anything, was prolong our ultimate deaths.

Nergal let out a roar of laughter. "You fool," he said, without looking behind him. "You can't kill me. But I *can* kill *her.*"

He squeezed my throat harder and the blackness began to weave its way in. I hiccupped tiny bits of air, but it wasn't enough. My lungs burned in my chest, straining for oxygen. It was no use, there was no air. He was killing me. I wished with everything I had left I could somehow take him with me, putting an end to his evil reign.

I stared into his face as I faded, expecting to find more glee at the moment of my death, but there was none. His eyes narrowed and his mouth opened wide, contorting in such a way I couldn't read it. Was the light in his eyes fading? Or was my lack of oxygen giving me another hallucination?

Suddenly, Nergal's clutch on my neck vanished and we both fell to the ground.

I was on the floor, but felt nothing. The haze was too thick as I fought to stay and see what was happening. The darkness wouldn't wait, and I fell into it.

CHAPTER TWENTY-SEVEN

I woke to the smell of lavender and musk. Instinctively, I knew from whom it came, and with my eyes closed, I inhaled deeply, trying to fill my whole being with it. Then I detected the pungent smell of sweat and...blood. I snapped open my eyes. Hunter was peering down at me, his hand stroking my face, as I lay across his lap. I couldn't tell for sure, but it seemed as if we were on the floor. I was no longer naked, thankfully. Someone had the decency to dress me in a robe of some kind.

Hunter smiled at me.

"Am I dead?" I asked.

He laughed. "No, Cassandra, you're very much alive." He brushed his thumb over my lips. "How do you feel?"

"Like I've just been through Hell. Where are we?" I moved to turn my head, but my neck felt like it had been wedged in a vise for days.

Hunter's hand gently stayed my face. "Just relax. We're in the hallway outside of the cell. I didn't want you waking up in there. You've been through enough. Your neck is probably going to take a while to heal."

I brought my hand to my neck, and when my fingers touched the tender flesh, the memories of those last moments came flooding back to me. "Nergal. Is he..."

"Shhh," he said, placing his finger to my lips. He leaned down and kissed me. His lips felt like heaven on mine, bringing with them the words I never thought I'd hear. "He's gone. It's over."

"Are you sure? But, how?" Just as I asked, I remembered the hazy image of a woman before I passed out.

"Anael. She came to save you...us."

"Anael was here? But Hadraniel would never have allowed her to come back. How did she even know?" My mind was spinning from the news. I felt like I was dreaming. Everything seemed to have worked out perfectly, but made no sense.

"She's still here, and I don't think she gave Hadraniel much of a choice after she found out what Nergal was doing to you." I opened my mouth to ask the obvious again, but he didn't give me the chance. "She knew because I told her, when I took your mother and Nora to the Elders."

I was shocked. "You went to the Elders? They let you in?"

"Your mother and Nora have a way with words."

"You made sure they were safe for me."

"I gave you my word."

"I know, but—"

"We can talk about all of this later. Right now, I only want to make sure you're okay, and get us out of here for good. You think you can walk?"

I hadn't moved anything but my head up until then, so I wiggled my toes to double check. I was achy as all get-out, but I had feeling in all the important places, so I nodded.

"Good," Hunter said. "Then let's get you up and out of here."

He lifted me with him as he stood, then gently set me on my feet, keeping his arm around my waist as I leaned into him. It took a minute before the dizziness cleared, and my legs were a bit shaky at first, but they slowly got stronger as I eased off Hunter. When I was balanced enough to stand on my own, Hunter turned me toward the long corridor. We moved past the doorway of the cell, and I painfully twisted my head to glance in. I saw Anael standing over a lifeless form on the floor, the Sword of Final Death hanging limply from the hand at her side.

I stopped and stared. Hunter urged me on, but I refused to move. I had an insatiable urge to see Nergal's dead eyes for myself. I was like a victim who insisted on confronting her predator to see justice was served before trying to move on. I needed proof it was over, that we were all still alive, while he lay rotting on the cold, stone floor.

"I want to see him."

"Trust me, Cassandra, he's dead. He'll never hurt you, or anyone else, again."

I turned and gazed into his eyes. "I need this. Please," I whispered.

He stared at me for a moment, and I gave him a look that told him I wasn't going anywhere but in that cell. He closed his eyes, and I knew I won.

"Fine, but one look, and then we get the hell out. That's it."

"Okay."

I moved into the room, and Hunter's arm tightened at my waist to pull me closer, but I felt viewing Nergal's dead body was something I had to do standing on my own two feet, not leaning on someone else, both figuratively and literally.

"I'm okay," I said, gazing into his eyes as I pulled away. He opened his mouth to argue, but decided better on it.

Turning back, I moved further into the room. Nergal's body mesmerized me, like a bystander drawn to a grisly scene. Even when Anael called out to me, I remained spellbound. I imagined Hunter must have said something to her, because she stepped away from Nergal, allowing me an unobstructed view.

My body tensed as I stood over him. He was flat on his back, legs outstretched, arms at his sides, his face turned away. I could only see half of his features, but I knew his eyes were closed. I don't know what I really expected, maybe veins marbling his skin, or his skin hardened to the point of cracking...hell, maybe even a skeletonized version of himself, but definitely not what I saw lying so peacefully on the concrete floor beneath me. He merely appeared as if he was sleeping. It reminded me of an old movie where the monster lay in wait for a helpless, brainless victim to enter and approach, just as I was now.

A chill blew across my neck, sending tremors through my entire body. The tremors turned into outright shakes, and I couldn't seem to get control of my body. I turned to Anael and my eyes were immediately drawn to the Sword still hanging from her hand at her side. Something inside compelled me to grab it, aching to feel it in my grasp, to feel the strength and power it could imbue me with. My body kept telling me I was desperate to have it, but my mind resisted the impulses.

I faintly heard a warning from Anael, and the sound broke my mind's hold on my body. I lunged for the Sword. It was in my hands before she even had a chance to react. Raising it over my head with both hands on the hilt, I went for Nergal, determined to rip him to pieces with it.

Someone hit me from behind, like a truck plowing into me. I landed on the floor hard, sending the Sword flying from my hands. My chin hit the ground as I watched the Sword slide across the room. The weight on my back was suffocating, and I gave a feeble attempt to buck it off, unsuccessfully. I knew it was Hunter, but I didn't know why he attacked me.

"Get...off...me," I said through clenched teeth.

He adjusted himself over me, redistributing his weight, but not enough to allow me up, or even move for that matter.

"Not until you calm down," he said.

"Cassandra," Anael said in a more soothing voice, "I know what you feel you have to do, but we can't let that happen."

"Why no—Hunter, would you get off me? I won't do anything. I just need to freaking breathe."

He got up, but pulled me with him, securing me in his hold, and keeping my back against his chest as we faced Anael.

"This isn't necessary," I told him. "I've calmed down."

"Yeah, well, I'm not willing to take a chance on this. Hear her out, and then I'll let you go."

I exhaled an audible sigh and gave Anael my full attention.

"Nergal is dead, but there's a way he can still live on," she said calmly, too calmly for the words that just came out of her mouth.

"What?"

"I hate to say it, but it's true. If that Sword"—she motioned across the room—"pierces his heart, his essence will be released to enter whomever it can latch onto. His essence carries all the evil he encompassed when he was alive. And for that reason, we need to get his body to the Elders. They can secure it where no one can get to it. The Sword will be protected there as well."

Shocked by her revelation, I stood gaping at Anael. After everything I'd just been through, that we'd all been through, the cockroach might live on? I felt sick. Any chance Nergal could be resurrected was like a dead weight on my soul. I didn't think I could hate him anymore than I already did, but hearing all of this ratcheted my hatred level to an all-new high.

"He really has a heart?" I asked.

"Yes, Cassandra, he does," she said. "It's dead, by all human standards, but it's still there. And, unfortunately, it still serves a purpose. A very evil purpose."

I wanted to cry, throw my body on the floor and have a full out temper tantrum, but I knew that wouldn't do any good. Plus, Hunter still had me pinned to him. There was nothing I could do to change things. But at least there *was* a way to keep him dead. I had to look at the bright side of this catastrophic situation and move on.

"Okay, so how do we get him to the Elders then?" I asked.

Hunter released me and came around to stand next to me.

"And what about all the others here that served him? Won't they be coming after us? What about Caleb? *Oh, God. My dad.* Is he still alive?" My heart started its frantic palpitations again. I didn't know what I'd do if the whole reason for my coming down here was in vain. I couldn't believe I'd waited so long to even find out what had happened to him.

"Your father is fine," Hunter told me. "We found him in another cell. He's still unconscious, but it doesn't look like Nergal did anything to him."

I closed my eyes and let out a sigh of relief.

"But you're right," he interrupted my moment of solace. "It won't be long before more of Nergal's demons come looking for him. We need to get out of here."

"What's the plan?" Anael asked Hunter.

"We'll all go to get Troy. I'll carry Nergal. You stay with Cassandra and Troy there while I go get Eric. I'll send him in to carry Nergal ou—"

Everything was happening so fast. "Wait. Eric's okay?"

"Yes, he was beaten up, but we heal fast."

Ah, yes, he had that whole demon-thing going on for him. Lucky him. I still felt like I'd been run over by a two-ton truck.

"You want us to meet you at the entrance then?" Anael asked, continuing with the plans. "I assume you're going to get Alison."

"Yes," Hunter said, stealing a glance at me.

My heart never failed to drop a notch or two from hearing that name. It didn't matter I knew Hunter cared only for me. The little green monster didn't rationalize, only reacted.

"What about Caleb? Did you find him?"

Hunter appeared to be getting impatient with all of my questions. I realized it wasn't the best time to play catch-up, but I couldn't help wanting to know.

"Yes, Cassandra. After I delivered your mother and Nora to the Elders, Anael and I went looking for him. It took awhile, but I finally got one of his crew to give up where he was hiding out. He was holding secret meetings in an old, abandoned insane asylum out in the middle of nowhere. Quite fitting, really. Nergal chained him up in one of the cells near his quarters when I brought him back. Unfortunately, we can't leave him here. Once his minions get wind Nergal is gone, they'll come and free him. We don't want Caleb out there with an army. We'll turn him over to the angels to do with what they will."

I understood everything he told me, and while I agreed, one thing still nagged at me. "You said it took awhile. How long were you gone?"

He and Anael exchanged a look I couldn't read before he turned back to me with a grim expression. "I was gone for the longest two months of my existence."

I stared back at him, confused. "But that can't be. I wasn't here for two months." I shook my head. They had to be wrong. It wasn't possible. Had I really been chained up that long?

"Yes, you were," Anael said with obvious pity.

"How...I don't remember..."

"You were probably out of it most of the time," Hunter said. "Thankfully."

He took me by the shoulders and pulled me against him. My head was turned into his chest, and I wrapped my arms around him in a daze while he held me tight. He kissed the top of my head. "I'm so sorry. I'm sorry it took me so long."

I was still trying to process everything. I hated knowing I'd mentally lost two months, but I knew I was better off not remembering what happened to me during that time. I didn't even want to think about the things Nergal might have done to me.

Like a victim of abuse, my conscious mind did what it had to in order to protect me. I was willing to let the puzzle remain as it was, even with a few pieces missing. "It's okay," I said, lifting my gaze to Hunter's. "You came back, and you're here now. That's all that matters."

He nodded.

"We really need to get going," Anael cut in.

Hunter didn't break our gaze. "You ready?"

"Yes. Let's get my dad so we can get the hell out of here once and for all."

CHAPTER TWENTY-EIGHT

My dad's cell wasn't too far from the one we were in. Nergal probably enjoyed knowing I was being tortured so close to *Daddy*. That was how his twisted mind worked. At least, my dad wasn't chained up, which surprised me. He was unconscious and lying unceremoniously in the middle of the room, as if someone had dropped him there.

I ran over and kneeled beside him. On instinct, I checked his pulse. Although it was faint, I gave a sigh of relief it was there. I couldn't wait to get him out. My two-month endurance was nothing compared to what I imagined he must have been through. Leaning down, I gently swept his unkempt hair away from his face and whispered into his ear, "I'm getting you out of here, Dad. We're going home now."

Hunter came in with Nergal hanging lifelessly over his shoulder. He moved to set him down, and I jumped up.

"Not here," I yelled. "Keep him away from my dad." I knew it was harsh, but I had so much pent-up hatred I could barely contain it. Passing up a chance to unleash my rage and fury onto the monster responsible caused my blood to boil when I saw him, regardless of whether he was dead or not. "Can we just get him out of here?"

Hunter understood the minute our eyes met and turned to confine Nergal to the corner of the room. I didn't notice Anael's hand on my shoulder until she said, "He's going to be okay...your dad. We're going to get him out of here. Eventually, he's going to wake up, and he'll be fine. Hunter only needs to leave Nergal here temporarily while he gets Eric and Alison. It's safer for him in case he runs into any of Nergal's demons."

"She's right, Cassandra," Hunter said, coming over and taking my hands in his. "I'll go get Eric first and send him here. He can carry Nergal out, and Anael can handle your dad. You can all go to the entrance where Anael's guards are waiting to take them back."

I glanced at Anael. She was so small and fragile-looking. "How are you going to carry my dad?"

"An angel's power can rival that of any demon. Isn't that right, Hunter?"

"Not *any* demon, but yes, they've been known to take out a demon or two," he said with a smirk.

The small respite of lightheartedness put my nerves at ease. I was sure they wouldn't be back to normal, however, until I was out of this hellhole. Not that I could remember what normal was. It seemed like an eternity since Hunter and I made love in the hotel room the night before we came to Hell.

"I'm going to go now," Hunter told me. "Will you be okay?"

I could see the familiar expression of worry in his eyes, since it had been there for far too long. *God, he was beautiful*. All I could think about was having everything over and putting a smile on his face. *A real smile*. Something rarely found on him, but something I vowed to see much more of.

I reached up on my toes and kissed his lips. "Yes. Go. I'll be fine. Just get them and come back as fast as you can."

"I promise," he said as he stroked my cheek before turning to leave.

After he was gone, I stood there, wondering what I could do. I felt like I should be doing something, but Anael assured me we could only wait. That allowed me the luxury of sinking my thoughts into the swamp of worries again. What if something happened to Hunter? How could I let him go alone? What if my dad never woke up? What if Nergal's guards found us? Would Anael and I be able to take them on?

I sat on the floor next to my dad, positioning myself between him and Nergal's body. I wasn't taking any chances. One thing my journey had taught me—nothing was ever as it seemed. I would not allow myself to get caught unprepared. I felt like I'd aged twenty years in only a short time. At least, I'd never be taken off guard again. Well, I hoped I wouldn't.

Anael stood in the center of the room, her feet apart, and hands on the hilt of the Sword, which rested blade-down toward the floor directly in front of her. She faced the doorway, stiff, poised, and ready. I would name her my guardian angel until Hunter returned. They joked about how strong she was as an angel, and I knew there was truth in it, especially with the Sword under her command, but I wondered if it should have been me standing there. I was, after all, the product of two supernatural powers. Wouldn't that make me a *super* supernatural?

"So, how did you manage to persuade Hadraniel to let you come?" I asked her, breaking the silence that seemed to drip off the walls. "And with some of his guards, if I heard correctly."

She turned to face me, but must have realized she wouldn't be able to keep watch at the same time, so she angled her body in order to do both. "I would have come, no matter what. I hope you know that." She paused, waiting for my acknowledgment, so I nodded. "We sold Hadraniel on the plan to kill Nergal and bring his body back. A chance to put his nemesis' corpse under his watchful confinement was something he couldn't pass up. He would finally be able to claim victory in this eternal war, and take control of the universe. He could make things right. The risk to me was great, but the reward was far greater. I had no doubt he would concede to it."

Anael's expression was sad at the last bit of information, and I imagined it was because her love for him still ran very deep. Yet, Hadraniel was willing to let her risk her soul for power. Even though the power meant a greater good, it still had to hurt.

"I'm sorry, Anael."

"Why?"

"Because if it weren't for me, you wouldn't be here. I came down to save my dad for me...well, for my mom and me, but it was entirely for selfish reasons."

"Don't you dare be sorry," she said, her green eyes blazing at me. "Don't you realize what you've done here, Cassandra?" When I gave her a puzzled look, she blew out a sigh. "My God, you killed Nergal."

"No, you killed Nergal," I argued.

"But I wouldn't have had the chance if it weren't for you. You sacrificed yourself for it to happen."

"But I didn't *know* it would happen. It's not like I chained myself up, knowing you'd arrive eventually."

"You downplay your worth. You are the key here, Cassandra. The universe works the way it's supposed to. You were meant to come down here, and I was meant to help you. Furthermore, Nergal *had* to die because of it."

"So, does that mean Hunter is part of this great universal plan? If the universe is on the side of good, what'll become of him once we get out of here? Will Hadraniel welcome Eric and him as they are? As demons from Hell? With open arms and gratitude for helping us?"

"You know he won't."

"Yeah, he made that clear the last time we were all together. You know, he may be the holiest angel there is, but in some ways, he's a lot like Nergal. Everything isn't as black and white as he would like to think. I'm a prime example. I'm shocked he's going to allow my dad inside his pristine castle."

For what now seemed like forever, all I could concentrate on was getting my dad and the rest of us out of Hell, away from Nergal, and away from evil. But I never thought beyond that. I expected a bright light shining at the end of that tunnel in the distance, pulling me ever closer to its warmth and goodness.

Now that I was closer, I began to see through the mist, and it wasn't as warm as I hoped it would be.

"You have to understand Hadraniel's position, Cassandra. He's got the weight of the universe on his shoulders. It's not only you and your family he needs to protect. It's not just the angels that need his safekeeping either. It's the families of billions of helpless humans who know nothing of our battles. Without him leading the angels, they won't stand a chance."

"I know, I know. I'm sorry." I dropped my head into my hands, wishing everything did not have to be so damn complicated. Running my fingers through my hair, I peered up at her. "I guess I'm just wondering what's really going to happen to me. I mean, I'm the issue here, aren't I? Hunter and Eric, I can turn, but me? I don't have the choice, so where does that leave me? Now that I've gone against the angels, what if he doesn't take me in? Will I be banned from seeing my parents? After all I've done to get my dad back, will I never be allowed to see him again because of my blood? God, if I turned Hunter, would we be separated too? I know I did the right thing, but why does the right thing always seem to be the wrong thing for *me*?"

I could feel my tears welling up, but I pushed them back. I would not cry. Not after everything I'd been through. It was not the time for a mental breakdown. "Woe is me, right? Sorry. I'm just tired and eager to get out of here. We can figure everything out rationally when we're out of this dismal place."

"Stop saying you're sorry," Anael said. "But you're right, we can figure all of this out later. Hadraniel will take you back. He has to. You are one of Heaven's greatest assets. With your abilities, we can end this war for good."

"Sure," I said, a little weary of being used as a pawn in the fight. "You know, Hunter told me he wouldn't let me turn him before we came down here."

"He did? Why?"

"He said he wouldn't be able to protect me without his powers. Do you think, now with Nergal being dead, he would do it?"

"Not until he knows every threat to you is eliminated."

Anael and I both jumped when a voice came from the door.

"Eric." I jumped up before launching myself at him. "You're okay. Thank God."

"Of course I am," he said. He was acting as if he hadn't just been released from the fires of Hell, literally. I drew back to scan him over. Aside from his clothing being torn, he appeared as strong and sturdy as ever.

"You know, sometimes I'm jealous I only have half of your blood."

"Don't be," he said flatly. "Hunter told me to grab Nergal and get you guys to the entrance." Eric, the demon of few words. Yep, he was fine. "Where is that piece of shit?" He pushed me aside and glanced around the cell. Once spotted, he wasted no time in going over and hauling Nergal up like a sack of potatoes.

"Right," Anael said, handing me the Sword, "let's get moving."

It never dawned on me Anael wouldn't be able to carry the Sword as well as my dad. My body pulsed as soon as it was in my hands. Some of the things I felt with it in my possession scared me. Did part of my blood crave it more than the other? I wanted to ask Anael if she got the same sensation, but I didn't want to alarm either her or Eric with my question. I could handle it. I *had* to handle it.

I set the Sword down to help Anael get my dad off the ground. It felt like I was tearing a limb from my body to even part with the Sword for a second. I did my best not to let my emotions show while lifting my dad's head and back so Anael could put one of her arms around him. Even knowing how strong she was, it amazed me to watch her lift him as if he were made of nothing. Once I knew she had him securely, I went to grab the Sword, but hesitated. Something inside me warned against it, contradicting my relentless desire to hold it once again.

"Ready, Cassandra?" Anael asked, glancing back as she moved to follow Eric out the door.

I snatched the Sword up and followed after them, trying my best to ignore the current of electricity that was lighting up my veins.

CHAPTER TWENTY-NINE

It didn't take us long to get to Anael's entrance. We walked single-file the entire way, with Eric in the lead and me bringing up the rear. My body was a tangle of nerves, jumping at every rustle and scrape that echoed throughout the corridor, ready to pounce on anything that tried to block our way to freedom. As big as the Sword was, I expected it to grow heavier in my hands, but it never did. Strangely, it felt more like an extension of my arm than a burden.

Unlike my entrance, Anael's opened up into a wide expanse of meadowland. Low grasses shimmied in a comfortable breeze, extending far beyond what my eyes could see. Blue skies with an occasional billowy cloud welcomed us. I heard water splashing in the distance, but didn't see the source of it.

Our entrances were like night and day. Mine was dark and foreboding, while hers seemed to lighten our spirits, bringing hope for greater things ahead. The instant I stepped into it and felt the warmth upon my face from a sun I could not see, relief flowed through me. Closing my eyes, I lifted my face and relished the sensation.

"I can take that for you if you'd like," a man's voice said, interrupting my daydream.

I opened my eyes slowly, allowing them to adjust to the brightness. Once they did, I saw a man in full angelic armor. It was the same kind I saw the day they saved me from Nergal's clutches long ago. He was standing before me and waiting expectantly. Peering around him, I saw at least a dozen more, two of whom were carrying my dad and Nergal. Anael was talking to the dark-haired one holding my dad, but Eric was standing close by my side.

"Miss?" he said again, and my focus returned to him.

"What?"

"I said, I can carry that for you if you'd like some relief."

"No, thank you. I'm fine. I'll carry it." As much as I wanted to relinquish every iota of responsibility I had over the fate of the world, I didn't trust it falling into the hands of anyone else yet. Anael came over, and the guard glanced at her. She nodded, and he walked back to join the rest of the guards.

"I instructed them to wait ten more minutes for Hunter to show, but if he doesn't, they will start back to the Sanctuary," she said.

"What? And leave him here? No. I won't leave without him, Anael."

"Me either," Eric added.

"Both of you, relax. I'm not leaving him either. If he doesn't show by then, they can start without us and we'll continue to wait."

The three of us waited in silence, while the guards talked amongst themselves. The ten minutes seemed to stretch on forever, with no sign of Hunter. My heart dropped further into my stomach with each passing second he didn't show. *Where was he?* Fear and scenarios of what could be wrong raced through my mind.

My eyes remained focused on the entrance opening, but I could see Anael periodically glancing over at the guards. I knew the ten minutes were up, probably more than ten minutes ago. A guard finally came over, and I heard her murmuring something to him before he walked back to the group behind me.

"The guards have got to get your father and Nergal out of here, Cassandra. It's too dangerous for them to continue to linger," she said. "I've told them to go ahead without us."

As if on cue, I could hear their footsteps fading away.

I nodded, but continued to stare straight ahead. The anticipation had me all keyed up, and my nerves couldn't take much more. I couldn't wait any longer.

"I'm going back for him," I said as I started for the opening.

"Whoa. Wait...Cassandra," Anael yelled from behind me, right before a muscled, solid arm spanned across my chest, stopping me short.

"I can't let you do that," Eric stated.

"And I can't stand around anymore. He could be in trouble in there. Something's wrong, Eric. He would have been here by now. I'm going." I shoved against his arm, but he wouldn't budge. I wasn't opposed to using more power on him if I had to, but I hoped it wouldn't come to that. I liked Eric. "Please." I peered directly into his eyes.

"If something happened to you, Hunter would make me eat that Sword, Cassandra."

"If something happens to him in there, and we don't do anything to help him, I'll kill you with my bare hands, *Eric*." There was no tenderness in my expression this time. The daggers in my eyes made it clear I was determined to go through with this, one way or another.

We stared at each other for a few moments before his arm finally dropped. I didn't give him time to think, I marched through the doorway, never looking back. When I heard both Eric and Anael following behind me, I gave a mental sigh of relief. After only a few steps, however, a hand clamped over my wrist, bringing me to an abrupt stop.

"Hell, Cassandra, at least, let me lead," Eric growled. I knew his ego was probably horribly bruised, so I let him step in front of me without a word. Besides, I had no idea where to go anyway.

Anael stayed behind me as we moved on. I gave her the Sword as soon as Eric took the lead. I didn't want to deal with all the crazy emotions it stirred up in me, not while I had Hunter to worry about. She removed the scabbard from Nergal's body earlier, buckling it at her waist, but she carried the Sword out in front of her, poised for an attack if anyone happened to jump out at us.

"Alison's quarters are just down there," Eric said, pointing toward the end of the hallway we occupied.

Our pace quickened, but Eric stopped a few doors away.

"Eric, what the hell..." I pushed myself off, after ramming him from behind.

"Son of a bi—" He charged toward the door we were in front of, and threw his whole body into it. At first, I couldn't see what caused him to act so violently, not until he pulled back and rammed into it once again. Through the slats of the door, I glimpsed Hunter standing against the far wall of the room, both hands raised above his head, shackled by chains to the wall.

Flashbacks of the first time I entered Hell and discovered Hunter half out of his mind and helpless sent my adrenaline pumping. I could hardly breathe at seeing him like that again. I screamed and charged at the door with Eric, not thinking or caring what the impact might do to my body. The power surging within me blocked out any pain it may have caused.

"Anael," Hunter shouted to us from inside. Eric and I both looked at him in surprise. I didn't realize he was conscious, and obviously, neither did Eric. Before I had a chance to let out the breath I was holding, I realized Anael was yelling at us at the same time.

"Get the hell out of the way," she screamed.

Confused, both Eric and I stepped toward the sides of the door. She closed her eyes and the door opened.

"Are you freaking kidding me?" I gawked at her.

"I used to be the Queen here, remember?" she said, walking past us into the room without further conversation.

I ran in behind her, along with Eric. "Hunter, are you okay?" I asked, scanning him over. He didn't appear to be hurt. There were no physical marks on him I could see. The only thing I *could* see was that he was pissed.

"I'm fine. Just get me out of these," he said, jiggling the chains.

Before I even had a notion of how to get him free, Anael hacked the chains with the Sword. They broke easily under its blade.

"What happened?" I asked, as Anael finished with the last chain.

"It was Caleb."

"What? I thought Caleb was chained up in some cell?"

"He was. This one. I was on my way to Alison's cell when I walked by and saw Alison trying to free him."

My jaw dropped. I couldn't help it. "Why would she try to free him?"

"I assumed she was confused at first. I yelled at her to stop, but she wouldn't even look at me. She kept trying to get him out of the chains. When I came into the room to pull her away, Caleb's flunkies grabbed me. There were too many of them, I couldn't take them all."

"Oh my God." I knew I shouldn't have let him go back by himself.

"It's okay. I'm not hurt. They didn't have time. All they wanted was to get out. They freed Caleb from the chains and put me in his place. Then they took off and left me here."

"Did he say anything?" Anael asked, worry etching into her forehead, her eyes wild with alarm. "Anything about what they might be planning?"

"I assume Nergal is with your guards?" he asked Anael before putting a strong arm around my waist.

"Yes, we told them to head to the Sanctuary without us so we could find you. It was too dangerous for them to stay out there any longer."

"I'm afraid the danger might be *with* them."

"What are you talking about?" Anael asked.

I angled my face up to his.

"When I told Caleb he wouldn't get far, that we'd hunt him down and take care of him the same way we took care of Nergal, he laughed at me. Then he told me he had friends in *high places*."

A light clicked on in my head as I remembered using a similar metaphor while talking to Nergal, only I was referring to demons. *But that meant…*

"He has an angel, or maybe more than one, working with him," Hunter said. "He's going after Nergal's body and the Sword. Caleb still has his eyes on becoming King of the Underworld. He made it clear he will stop at nothing to get it. I have no doubts about him this time. He had a big following with him, and I can imagine there are even more outside of Hell. He's been planning this for a long time. We were merely a setback in his plans."

I unleashed a long growl that came from deep within my core. "I can't believe this. I should have killed him when I had the chance. How do we stop this from happening? How do we keep Nergal's body out of Caleb's grimy paws if we don't even know who he's working with?"

"We hunt him down," Eric said, eyes narrowed. His features were tense, and I could hear the determination in every word.

Hunter and Anael nodded their agreement.

"Cassandra and I can keep an eye on Nergal and the Sword at the Sanctuary," Anael offered.

"No," Hunter said. "She stays with us."

"But she'll be safer at the Sanctuary. We'll be there to protect her."

"Nergal and the Sword weren't the only things Caleb told me he was going back for."

My heart skipped when he gazed into my eyes. I knew before he even said the words.

"But why would he come back for me? He's got Ali..." I stopped myself before dropping another blow on Hunter.

"He told me to keep his queen warm for him until he came back."

I sucked in a breath, utterly shocked by Caleb's resolve to make me his queen.

"I am only telling you this so you know why I won't let you out of my sight until he is captured and killed. I don't care how long it takes. Do you understand, Cassandra? You are not to go anywhere without me."

His eyes were angry, even possessive as they stared back at me. With his jaw set, he waited for me to reply. When I didn't, his fingers dug into my waist. "Cassandra," he demanded.

"Yes," I told him, half-dazed. "I understand." *Would this never end?* Was I destined forever to hunt *and* be hunted? I didn't want to live out the rest of my days constantly looking over my shoulder, wondering on whose side I was being pawned next. I made a promise to myself right then and there, that I would do whatever it took to no longer be that pawn. "But when we find him, Hunter, I want to be the one to kill him."

"It'll be my pleasure to stand by and watch," he said.

"We have to go," Anael said. "Hopefully this mole, if there really is one, didn't come with us. We may already be too late."

With that, the race began. As we hurried to get to the entrance, thoughts of my dad being caught in an unexpected line of fire while still unconscious moved me faster through the corridors. I was also running to get out of the nightmare I'd been trapped in for the last few months. Relieved to finally be done with it, I now wondered what lay ahead for us. Was I leaving one Hell only to find myself in another with a mere change of scenery? One thing I knew I could count on—this time, Hunter would be by my side.

EPILOGUE

Three months ago, we delivered my dad and Nergal to the gates of the Sanctuary where the Elders stayed. The gates were as far as Hunter, Eric and I were allowed to go. Despite the argument from Anael, my mom, and Nora, begging Hadraniel to let us seek protection there, he adamantly refused. Apparently, anything of the hellish variety was not welcome there. I may have been his descendent, but my little journey to Sheol was not to be forgiven. Not yet, anyway.

Eric chose to stay on as a Seeker until Caleb was found and dealt with. He was staying with Hunter in the apartment next to mine for the time being. Since Nora learned he wanted to turn, she opted to stay with us as well. Hunter and I stayed in his apartment, while Nora and Eric shared ours. We weren't around very much to make any real arrangements. Most of the time we were out, canvassing places we thought Caleb might be. The search for him, however, ended up becoming a crapshoot since we had no clues where he went. All of his demon cronies disappeared as well. Caleb and his new coalition, which now included Alison, were ghosts, but I knew they would reappear eventually. Caleb was incapable of keeping a low profile for too long. He didn't have it in him.

Hunter didn't seem visibly affected by Alison's betrayal. I tried to talk to him about it several times, but all he said was the Alison he knew and cared for from the past no longer existed. The new Alison was just another enemy in our war with Hell, and his only concern was to find and destroy them, while keeping me safe. I thought Caleb's obsession to have me as his queen might have fizzled out with her at his side, but Hunter didn't agree. He said Caleb had much more vested interest in me than a sexual relationship, and he was a poor loser.

With Caleb's threat came Hunter's fanatical security. I wasn't allowed to do anything without him. I loved him with everything I was, but Hunter as a six-foot-five-inch shadow suffocated me. Now, more than ever, I anxiously wanted to end the war with Hell, Caleb rebellion and all. I still hoped I could turn Hunter and live a normal life together. Someday, maybe. For now, at least, my family and friends were close and safe.

It was great having Nora to talk to again. She filled me in on Eric and her, telling me how it all started. She said he was so in love with her, he couldn't wait to be turned. She couldn't wait either. The blue of our eyes still freaked her out, but in some ways, I think she envied our power. I'd catch her eyes glued on us with fascination whenever Eric and Hunter trained me to use my powers more effectively.

My dad finally emerged from his Guardian coma after almost a month at the Sanctuary. Memories of everything stayed with him, so it was quite the reunion when he saw my mom. They were staying with the Heavenly Council, rekindling their love, or so I assumed. I only got to see them together a few times. Between going away to find Caleb and being forbidden inside the angelic dwellings, it was pretty hard to for us get together. The few times we did, my dad looked good. *Really* good. Just like he did in the pictures I saw growing up. I longed to sit down with him and tell him about my life, what we missed together. It was another part of the dream I could only cling to.

Mom was the happiest I'd seen in a long time, aside from worrying about me. She doted over my dad like a teenager with a crush during the times I saw them. It was nice to see her that way. After so many years of doing everything on her own, making sure I stayed safe and happy, she deserved some happiness for herself. Her Guardian visions continued once she got her blood pressure regulated again after all of the craziness we endured. Same with Nora. Neither of them was allowed to go out on their missions alone, however. My mom was assigned to one of the guards from Hadraniel's army, while Eric always accompanied Nora on hers. The angels frowned upon Eric's demonic presence at these rescues, but they didn't try to intercede with the arrangement. Maybe knowing Eric was determined to become a Guardian again softened their shells.

There was no softening when it came to Hunter, though. Even after everything he'd done for us, Hadraniel would not let up on him. I assumed it was because Hunter still showed no intentions of being turned. Or maybe it was an alpha clash. They were both natural leaders, unwilling to take orders from anyone. It was uncanny how similar they were. They'd be quite a force ruling over an army together, I imagined.

Hadraniel's army began waging active battles over the scattered demon forces. After Nergal's absence became known in Sheol, the Seekers and demons spread out into small rebellious groups. They took it upon themselves to persist in their hellish ways individually, stealing souls and spreading evil as sporadically as before. Without someone ruling over them, it seemed like they'd fallen into free-for-all mode, as we suspected. Nergal's Underworld quarters were abandoned, and all the work done down there ceased after the angel army swept through and cleaned house.

I made Anael stay in constant contact with me regarding Nergal's status. Having the threat of a traitor amongst the angels hanging over our heads, I refused to let down my guard, even though I wasn't allowed in the Sanctuary. Every day, she'd call to let me know she'd physically seen Nergal's dead body still secured in his prison. I wasn't sure if Hadraniel knew she was keeping tabs on him for me or not, nor did I care. Essentially, I felt it was my right to know, since I was the main reason he was locked away for good. Hadraniel suspected there might be a mole in their midst, but also suggested it might only be a rumor.

I knew better. I learned from my mistakes. Caleb was a cocky, devilish bastard who would do anything to seize ultimate power, and that meant he was dangerous and unpredictable. I had no doubt there was a mole, and it would only be a matter of time before it made a mistake and came out of its hole.

When Anael told me Hadraniel requested our presence at the Sanctuary three months after placing Nergal under the angels' protection, I knew the time had come. My invitation there was surprising enough, but he specifically asked for Hunter and Eric as well. Dread hung over us like a dark storm cloud as we made our way there.

When we approached the black, wrought-iron gates, they opened and two stone-faced guards appeared on either side of us. The brick path leading to the Sanctuary seemed long and circuitous before it ended at the great mansion's steps. It made me feel like Dorothy again, on her way to see the Wizard. When we reached the steps, I peered up at the massive stone building, its Romanesque architecture both beautiful and daunting. Taller than it was wide, several huge towers disappeared into the sky above and rose over the arcades between them. Their arched windows appeared black against the gray-colored stone throughout its thick walls.

Anael waited in front of the huge wooden door that stood open, welcoming us, in a dark, creepy-castle kind of way. When we met her at the top of the stairs, she nodded and motioned us inside ahead of her. Her face was grim, and with a look, I tried to coax something out of her as to what we should expect, but she gave nothing away either through words or expressions. No conversations, only a thick, dismal sense of anticipation, which made me feel like we were prisoners, awaiting our sentences.

We weren't in the foyer long enough for me to take in any details besides the pristine whiteness of it. It appeared even brighter when I spotted the huge crystal chandelier that hung from the ceiling. We were ushered into a living room that opened up to the left. The room was huge and designed for comfort. Plump, cushioned sofas and chairs in rich maroons and golds urged us to relax in their luxury, while our feet sunk into the plush carpeting. Long, maroon drapes covered the wall-length windows, shutting out cloudy skies that seemed to follow us to the Sanctuary. The room was dark except for the huge fireplace at the opposite wall and some strategically placed lamps. My eyes were drawn to the fire, flickering quietly in the hearth, causing a chill to run through me, despite the warmth it radiated.

"Thank you for coming," Hadraniel's voice said from my right, jarring me from old, nightmarish memories. We all turned toward him as he emerged with a tumbler of clear liquid from a service bar set against the far wall.

I couldn't suppress a small gasp as I looked at him. He was dressed casually in lightweight lounge pants and a V-neck shirt, something I didn't expect. Every other time I'd seen him, he was either in full battle gear, with armor covering his muscled body, or wearing some kind of regal-looking suit. Although this outfit appeared much looser, there was no mistaking the definition of his body beneath when he walked. He was big and broad, and power emanated from him. His facial features, handsome enough to make every male model drown in jealousy, could never be mistaken for anything other than strength and leadership. Hadraniel had the ability to keep an entire room transfixed on him until he left.

"Please have a seat," he said. "Can I get any of you something to drink?"

"I'd just as soon get to the point of this meeting, if you don't mind," Hunter said, his words sounding stiff, as if he preferred not speaking at all. "I assure you, I don't enjoy being here as much as you bristle at my appearance in your cozy little quarters. Obviously, you need something from us."

So much for playing nice.

"Very well," Hadraniel said. "Nergal's body has been stolen."

We all knew it was coming. We even talked about it on the way over. But knowing it actually happened didn't stop our collective gasps...well, at least, Nora's and mine. Eric and Hunter remained stone-faced, as if Hadraniel just announced the sun would rise and set daily. Not a flinch or a grimace. I *really* wanted to learn how to do that.

"So, you didn't want to listen to us before when we told you there was a mole in your alliance," Hunter said. "You didn't even want to allow one of your own blood anywhere near you because her eyes have a touch of blue. And now, you...*what*...need us? Tell me, Oh Holy One, how can we solve *your* dilemma?"

"I wouldn't get so cocky if I were you, demon. Let's not forget whom Caleb promised to come after, and I'm certain you don't want that to happen. Not to mention the fact he could also have the power to be your ruler. Please correct me if I have any of this wrong." Hadraniel glared at Hunter.

"He still doesn't have the Sword, or did you let that slip away too?"

"No, the Sword is still here, under heavy guard."

"What do you want from us, Hadraniel?" I asked, trying to end their pissing match. "You want us go out and find Caleb?"

"Not you, Cassandra. Only them." He nodded toward Hunter and Eric. "You will stay here."

"I'll be fine with them," I argued. "Besides, I've already proven I'm stronger than Caleb. He's no match for my powers."

"I'm not worried about that," he told me.

"Then why should I stay here? I belong with them. You made that clear in the last few months."

He didn't answer me, only stared, as if waiting for me to piece together some mystery. I felt like an idiot. What was he up to?

I glanced over at Hunter. He narrowed his eyes at Hadraniel, apparently as confused as I. Then his eyes widened and lips parted.

"Will someone please tell me what the hell is going on?" I turned to Anael, but she lowered her head.

"That is not going to happen, Hadraniel," Hunter said. "She stays with me."

"You know it's the best way," Hadraniel retorted.

Anael moved to stand in front of Hunter and placed a hand on his arm. "I won't let anything happen to her, Hunter. You know I won't. She's my blood."

"Would someon—" I started.

"As she is his," Hunter said, referring to Hadraniel. "But that won't stop him from trying to use her as bait."

"We won't let Caleb get that close," Anael said.

"Wait, what?" I interrupted. Christ, did everyone have a hidden agenda but me? "How about letting me in on what is obviously about me? Maybe I can make my own adult decisions. Would that be okay with all of you?"

Hunter turned to me, his eyes blazing with determination. "No, it's not okay with me when it involves being away from you, and you being offered as bait." He pounced on Anael. "I can't believe you would even consider it after everything she's been through."

"It's not as if she's going to be strung up in chains here," Hadraniel said, his voice rising. "Unlike you, I do have a soul."

I stepped in front of Hadraniel before Hunter and Eric could reach him, although they tried. I wasn't powerful enough to stop either of them...well, maybe Eric, but I knew they wouldn't plow through me.

"Stop. All of you," I commanded. Once everyone appeared calm, I turned to Hadraniel. "Why can't we all wait for him to come if you're so sure he'll come after me? Why should Hunter and Eric bother searching for him?"

"Because he doesn't like demons in his house," Nora said, surprising me as she moved between Hunter and Eric to stand next to me and face Hadraniel. *Go, Nora.* We must have started wearing off on her. Hadraniel's bored expression said he could care less she'd gotten a backbone, and he failed to acknowledge she was right about his shitty way of using me.

I moved closer to him, pulling my spine straighter so I could stare him in the eyes more easily. One of his eyebrows shot up at my boldness, but he didn't move.

In the last year, I discovered I was the descendent of one of the most powerful angels, my blood was mixed with that of a demon, my dad was alive, and I could turn Seekers back into Guardians. I'd also fallen in love with a demon, was held in captivity and tortured in *God only knew what kind of ways* by the Devil, and managed to help kill said Devil. I'd been through more in the last year than some in one existence. After everything I'd learned and experienced, a piece of me hardened, slowly wrapping around my vulnerability with a protective shell.

The man standing before me could no longer intimidate me.

"Well, I guess you're just going to have to get used to them, *Grandpa.* That's if you want me to be your sacrificial lamb."

He studied me for a moment, testing to see if I would break under his penetrating gaze. I kept my eyes on his and challenged him right back.

"Very well. They can stay as long as you are here. But if I see any indication that appears remotely demonic coming from them, you're all out."

"Agreed," I said.

"Fine. Anael, please show them to the guest quarters," Hadraniel said before leaving the room. He made his position clear by turning his nose up at Hunter and Eric on his way out.

Oh, this was going to be interesting. Even after all I'd been through, it might be the most challenging situation yet. Two demons living amongst the Holiest of Holies, building a bridge to work together in order to capture the one thing that could destroy them all—Caleb. And me, the half-demon, stuck smack dab in the center of it all once again.

Reviews help readers decide if a book is right for them. If this story worked for you, please consider leaving an honest review. Just a few words make a real difference.

Thank you!

Read on for a sneak peek of Angel of Fate, the final book in the Fate Trilogy.

CHECK OUT A SNEAK PEEK
OF THE 3RD AND FINAL BOOK IN
THE FATE TRILOGY

CHAPTER ONE

"I have a surprise for you," I whispered into Hunter's ear as I lay over his naked torso.

A rumbling moan echoed from deep within his throat, and he hardened even more beneath me.

"Do you, now?" his low, seductive voice purred back.

Straddling him, I sat up on my knees and grinned as his mouth lifted on one side in a sexy smile, his blue eyes glowing with passion. Sweat glistened on his muscled chest from heat radiating within, causing his scent to invade me like a pheromone.

So many times before, my insides would have melted from a mere glance at him like this. Even without looking, the energy pulsating from him would have drawn me in.

Not this time.

"Stay right there," I told him, meeting his sexy smile with one of my own.

I reached over the side of the bed, my hip movement causing him to moan again. Knowing the effect I had on him always brought a smile to my face.

Complete control.

Reaching between the mattress and box springs, my fingers slid across until I felt metal brush against my fingertips. I leaned over the edge of the bed, grasped the hilt of the Sword, and pulled it out.

The energy hit me like a jolt of electricity, sending volts up my arms, around my shoulders and into my chest, where they zoned in on my heart, deadening it with every shock. Completely transfixed by the beauty of the Sword in my hands, I sat for a moment, reveling in the fact it was a part of me, the source of my whole being.

And now together, the Sword and I would clear the way for absolute power and domination.

The man before me who thought himself my soul mate for the last year, had given up the very essence of his being to stay with me, to save me from my own evil fate. But Fate couldn't be molded or shaped. It was unyielding, fixed. I had become who I was meant to be, and there was nothing or no one who could change that.

I had no soul mate because I no longer had a soul.

Hunter would never concede to Fate, so this would be his.

Raising the Sword and tilting the tip forward, I aimed it for Hunter's heart. Our gazes locked over the shiny steel of the blade. His eyes narrowed, no longer blazed with passion. A muscle twitched near his jaw, but the rest of his gorgeous body remained motionless. Surely he was fighting every instinct to defend himself. Or did he know he didn't stand a chance? That was the beauty of Hunter—his demeanor never gave him away. His enemies never noticed him coming. It was a valuable lesson I'd learned from him.

I gripped the Sword tighter and inched it closer to his skin. Hunter's eyes never wavered from mine.

"Fight it, Cassandra."

"You can't fight destiny," I told him.

"Your destiny is with me."

Stilling the Sword above him, I said, "My destiny is where you should have left me."

His gaze intensified as if it were trying to penetrate my soul even though he no longer had that luxury. Time stood still and what might have been hours was only a few moments. In lazy defiance, he added, "I have no regrets."

One edge of my upper lip eased into a grin. My eyes burned with new luminosity, flares of light reaching out like sparks spitting from an open wire. I was in my true form.

"Neither do I." My words echoed with finality.

Before his eyes closed, he inhaled, cutting off the connection between us as if he were already at peace with his Final Death. That's when I plunged the blade straight into his heart.

***

I jolted up in bed from a resounding scream that had penetrated my sleep. As I scanned the room, images from my nightmare returned in waves. The scream had been my own, and my body shook, but it wasn't enough to rid the dread of what had happened and how it consumed my thoughts.

Past experience told me my recurring nightmares weren't like everyone else's. It wasn't merely my mind's way of playing creative genius with random pieces of my day while I slept. No, mine were warnings. Premonitions.

Fingers lightly brushed my arm, and I quivered from the touch. Gentle lips kissed my bare shoulder, and I exhaled the breath I didn't realize I was holding. The combination released tension throughout my body, urging it to relax. Everything appeared as it should be. Hunter was there... alive... and I loved him. These thoughts had become routine every time I woke from the nightmare. Groping at scattered beliefs to confirm it could never happen, no matter what the past had taught me, I told myself, not this time, not this one. *This time*, I wouldn't let it happen.

"Another one?" he asked, still at my shoulder.

I couldn't look at him. Not yet. Dreams or not, it was too difficult to meet his eyes knowing I'd just killed him. Instead, I simply nodded.

He kissed my shoulder again, this time with more tenderness than usual, but I still couldn't shake the imprint from my mind. Lately, more kisses were required to provide enough relief for me to completely warm back up. We'd played out this same scene too many times during the last month. Each time the emotions from my nightmare appeared closer to the surface, more powerful, lingering longer.

And still, I wouldn't tell him the truth.

"Do you remember anything more?"

I shook my head. "No. They're just more... intense."

"It's going to take time, Cassandra. Your mind is only trying to deal with what you've been through. Who knows what that monster did to you down there. But you're safe now. I'm here."

Hunter thought my dreams were about Nergal holding me captive in Hell. I'd blacked out during most of that ordeal, losing all track of the time, but almost wished the nightmares *were* about that. It might make looking him in the eye each morning much easier. I continued letting him believe I was reliving that nightmare, choosing my own secret hell instead.

How could I tell him I dreamt about killing him every night? He understood my dreams always ended up being some whacked out form of a prophecy, so what would I say? "I think I'm going to kill you soon because every night I stab you through the heart with the Sword of Final Death"? No way. We were finally able to be together. *Together*, really together. No one in our way. Neither of us chained to something in Hell. Free to sleep every night in each other's arms. It was wonderful, except for the terrifying nightmares that invaded the bliss while I slept, or when the occasional image popped into my head when we were together. But my time with him was precious, and I wasn't about to change that.

I finally got the nerve to look back at him over my shoulder. Our gazes locked instantly as if they were connected to an invisible beam magnetically drawing them to one another. We stayed that way, taking each other in.

God, he was beautiful. This man, who to everyone else was a feral predator, a lion who only needed to look at you to cause you to unravel, was a pussycat when it came to me. But it hadn't always been that way with us. First, he wanted to kill me, and then he wanted to claim me. Now, he only wanted to love and protect me.

I'd been as bad in the beginning, trying to fight the draw between us, afraid of what he was and what he might make me. But eventually we both realized when it came to the heart, there were no sides. Black and white, good and evil, they all melded together until neither of us cared what it was anymore as long as it was by our side at night.

Of course, I understood I was riding a thin line lying to him, and eventually it would reach a breaking point. Most of the time, Hunter was able to read my mind, but so far, there were no telltale signs he knew. That meant he was either playing along or his telepathic abilities were on the fritz. More than likely, his mind-reading skills were temporarily down. Based on my previous experience with him, Hunter didn't *play along* with anything or anyone. He was a blatant kind of guy, and by blatant, I mean unrepentant, audacious, cocky, fearless, pretty much in-your-face. Hunter got what he wanted, no matter the cost or consequences. Heaven help me if he thought for a minute I was lying to him.

I wondered why he didn't have all his powers, though, but assumed it was because he was a demon living under the roof of the angels. Maybe Hadraniel snuffed out Hunter's power to avoid a war every time an angel had bad thoughts about us, which was pretty much every time they set eyes on us.

Lying wasn't my strong suit. Avoiding was another story. Avoiding, I did well.

"I just want all this over with because I hate living here. The way they look at me every time I enter a room, I feel like I

need to check my shoes for shit." By they, I meant the angels...
but he knew that.

"You know, I'd be more than happy to take care of that for
you," he said with a sparkle in his eyes. "Just say the word. I'm
only here for you, you know. If it were up to me, I'd take you
away from all of this, somewhere where it's just you and I." He
brought his lips to my shoulder again and proceeded to trail a
luscious line of kisses across it and then up my neck. A new kind
of shiver overtook me. "Where I'd ravish you all day." He gave
me a solitary kiss. "Every day." Wow. Another mind-blowing
kiss.

A moan escaped my lips. Hunter also had a delectable way
of taking my mind off of everything—nightmares, monsters—the
world.

"Hmmm... if Caleb doesn't show up soon, I may take you
up on tha—"

A loud knock on the door interrupted me. Hunter growled
his distaste. I was about to get up, but he ignored whoever was
there and started feasting on my neck again. Apparently,
whoever was at the door didn't warrant acknowledgment. With
the pure pleasure he was dishing out, he left me no choice but to
agree.

Two more loud knocks boomed, echoing through the
room, but Hunter still couldn't be distracted.

"Hunter, we should probably see who it is."

His tongue started on my ear.

"Hunter... really," I released on a breath.

He growled again, this time a long, low one, reminiscent of
defeat instead of rebellion.

I silently cried over the loss of his lips on me as he shouted
across the room, "I'll be right there, Eric. Meet me in the foyer
downstairs."

"You knew who it was all along?"

He pulled me onto his lap to face him, a sexy smirk playing on his lips. "I know everything."

"Oh yeah, smart guy?" I laughed. "Then when is Caleb going to show up so we can finally get on with our lives?"

I'd meant it to be playful, but Hunter's smile quickly disappeared. He placed his finger underneath my chin, easing my face up so I'd look him in the eyes. "I'll find Caleb," he said, his tone leaving no doubt this was nothing more than fact. "I'm going to find him, and I'm going to kill him. And then we'll go far away from all of this where I can fill your world with everything you've ever fantasized about, leaving no room for nightmares. I promise you, Cassandra."

He melted me. He did. Hunter was the only one in the world who had the power to change my fate. My nightmares didn't stand a chance as long as I had him. I loved him beyond words, beyond actions. It was a love that could only be experienced to be believed. The emotional side was so intense and sometimes it held me paralyzed, unable to move or utter a word. I could only gaze upon him and let the feelings pulse within me like a racing heartbeat trying to return to a steady tempo.

He slid his thumb over my bottom lip, bringing my attention back. I kissed the tip of it.

"I believe you," I whispered.

He smiled. "Too bad. I was hoping I needed to convince you." His gaze lazily slid down my neck to my bare chest. His finger followed.

My eyes closed of their own accord, and I moaned, leaning into his hand, as it cupped one of my breasts.

"Isn't Eric waiting for you?" I said on a pant.

"Yes." His lips were at my neck again. I could feel he was more than ready for me as I moved my hips against him.

"Is it important?"

"We have a lead on Caleb."

It took a moment for the words to sink in since they were muffled against my neck. I snapped back, grabbing his busy hands at the same time.

"Hunter."

While trying to make eye contact with him, his still heavy with passion and focused on my other body parts, I took his hands and shoved them hard against his chest. "Hunter."

Finally, I got his attention. He read the look on my face and sighed as he leaned his forehead against mine. "Caleb is going to experience pain like he's never felt. Only then will I let him die," he said, and then gently lifted me off his lap. As he got off the bed, I covered myself with a sheet.

Watching him dress, I asked, "What's this lead?"

He sat on the bed to put his boots on. "Some rogue the angels captured. Supposedly he worked with Caleb and knows where he is. Same shit, different demon. We'll see if he's legit."

Word had made it out months ago the angels were looking for Caleb and would pay dearly to get him, something the demons banked on when they were captured. Every one of them claimed they knew where he was, but up to this point, none of the leads had panned out. The demons were merely using desperate attempts to escape their demise.

Hunter insisted that he, Eric, and a few other loyal demons were present when the angels questioned those captured. The angels had a tendency to be a little trigger-happy when it came to demons. Hadraniel refused to have his angels bring any demons back to the Sanctuary to be questioned, so Hunter and the group had to go out whenever one popped up.

"How long will you be gone?"

"Not long. I'll be back by dinner."

I almost laughed at the unintentional normalcy of his answer, as if we were some old married couple. He was going out for bowling and beers with the boys, instead of reading the mind of some demon from Hell who allegedly had knowledge of the self-proclaimed king of the Underworld. The truth was, I was getting tired of being the little woman stuck at home, waiting for the men of the house to get back from taking care of business.

"Let me go this time," I said.

One look at his face and I immediately knew the answer. I'd seen it so many times in the last few months, words no longer needed to follow it. I rolled my eyes and turned away from him.

"We talked about this, Cassandra."

"Yeah, yeah. I know. It could be a trap. They might be waiting for me... blah, blah, blah." I faced him again, bracing myself on the bed with one hand while holding the sheet against me with the other. A tirade didn't produce the desired results while body parts jiggled. And a rant was exactly what I was about to let loose on him. "Maybe that's what we need. It's probably the only way we are going to get to Caleb. Did you guys ever think of that? It's obvious he's not coming to the Sanctuary. He's been gone three months. Ninety days that I've been cooped up in this godforsaken place to do nothing but sit here like some lamb roped up to a pole in the ground. It's not fair, Hunter." Yeah, I knew I sounded like a spoiled child, but if they were going to treat me like one, I might as well give them the full treatment.

"You're safer here."

God, sometimes I hated his simplicity.

"I'm safe with you. You said so three months ago."

"And at that time, I believed it. But now, I don't know that I'm enough to keep you safe."

"What are you talking about? Of course, you are."

"Caleb is building an army, Cassandra. It's not just the few demons I believed were stupid enough to follow him. He's promising rogues the chance to rule the world with him if they help recover two things—the Sword and you. One of those things I'm not willing to lose for pride. I may be one of the strongest demons, but I can't fight off an army. And I'm no good to you if they get to me. Here, I have an army to fight with... one that has the same goal. Regardless of our hatred for the angels, we have the same goals right now."

"But we don't even know if Caleb still wants me. Maybe he's moved on and found a new queen. Maybe—"

Hunter jumped up from the bed and glared down at me. "I'm not willing to take a chance with you on *maybes*. Ever. You're to stay here where I can keep you safe. Is that understood?"

I clenched my teeth and mimicked his glare. He was the most stubborn man I'd ever known, but I also understood I'd never win this fight. We'd had the discussion before. His resolve hadn't budged an inch. Especially with everyone else siding with him. Not one person under this roof would see my side of it. Not my mom, dad, or even Nora.

"Fine," I yelled, turning my back on him. "Go save the world while I sit here and learn to knit or something."

The mattress lowered near me, and before I knew what was happening, Hunter spun me around by the shoulders to face him. His face was inches from mine as he held me in place.

"My only care in this world is you. The rest of it can go to Hell. I don't give a shit. But I will not lose you, Cassandra."

His kiss was demanding, possessive, harsh against my lips until I melted into it. Then it turned soft and sweet, a mark of love.

I knew it was his love for me making him obstinate about this. Caleb had promised he would come for the Sword and me. He wasn't one to forget his demented goals, regardless of how much I tried to convince myself and everyone else otherwise. But none of that changed the fact I was going stir-crazy being stuck day after day, not knowing when or if anything would ever happen. It also didn't stop the moments of resentment I'd had frequently toward everyone in the Sanctuary. A passing reaction? Maybe, but I couldn't seem to control it anymore. After

Hunter left, I decided to burn off some of that pent-up frustration by beating the shit out of something.

More books by L.J. Kentowski

Fate Trilogy:

Guardian Of Fate (Book 1)
Seeker Of Fate (Book 2)
Angel Of Fate (Book 3)

Lexie Pearce Series:

Descended in Vengeance (Book 1)

Heart of Seeton Series:

Love Owned (Book 1)
Full Potential (Book 2)

Learn more about these books at
http://www.laurakentowski.com/

<u>Get a FREE Urban Fantasy Short Story!</u>
When you sign up for my VIP Newsletter, you'll receive access to release news, upcoming events, and exclusive content and giveaways!
As a thank you for joining, you'll also receive a FREE bonus short story companion to the Lexie Pearce Series!
Get started here:
https://preview.mailerlite.io/forms/1675703/160480288834588588/share

ABOUT THE AUTHOR

L.J. Kentowski lives with her husband and son in the Midwest, where to keep from freezing her tail off for nine months out of the year, she bundles up in front of a fire, writes stories, eats Twizzlers, and tries to ignore the Great Dane on her lap while she types.

Her first series is an Adult Urban Fantasy/Paranormal Romance trilogy, *The Fate Series*, filled with Angels, Demons, and the In-Betweens.

To learn more about L.J.'s books, visit her at the following places:

Newsletter (free newsletter announcing book releases and special contests)
Website
Facebook
Pinterest

Instagram